CANDIDE
AND
ZADIG

VOLTAIRE

CANDIDE

AND

ZADIG

TRANSLATED FROM THE FRENCH BY
ROBERT BRUCE BOSWELL

KÖNEMANN

❦ Notes (on pp. 225 to 264)
are keyed thus in the margin

© 1998 for this edition
Könemann Verlagsgesellschaft mbH
Bonner Straße 126, D–50968 Köln

Series editor: Michael Hulse
Volume editor: Chris Miller
Cover design: Peter Feierabend
Layout and typesetting: Birgit Beyer
Printed in Hungary
ISBN 3-8290-0885-6
10 9 8 7 6 5 4 3 2 1

CONTENTS

ZADIG

OR

DESTINY

AN EASTERN TALE

CERTIFICATE OF APPROVAL.—I, the undersigned, who have ✑ succeeded in making myself pass for a man of learning and even of wit, have read this manuscript, and found it, in spite of myself, curious and amusing, moral and philosophical, and worthy even of pleasing those who hate romances. So I have disparaged it, and assured the cadi that it is an abominable ✑ work.

*Dedicatory Epistle of Zadig
to the Sultana Sherah,
by Sadi
The 10th day of the month Shawal,
in the year 837 of the Hegira*

Delight of the eyes, torment of the heart, and lamp of the soul,
I kiss not the dust of thy feet, because thou dost scarcely ever
walk, or only on Persian carpets or over rose leaves. I present
thee with the translation of a book written by an ancient sage,
to whom, being in the happy condition of having nothing to
do, there occurred the happy thought of amusing himself by
writing the story of Zadig, a work that means more than it
seems to do. I beseech thee to read it and form thy judgment
on it; for although thou art in the springtime of life, and
courted by pleasures of every kind; although thou art fair, and
thy talents add to thy beauty; and although thou art loaded
with praises from morning to night, and so hast every right to
be devoid of common sense, yet thou hast a very sound
intelligence and a highly refined taste, and I have heard thee
argue better than any old dervish with a long beard and
pointed cap. Thou art cautious yet not suspicious; thou art
gentle without being weak; thou art beneficent with due
discrimination; thou dost love thy friends, and makest to
thyself no enemies. Thy wit never borrows its charm from the
shafts of slander; thou dost neither say nor do evil, in spite of
abundant facilities if thou wert so inclined. Lastly, thy soul has
always appeared to me as spotless as thy beauty. Thou hast
even a small stock of philosophy, which has led me to believe
that thou wouldst take more interest than any other of thy sex
in this work of a wise man.

It was originally written in ancient Chaldee, which neither
thou nor I understand. It was translated into Arabic for the
entertainment of the famous Sultan Oulook, about the time
when the Arabs and Persians were beginning to compose "The
Thousand and One Nights," "The Thousand and One Days,"

11

etc. Oulook preferred to read "Zadig"; but the ladies of his harem liked the others better.

"How can you prefer," said the wise Oulook, "senseless stories that mean nothing?"

"That is just why we are so fond of them," answered the ladies.

I feel confident that thou wilt not resemble them, but that thou wilt be a true Oulook; and I venture to hope that when thou art weary of general conversation, which is of much the same character as "The Arabian Nights Entertainment," except that it is less amusing, I may have the honour of talking to thee for a few minutes in a rational manner. If thou hadst been Thalestris in the time of Alexander, son of Philip, or if thou hadst been the Queen of Sheba in the days of Solomon, those kings would have travelled to thee, not thou to them.

I pray the heavenly powers that thy pleasures may be unalloyed, thy beauty unfading, and thy happiness everlasting.

CHAPTER I

The Man of One Eye

In the time of King Moabdar there lived at Babylon a young man named Zadig, who was born with a good disposition, which education had strengthened. Though young and rich, he knew how to restrain his passions; he was free from all affectation, made no pretension to infallibility himself, and knew how to respect the foibles of others. People were astonished to see that, with all his wit, he never turned his powers of raillery on the vague, disconnected, and confused talk, the rash censures, the ignorant judgments, the scurvy jests, and all that vain babble of words which went by the name of conversation at Babylon. He had learned in the first book of Zoroaster that self-conceit is a bladder puffed up with wind, out of which issue storms and tempests when it is pricked. Above all, Zadig never prided himself on despising women, nor boasted of his conquests over them. Generous as he was, he had no fear of bestowing kindness on the ungrateful, therein following the noble maxim of Zoroaster: *When thou eatest, give something to the dogs, even though they should bite thee*. He was as wise as man can be, for he sought to live with the wise. Instructed in the sciences of the ancient Chaldeans, he was not ignorant of such principles of natural philosophy as were then known, and knew as much of metaphysics as has been known in any age, that is to say, next to nothing. He was firmly persuaded that the year consists of 365 days and a quarter, in spite of the latest philosophy of his time, and that the sun is the centre of our system; and when the leading magi told him with contemptuous arrogance that he entertained dangerous opinions, and that it was a proof of hostility to the government to believe that the sun turned on its own axis and that the year had twelve months, he held his peace without showing either anger or disdain.

Zadig, with great riches, and consequently well provided with friends, having health and good looks, a just and well-disciplined mind, and a heart noble and sincere, thought that he might be happy. He was to be married to Semira, a lady whose beauty, birth, and fortune rendered her the first match in Babylon. He felt for her a strong and virtuous attachment, and Semira in her turn loved him passionately. They were close upon the happy moment which was about to unite them, when, walking together towards one of the gates of Babylon, under the palm trees which adorned the banks of the Euphrates, they saw a party of men armed with swords and bows advancing in their direction. They were the satellites of young Orcan, the nephew of a minister of state, whom his uncle's hangers-on had encouraged in the belief that he might do what he liked with impunity. He had none of the graces nor virtues of Zadig; but, fancying he was worth a great deal more, he was provoked at not being preferred to him. This jealousy, which proceeded only from his vanity, made him think that he was desperately in love with Semira, and he determined to carry her off. The ravishers seized her, and in their outrageous violence wounded her, shedding the blood of one so fair that the tigers of Mount Imaus would have melted at the sight of her. She pierced the sky with her lamentations. She cried aloud:

"My dear husband! They are tearing me from him who is the idol of my heart."

Taking no heed of her own danger, it was of her beloved Zadig alone that she thought, who, meanwhile, was defending her with all the force that love and valour could bestow. With the help of only two slaves he put the ravishers to flight, and carried Semira to her home unconscious and covered with blood. On opening her eyes she saw her deliverer, and said:

"O Zadig, I loved you before as my future husband, I love you now as the preserver of my life and honour."

Never was there a heart more deeply moved than that of Semira; never did lips more lovely express sentiments more touching, in words of fire inspired by gratitude for the greatest of benefits and the most tender transports of the most honourable love. Her wound was slight, and was soon cured; but Zadig was hurt more severely, an arrow had struck him near the eye and made a deep wound. Semira's only prayer to Heaven now was that her lover might be healed. Her eyes were bathed in tears night and day; she longed for the moment when those of Zadig might once more be able to gaze on her with delight; but an abscess which attacked the wounded eye gave every cause for alarm. A messenger was sent as far as Memphis for Hermes, the famous physician, who came with a numerous train. He visited the sick man, and declared that he would lose the eye; he even foretold the day and the hour when this unfortunate event would happen.

"If it had been the right eye," said he, "I might have cured it, but injuries to the left eye are incurable."

All Babylon, while bewailing Zadig's fate, admired the profound scientific research of Hermes. Two days afterwards the abscess broke of itself, and Zadig was completely cured. Hermes wrote a book, in which he proved to him that he ought not to have been cured; but Zadig did not read it. As soon as he could venture forth, he prepared to visit her in whom rested his every hope of happiness in life, and for whose sake alone he desired to have eyes. Now Semira had gone into the country three days before, and on his way he learned that this fair lady, after loudly declaring that she had an insurmountable objection to one-eyed people, had just married Orcan the night before. At these tidings he fell senseless, and his anguish brought him to the brink of the grave; he was ill for a long time, but at last reason prevailed over his affliction, and the very atrocity of his treatment furnished him with a source of consolation.

"Since I have experienced," said he, "such cruel caprice from a maiden brought up at the court, I must marry one of the townspeople."

He chose Azora, who came of the best stock and was the best behaved girl in the city. He married her, and lived with her for a month in all the bliss of a most tender union. The only fault he remarked in her was a little giddiness, and a strong tendency to find out that the handsomest young men had always the most intelligence and virtue.

CHAPTER II

The Nose

One day Azora returned from a walk in a state of vehement indignation, and uttering loud exclamations.

"What is the matter with you, my dear wife?" said Zadig; "who can have put you so much out of temper?"

"Alas!" she replied, "you would be as indignant as I, if you had seen the sight which I have just witnessed. I went to console the young widow Cosrou, who two days ago raised a tomb to her young husband beside the stream which forms the boundary of this meadow. She vowed to Heaven, in her grief, that she would dwell beside that tomb as long as the stream flowed by it."

"Well!" said Zadig, "a truly estimable woman, who really loved her husband!"

"Ah!" returned Azora, "if you only knew how she was occupied when I paid her my visit!"

"How then, fair Azora?"

"She was diverting the course of the brook."

Azora gave vent to her feelings in such lengthy invectives, and burst into such violent reproaches against the young widow, that this ostentatious display of virtue was not altogether pleasing to Zadig.

He had a friend named Cador, who was one of those young men in whom his wife found more merit and integrity than in others; Zadig took him into his confidence, and secured his fidelity, as far as possible, by means of a considerable present.

Azora, having passed a couple of days with one of her lady friends in the country, on the third day returned home. The servants, with tears in their eyes, told her that her husband had died quite suddenly the night before, that they had not dared to convey to her such sad news, and that they had just buried Zadig in the tomb of his ancestors at the end of the garden. She wept, and tore her hair, and vowed that she would die. In the evening Cador asked if she would allow him to speak to her, and they wept in company. Next day they wept less, and dined together. Cador informed her that his friend had left him the best part of his property, and gave her to understand that he would deem it the greatest happiness to share his fortune with her. The lady shed tears, was offended, allowed herself to be soothed; the supper lasted longer than the dinner, and they conversed together more confidentially. Azora spoke in praise of the deceased, but admitted that he had faults from which Cador was free.

In the middle of supper, Cador complained of a violent pain in the spleen. The lady, anxious and attentive, caused all the essences on her toilet table to be brought, to try if there might not be some one among them good for affections of the spleen. She was very sorry that the famous Hermes was no longer in Babylon. She even condescended to touch the side where Cador felt such sharp pains.

"Are you subject to this cruel malady?" she asked in a tone of compassion.

"It sometimes brings me to the brink of the grave," answered Cador; "and there is only one remedy which can relieve me: it is to apply to my side the nose of a man who has been only a day or two dead."

"What a strange remedy!" said Azora.

"Not more strange," was his reply, "than the scent-bags of Mr. Arnoult being an antidote to apoplexy."

That reason, joined to the distinguished merit of the young man, at last decided the lady.

"After all," said she, "when my husband shall pass from the world of yesterday into the world of tomorrow over the bridge Chinavar, the angel Azrael will not grant him a passage any the less because his nose will be a little shorter in the second life than in the first."

She then took a razor, and went to her husband's tomb; after she had watered it with her tears, she approached to cut off Zadig's nose, whom she found stretched at full length in the

17

tomb, when he suddenly got up, and, holding his nose with one hand, stopped the razor with the other.

"Madam," said he, "do not cry out so loudly another time against young Cosrou; your intention of cutting off my nose is as bad as that of turning aside a stream."

CHAPTER III

The Dog and the Horse

Zadig found by experience that the first month of marriage is, as it is written in the book of the Zendavesta, the moon of honey, and that the second is the moon of wormwood. He was some time afterwards obliged to put away Azora, who became too unmanageable to live with, and he sought for happiness in the study of nature.

"There is no delight," he said, "equal to that of a philosopher, who reads in this great book which God has set before our eyes. The truths which he discovers are his own: he nurtures and educates his soul, he lives in peace, he fears no man, and no tender spouse comes to cut off his nose."

Full of these ideas, he retired to a country house on the banks of the Euphrates. There he did not spend his time in calculating how many inches of water flowed in a second under the arches of a bridge, or whether a cubic line of rain fell in the month of the mouse more than in the month of the sheep. He did not contrive how to make silk out of cobwebs, nor porcelain out of broken bottles; but he studied most of all the properties of animals and plants; and soon acquired a sagacity that showed him a thousand differences where other men see nothing but uniformity.

One day, when he was walking near a little wood, he saw one of the queen's eunuchs running to meet him, followed by several officers, who appeared to be in the greatest uneasiness, and were running hither and thither like men bewildered and searching for some most precious object which they had lost.

"Young man," said the chief eunuch to Zadig, "have you seen the queen's dog?"

Zadig modestly replied: "It is a bitch, not a dog."

"You are right," said the eunuch.

"It is a very small spaniel," added Zadig; "it is not long since she has had a litter of puppies; she is lame in the left forefoot, and her ears are very long."

"You have seen her, then?" said the chief eunuch, quite out of breath.

"No," answered Zadig, "I have never seen her, and never knew that the queen had a bitch."

Just at this very time, by one of those curious coincidencies which are not uncommon, the finest horse in the king's stables had broken away from the hands of a groom in the plains of Babylon. The grand huntsman and all the other officers ran after him with as much anxiety as the chief of the eunuchs had displayed in his search after the queen's bitch. The grand huntsman accosted Zadig, and asked him if he had seen the king's horse pass that way.

"It is the horse," said Zadig, "which gallops best; he is five feet high, and has small hoofs; his tail is three and a half feet long; the bosses on his bit are of gold twenty-three carats fine; his shoes are silver of eleven pennyweights."

"Which road did he take? Where is he?" asked the grand huntsman.

"I have not seen him," answered Zadig, "and I have never even heard anyone speak of him."

The grand huntsman and the chief eunuch had no doubt that Zadig had stolen the king's horse and the queen's bitch, so they caused him to be brought before the Assembly of the Grand Desterham, which condemned him to the knout, and to pass the rest of his life in Siberia. Scarcely had the sentence been pronounced, when the horse and the bitch were found. The judges were now under the disagreeable necessity of amending their judgment; but they condemned Zadig to pay four hundred ounces of gold for having said that he had not seen what he had seen. He was forced to pay this fine first, and afterwards he was allowed to plead his cause before the Council of the Grand Desterham, when he expressed himself in the following terms:

"Stars of justice, fathomless gulfs of wisdom, mirrors of truth, ye who have the gravity of lead, the strength of iron, the brilliance of the diamond, and a close affinity with gold, inasmuch as it is permitted me to speak before this august assembly, I swear to you by Ormuzd that I have never seen the queen's respected bitch, nor the sacred horse of the king of kings. Hear all that happened: I was walking towards the little wood where later on I met the venerable eunuch and the most illustrious grand huntsman. I saw on the sand the footprints of an animal, and easily decided that they were those of a little dog. Long and faintly marked furrows, imprinted where the sand was slightly raised between the footprints, told me that it was a bitch whose dugs were drooping, and that consequently she must have given birth to young ones only a few days before. Other marks of a different character, showing that the surface of the sand had been constantly grazed on either side of the front paws, informed me that she had very long ears; and, as I observed that the sand was always less deeply indented by one paw than by the other three, I gathered that the bitch belonging to our august queen was a little lame, if I may venture to say so.

"With respect to the horse of the king of kings, you must know that as I was walking along the roads in that same wood, I perceived the marks of a horse's shoes, all at equal distances. 'There,' I said to myself, 'went a horse with a faultless gallop.' The dust upon the trees, where the width of the road was not more than seven feet, was here and there rubbed off on both sides, three feet and a half away from the middle of the road. 'This horse,' said I, 'has a tail three feet and a half long, which, by its movements to right and left, has whisked away the dust.' I saw, where the trees formed a canopy five feet above the ground, leaves lately fallen from the boughs; and I concluded that the horse had touched them, and was therefore five feet high. As to his bit, it must be of gold twenty-three carats fine, for he had rubbed its bosses against a touchstone, the properties of which I had ascertained. Lastly, I inferred from the marks that his shoes left upon stones of another kind, that he was shod with silver of eleven pennyweights in quality."

All the judges marvelled at Zadig's deep and subtle discernment, and a report of it even reached the king and queen. Nothing but Zadig was talked of in the antechambers, the presence chamber, and the private closet; and, though several of the magi were of opinion that he ought to be burned as a wizard, the king ordered that he should be released from the fine of four hundred ounces of gold to which he had been condemned. The registrar, the bailiffs, and the attorneys came to his house with great solemnity to restore him his four hundred ounces; they kept back only three hundred and ninety-eight of them for legal expenses, and their servants too claimed their fees.

Zadig saw how very dangerous it sometimes is to show oneself too knowing, and resolved on the next occasion of the kind to say nothing about what he had seen.

Such an opportunity soon occurred. A state prisoner made his escape, and passed under the windows of Zadig's house, who, on being questioned, answered nothing; but it was proved that he had looked out of the window. For this offence he was condemned to pay five hundred ounces of gold, and he thanked his judges for their leniency, according to the custom of Babylon.

"Good Heavens!" said Zadig to himself, "what a pity it is when one takes a walk in a wood through which the queen's bitch and the king's horse have passed! how dangerous it is to stand at a window! and how difficult it is to be happy in this life!"

CHAPTER IV

The Envious Man

Zadig sought consolation in philosophy and friendship for the unkindness with which fortune had treated him. In one of the suburbs of Babylon he had a house tastefully furnished, where he had gathered all the arts and pleasures that were worthy of a gentleman. In the morning his library was open to all men of learning; in the evening his table was surrounded by good company. But he soon discovered what danger there is in entertaining the learned. A hot dispute arose over a law of Zoroaster, which prohibited the eating of a griffin.

"How can a griffin be forbidden," said some, "if no such creature exists?"

"It must exist," said the others, "since Zoroaster forbids it to be eaten."

Zadig endeavoured to bring them to an agreement by saying:

"If there are griffins, let us refrain from eating them; and if there are none, there will be all the less danger of our doing so. Thus, in either case alike, Zoroaster will be obeyed."

A learned scholar who had composed thirteen volumes on the properties of the griffin, and who was moreover a great magician, lost no time in bringing an accusation against Zadig before an archimagian named Yebor, the most foolish of the Chaldeans, and consequently the most fanatical. This man would fain have impaled Zadig for the greater glory of the Sun, and would have recited the breviary of Zoroaster in a more complacent tone of voice for having done it; but his friend Cador (one friend is worth more than a hundred priests) sought out old Yebor, and addressed him thus:

"Long live the Sun and the griffins! Take good heed that you do no harm to Zadig; he is a saint; he keeps griffins in his back-yard, and abstains from eating them; and his accuser is a heretic, who dares to maintain that rabbits have cloven feet and are not unclean."

"In that case," said Yebor, shaking his bald head, "Zadig must be impaled for having thought wrongly about griffins, and the other for having spoken wrongly about rabbits."

Cador settled the matter by means of a maid of honour, who had borne Yebor a child, and who was held in high esteem in the college of the magi. No one was impaled, though a good many of the doctors murmured threat, and prophesied the downfall of Babylon in consequence.

Zadig exclaimed: "On what does happiness depend! Everybody in this world persecutes me, even beings that do not exist."

He cursed all men of learning, and determined to live henceforth only in the best society. He invited to his house the most distinguished men and the most charming women in Babylon; he gave elegant suppers, often preceded by concerts, and enlivened by interesting conversation, from which he knew how to banish that straining after a display of wit, which is the surest way to have none and to mar the most brilliant company. Neither the choice of his friends, nor that of his dishes, was prompted by vanity; for in everything he preferred being to seeming, and thereby he attracted to himself the real respect to which he made no claim.

Opposite Zadig's house lived Arimaze, a person whose depraved soul was painted on his coarse countenance. He was consumed with malice, and puffed up with pride, and, to crown all, he set up for being a wit and was only a bore. Having never been able to succeed in the world, he took his revenge by railing at it. In spite of his riches, he had some trouble in getting flatterers to flock to his house. The noise of the carriages entering Zadig's gates of an evening annoyed him, the sound of his praises irritated him yet more. He sometimes went to Zadig's parties, and sat down at his table without being invited, where he spoiled all the enjoyment of the company, just as the harpies are said to infect whatever food they touch. One day a lady whom he was anxious to entertain, instead of accepting his invitation, went to sup

By heinous crimes
Set on the throne,
In peaceful times
One foe alone.

The Envious Man was happy for the first time in his life, for he had in his hands the means of destroying a virtuous and amiable man. Full of such cruel joy, he caused this lampoon written by Zadig's own hand to be brought to the king's notice, who ordered him to be sent to prison, together with his two friends and the lady. His trial was soon over, nor did his judges deign to hear what he had to say for himself. When he was brought up to receive sentence, the Envious Man crossed his path, and told him in a loud voice that his verses were good for nothing. Zadig did not pride himself on being a fine poet, but he was in despair at being condemned as guilty of high treason, and at seeing so fair a lady and his two friends kept in prison for a crime that he had never committed. He was not allowed to speak, because his note-book spoke for him. Such was the law of Babylon. He was then forced to go to his execution through a crowd of inquisitive spectators, not one of whom dared to commiserate him, but who rushed forward in order to scrutinise his countenance, and to see whether he was likely to die with a good grace. His relations alone were distressed; for they were not to be his heirs. Three quarters of his estate were confiscated for the king's benefit, and the Envious Man profited by the other quarter.

Just as he was preparing for death, the king's parrot escaped from its perch, and alighted in Zadig's garden, on a thicket of roses. A peach had been carried thither by the wind from a tree hard by, and it had fallen on a piece of writing paper, to which it had stuck. The bird took up both the peach and the paper, and laid them on the monarch's knees. The king, whose curiosity was excited, read some words which made no sense, and which appeared to be the ends of four lines of verse. He loved poetry, and princes who love the muses never find time

with Zadig. Another day, when he was talking with him in t[h]
palace, they came across a minister who asked Zadig
supper without asking Arimaze. The most inveterate hatre[d]
are often founded on causes quite as trivial. This person, w[h]
went by the name of "the Envious Man" in Babylon, wishe[d]
to ruin Zadig because people called him "the Happy ma[n]
Opportunities for doing harm are found a hundred times
day, and an opportunity for doing good occurs once a ye[a]
as Zoroaster has observed.

On one occasion the Envious Man went to Zadig's hous[e]
and found him walking in his garden with two friends and
lady, to whom he was addressing frequent compliment[s]
without any intention other than that of making himse[lf]
agreeable. The conversation turned upon a war, which th[e]
king had just brought to a prosperous termination, again[st]
the prince of Hyrcania, his vassal. Zadig, who had displaye[d]
his valour during the short campaign, had much to say i[n]
praise of the king, and still more in praise of the lady. He too[k]
out his note-book, and wrote down four lines, which he mad[e]
on the spur of the moment, and which he gave to his fa[ir]
companion to read. His friends entreated him to be allowed [a]
sight of them; but his modesty, or rather a natural regard f[or]
his reputation, made him refuse. He knew that such im[-]
promptu verses are never of any value except in the eyes [of]
her in whose honour they have been composed, so he tore i[n]
two the leaf on which he had just written them, and threw th[e]
pieces into a thicket of roses, where his friends looked f[or]
them in vain. A shower came on, and they betook themselve[s]
indoors. The Envious Man, who remained in the garde[n]
searched so diligently that he found one fragment of the lea[f]
which had been torn in such a way that the halves of each lin[e]
that were left made a continuous sense, and even a rhyme[d]
verse, in shorter metre than the original; but by an accide[nt]
still more strange, these short lines were found to contain th[e]
most opprobrious libel against the king. They read thus:

hang heavy on their hands. His parrot's adventure set him thinking. The queen, who remembered what had been written on the fragment of the leaf from Zadig's note-book, had it brought to her.

Both pieces were put side by side, and were found to fit together exactly. The verses then read as Zadig had made them:

By heinous crimes I saw the earth alarm'd,
Set on the throne one king all evil curbs;
In peaceful times now only Love is arm'd,
One foe alone the timid heart disturbs.

The king immediately commanded that Zadig should be brought before him, and that his two friends and the fair lady should be let out of prison. Zadig prostrated himself with his face to the ground at their majesties' feet, asked their pardon most humbly for having made such poor rhymes, and spoke with so much grace, wit, and good sense, that the king and queen desired to see him again. He came again accordingly, and won still greater favour. All the property of the Envious Man who had accused him unjustly was given to Zadig, but he restored it all, and the Envious Man was touched, but only with the joy of not losing his wealth after all. The king's esteem for Zadig increased every day. He made him share all his pleasures, and consulted him in all matters of business. The queen regarded him from that time with a tender complacency that might become dangerous to herself, to her royal consort, to Zadig, and to the whole State. Zadig began to think that it is not so difficult after all to be happy.

CHAPTER V

The Prize of Generosity

The time was now arrived for celebrating a high festival, which recurred every five years. It was the custom at Babylon to announce in a public and solemn manner, at the end of such a period, the name of that citizen who had done the most generous act during the interval. The grandees and the magi were the arbitrators. The chief satrap, who had the city under his charge, made known the most noble deeds that had been performed under his government. The election was made by vote, and the king pronounced judgment. People came to this festival from the farthest corners of the earth, and the successful candidate received from the monarch's hands a cup of gold decorated with precious stones, the king addressing him in these terms:

"Receive this reward of generosity, and may the gods grant me many subjects who resemble you."

The memorable day then was come, and the king appeared upon his throne, surrounded by grandees, magi, and deputies, sent by all nations to these games, where glory was to be gained, not by the swiftness of horses nor by strength of body, but by virtue. The chief satrap proclaimed with a loud voice the actions that might entitle their authors to this inestimable prize. He said nothing about the magnanimity with which Zadig had restored all his fortune to the Envious Man; that was not considered an action worthy of disputing the prize.

First, he presented a judge who, after having given judgment against a citizen in an important law-suit, under a mistake for which he was in no way responsible, had given him all his own property, which was equal in value to what the other had lost.

He next brought forward a young man, who, being over head and ears in love with a damsel to whom he was engaged to be married, had resigned her to a friend who was nearly

28

dying for love of her, and had moreover resigned the dowry as well as the damsel.

Then he introduced a soldier, who in the Hyrcanian war had given a still nobler example of generosity. Some of the enemy's troops were laying hands on his mistress, and he was defending her from them, when he was told that another party of Hyrcanians, a few paces off, were carrying away his mother. With tears he left his mistress, and ran to rescue his mother; and when he returned to the object of his love, he found her dying. He was on the point of slaying himself, but when his mother pointed out that she had no one but him to whom she could look for succour, he was courageous enough to endure to live on.

The arbitrators were inclined to give the prize to this soldier; but the king interposed, and said:

"This man's conduct and that of the others is praiseworthy, but it does not astonish me; whereas yesterday Zadig did a thing that made me marvel. Some days before, my minister and favourite Coreb had incurred my displeasure and been disgraced. I uttered violent complaints against him, and all my courtiers assured me that I was not half severe enough; each vied with his neighbour in saying as much evil as he could of Coreb. I asked Zadig what he thought of him, and he dared to say a word in his favour. I am free to confess that I have heard of instances in our history of men atoning for a mistake by the sacrifice of their goods, giving up a mistress, or preferring a mother to a sweetheart, but I have never read of a courtier speaking a good word for a minister in disgrace, against whom his sovereign was bitterly incensed. I award twenty thousand pieces of gold to each of those whose generous acts have been recounted; but I award the cup to Zadig."

"Sire," said he, "it is Your Majesty alone who deserves the cup, for having done a deed of unprecedented magnanimity, in that, being a king, you were not angry with your slave when he ran counter to your passion."

The king and Zadig were regarded with equal admiration. The judge who had given away his fortune, the lover who allowed his friend to marry his mistress, and the soldier who had preferred his mother's safety to that of his sweetheart, received at the monarchs' hands the presents he had assigned, and saw their names written in the Book of the Generous, but Zadig had the cup. The king gained the reputation of a good prince, which he did not keep long. The day was celebrated with feasts that lasted longer than the law directed, and its memory is still preserved in Asia. Zadig said:

"At last, then, I am happy." But he was deceived.

CHAPTER VI

The Minister

The king had lost his prime minister, and chose Zadig to fill his place. All the fair ladies in Babylon applauded the choice; for since the foundation of the empire there had never been known such a young minister. All the courtiers were offended; and the Envious Man spat blood on hearing the news, while his nose swelled to an enormous size. Zadig, having thanked the king and queen, proceeded to thank the parrot also.

"Beautiful bird," he said, "it is you who have saved my life, and made me prime minister: the bitch and the horse belonging to Their Majesties did me much harm, but you have done me good. On what slight threads do human destinies depend! But," added he, "a happiness so strangely acquired will, perhaps, soon pass by."

"Ay," replied the parrot.

Zadig was startled at the response; but, being a good naturalist, and not believing that parrots were prophets, he soon recovered himself.

Applying all his energies to the duties of his office, he made everybody feel the sacred power of the laws, but made no one feel the weight of his dignity. He did not interfere with the free expression of opinion in the divan, and each vizier was welcome to hold his own without displeasing him. When he acted as judge in any matter, it was not he who pronounced sentence, it was the law; but when the law was too harsh, he tempered its severity; and when there were no laws to meet the case, his sense of equity supplied him with decisions that might have been taken for those of Zoroaster.

It is from Zadig that the nations of the world have received the grand maxim: "It is better that a guilty man should be acquitted than that an innocent one should be condemned." He held that laws were made as much for the sake of helping as of intimidating the people. His chief skill lay in revealing the truth which all men try to darken. From the very beginning of his administration he put this great talent to good use. A famous merchant of Babylon had died in India, and made his two sons heirs to equal portions of his estate, after having given their sister in marriage; and he left a present of thirty thousand gold pieces to that one of his two sons who should be judged to have shown the greater love towards himself. The elder built him a tomb, the second increased his sister's dowry with a part of his own inheritance. Everybody said: "It is the elder son who has the greater love for his father, the younger loves his sister better; the thirty thousand pieces belong to the elder."

Zadig sent for the two brothers, one after the other. He said to the elder:

"Your father is not dead; he has been cured of his last illness, and is returning to Babylon."

"God be praised!" answered the young man, "but his tomb has cost me a large sum of money."

Zadig then said the same thing to the younger brother.

"God be praised!" answered he; "I will restore to my father all that I have, but I hope that he will leave my sister what I have given her."

"You shall restore nothing," said Zadig, "and you shall have the thirty thousand pieces; it is you who love your father best."

A very rich young lady had promised her hand to two magi, and, after having received a course of instruction for some months from each of them, found herself likely to become a mother. Both still wishing to marry her, she said she would take for her husband the one who had put her in a position to present the empire with a citizen.

"It is I who have done that good work," said one of them.

"It is I who have had that privilege," said the other.

"Well," answered she, "I will recognise that one as the father of the child who can give him the best education."

She was brought to bed of a son. Each of the two magi wished to bring it up, and the case was referred to Zadig, who summoned the magi to his presence.

"What will you teach your pupil?" he asked of the first.

"I will instruct him," said the learned professor, "in the eight parts of speech, in logic, astrology, demonology, the difference between substance and accident, abstract and concrete, the doctrine of the monads and the pre-established harmony."

"For my part," said the other, "I will endeavour to render him just and worthy of having friends."

Zadig exclaimed: "Whether you are his father or not, you shall marry his mother."

Day after day complaints reached court of the governor of Media, whose name was Irax. He was a high and mighty personage, not a bad fellow at bottom, but spoiled by vanity and self-indulgence. He seldom suffered anyone to speak to him, and never to contradict him. Peacocks are not more conceited than he was, nor doves more voluptuous, nor turtles more indolent; every breath he drew was devoted to vain glory and false pleasures. Zadig undertook to reform him.

He sent him, in the king's name, a skilful musician with a dozen singers and two dozen fiddlers, also a butler with half a dozen cooks and four chamberlains, who were never to leave him alone. By the king's orders the following ceremonies were strictly observed, and this is how matters were carried on.

The first day, as soon as the pleasure-loving Irax was awake, the musical conductor entered his chamber followed by the singers and fiddlers: a cantata was sung which lasted two hours, and every three minutes there was this refrain:

Whose merits e'er attain'd such height?
    Who with such grace was e'er endow'd?
Has not his Highness every right
    To feel self-satisfied and proud?

After this cantata was performed, one of the chamberlains made him a speech, three quarters of an hour long, in which he praised him expressly for all those good qualities in which he was most deficient. The oration finished, he was escorted to

33

the table to the sound of musical instruments. The dinner lasted three hours; whenever he opened his mouth to speak, the first chamberlain said: "Whatever he says will be right." Scarcely had he spoken four words, when the second chamberlain would exclaim: "He is right." The two other chamberlains burst into fits of laughter at all the witticisms which Irax uttered, or which they attributed to him. After dinner he was favoured with a repetition of the cantata.

This first day seemed to him delightful; he thought that the king of kings was honouring him according to his deserts. The second appeared a little less agreeable, the third palled upon him considerably, the fourth was intolerable, and the fifth absolute torture. At last, rather than hear the continual refrain:

Has not his Highness every right
To feel self-satisfied and proud?

rather than hear the perpetual assurance that whatever he said was right, rather than be harangued every day at the same hour, he wrote to the court entreating the king to be good enough to recall his chamberlains, his musicians, and his butler; and he promised to be less vain and more industrious in future. He was henceforth less tolerant of flattery, gave fewer entertainments, and was all the happier; for, as the Sadder has said:

"Continual pleasure is no pleasure."

CHAPTER VII

Settling Disputes and Giving Audience

Thus it was that Zadig daily showed the shrewdness of his intellect and the goodness of his heart. He was admired, yet he was also loved. He passed for the most fortunate of men; all the empire resounded with his name, all the women ogled him, and all the citizens extolled his justice; the men of science regarded him as their oracle, and even the priests confessed that he knew more than the old archimagian Yebor. Far from wishing to prosecute him for his opinions on the subject of griffins, they believed only what seemed credible to him.

Now there was a great controversy in Babylon, which had lasted fifteen hundred years, and had divided the empire into two bigoted sects; one maintained that the temple of Mithras should never be entered except with the left foot foremost; the other held this practice in abomination, and always entered with the right foot first. The rival sects waited impatiently for the day on which the solemn feast of the holy fire was to be held, to know which side would be favoured by Zadig. All had their eyes fixed on his two feet, and the whole city was in agitation and suspense. Zadig leaped into the temple with both his feet together, and afterwards proved in an eloquent discourse that the God of heaven and earth, who is no respecter of persons, cares no more for the left leg than for the right. The Envious Man and his wife contended that there were not enough figures of speech in his discourse, that he had not made the mountains and hills skip about freely enough.

"He is dry and wants imagination," they said; "one does not see the ocean fly before him, nor the stars fall, nor the sun melt like wax; he lacks the fine oriental style."

Zadig was content with having the style of a reasonable man. He was a favourite with all classes, not because he was in the right road, nor because he was reasonable, nor even because he was amiable, but because he was grand vizier.

He also happily put an end to the hot dispute between the white and the black magi. The white asserted that it was impious, when praying to God, to turn towards the east in winter; the black were confident that God abhorred the prayers of those who turned towards the west in summer. Zadig directed that men should turn to whatever quarter of the compass they pleased.

He likewise found out the secret of dispatching all his business, both public and private, in the morning, and he employed the rest of the day in providing Babylon with refined entertainments. He caused tragedies to be represented which moved the audience to tears, and comedies that made them laugh; a custom which had long passed out of fashion, and which he had the good taste to revive. He did not pretend to know more about their art than the actors themselves; he rewarded them with gifts and distinctions, and was not secretly jealous of their talents. In the evenings he diverted the king much, and the queen still more.

"A great minister!" said the king.

"A charming minister!" said the queen.

Both of them agreed that it would have been a thousand pities if Zadig had been hanged.

Never was statesman in office obliged to give so many audiences to the ladies. The greater number came to speak to him about no business in particular for the sake of having particular business with him. The wife of the Envious Man presented herself among the first; she swore by Mithras and the Zendavesta, and the holy fire, that she detested the conduct of her husband; then she told him in confidence that this husband of hers was jealous and treated her brutally, and gave him to understand that the gods punished him by refusing him the precious effects of that holy fire whereby alone man is made like the immortals. She ended by dropping her garter. Zadig picked it up with his customary politeness, but did not offer to fasten it again round the lady's knee, and this little fault, if it can be considered such, was the cause of the most dreadful misfortunes. Zadig thought no more about the incident, but the Envious Man's wife thought about it a great deal.

Other ladies continued to present themselves every day. The secret annals of Babylon assert that he yielded to temptation on one occasion, but that he was astonished to find that he enjoyed his mistress without pleasure, and that his mind was distracted even in the midst of the tenderest embraces. The fair one to whom he gave, almost unconsciously, these tokens of his favour was a lady in waiting to Queen Astarte. This amorous daughter of Babylon consoled herself for his coldness by saying to herself:

"That man must have a prodigious amount of business in his head, since his thoughts are absorbed with it even when he is making love."

Zadig happened at a moment when many people say nothing and others only utter terms of endearment, to suddenly exclaim: "The queen!" The fair Babylonian fancied that he had at last recovered his wits at a happy moment, and that he was addressing her as his queen. But Zadig, still absent-minded, proceeded to utter the name of Astarte. The lady, who in this agreeable situation interpreted everything in a flattering sense, imagined that he meant to say: "You are more beautiful than Queen Astarte." She left the seraglio of Zadig with magnificent presents, and went to relate her adventure to the Envious Woman, who was her intimate friend. The latter was cruelly piqued at the preference shown to the other.

"He did not even condescend," said she, "to replace this garter which I have here, and which I will never use again."

"Oh!" said her more fortunate friend, "you wear the same garters as the queen! Do you get them from the same maker?"

The Envious Woman fell into a brown study, and made no reply, but went and consulted her husband, the Envious Man.

Meanwhile Zadig became aware of his constant absence of mind whenever he gave an audience or administered justice; he did not know to what to attribute it; it was his only subject of annoyance.

He had a dream, in which he seemed to be lying at first on a heap of dry herbs, among which were some prickly ones which made him uncomfortable, and that afterwards he reposed luxuriously upon a bed of roses, out of which glided a snake that wounded him in the heart with its pointed and poisoned tongue.

"Alas!" said he, "I lay a long time on those dry and prickly herbs; I am now on the bed of roses; but who will be the serpent?"

CHAPTER VIII

Jealousy

Zadig's ill-luck arose out of his very happiness, and was mainly due to his merits. He had daily interviews with the king and with Astarte, his august consort. The charm of his conversation was doubled by that desire to please which is to the mind what ornaments are to personal beauty; his youth and graceful manners insensibly made an impression upon Astarte, of the strength of which she was not at first aware. Her passion grew up in the bosom of innocence. Astarte gave herself up without scruple and without fear to the pleasure of seeing and hearing a man who was so dear to her husband and to the State; she never ceased singing his praises to the king; she was perpetually speaking about him to her women, who even went beyond her in their commendations; everything served to fix more deeply in her heart the arrow of which she was unconscious. She bestowed presents upon Zadig, into which more love-making entered than she supposed; she meant to speak to him as a queen satisfied with his services, but the expressions she used were sometimes those of a woman of tender sensibility.

Astarte was much more beautiful than that Semira who had such a detestation of one-eyed men, or that other woman who had intended to cut off her husband's nose. Astarte's familiar manner, her soft speeches at which she began to blush, her eyes which, despite her efforts to turn them away, were ever fixed upon his own, kindled in Zadig's heart a fire which filled him with astonishment. He fought against his feelings; he called to his aid the philosophy which had never before failed him; he drew from it nothing but a clearer perception of his folly, and received no relief. Duty, gratitude, and outraged majesty presented themselves to his view as so many avenging deities; he struggled, and he triumphed; but this victory, which had to be repeated every moment, cost him groans and tears.

He no longer dared to address the queen with that delightful freedom which had had such charms for both of them; a cloud overshadowed his eyes; his conversation was constrained and abrupt; his eyes were downcast, and when, in spite of himself, they turned towards Astarte, they encountered those of the queen moistened with tears from which there shot forth arrows of flame. They seemed to say to each other:

"Our adoration is mutual, yet we are afraid to love; we are both consumed with a fire which we condemn."

When Zadig left her side it was with bewilderment and despair, his heart oppressed with a burden which he was no longer able to support: in the violence of his agitation he let his friend Cador penetrate his secret, like a man who, after having endured the most excruciating pains, at last makes his malady known by a cry which a keener spasm than any before wrings from him, and by the cold sweat which pours over his forehead.

Cador addressed him as follows:

"I have already divined the feelings that you would fain hide from yourself; the passions have symptoms which cannot be misinterpreted. Judge, my dear Zadig, since I have been able to read your heart, whether the king is not likely to discover there a sentiment that may give him serious offence. He has no other fault but that of being the most jealous of men. You resist your passion with more vigour than the queen can contend against hers, because you are a philosopher, and because you are Zadig. Astarte is a woman; she lets her looks speak for her with all the more imprudence that she does not yet believe herself blameworthy. Assured of her innocence, she unfortunately neglects appearances which it is necessary to observe. I shall tremble for her so long as she has nothing wherewith to reproach herself. If you came to a common understanding, you would be able to throw dust into all eyes; a growing passion, forcibly checked, gives evident tokens of its existence; but love when gratified can easily conceal itself."

Zadig shuddered at the suggestion of betraying the king, his benefactor; and he was never more faithful to his prince than when guilty of an involuntary crime against him. Meanwhile the queen pronounced the name of Zadig so often, she blushed so deeply as she uttered it, she was sometimes so animated, and at other times so confused when she addressed him in the king's presence, and she was seized with so profound a fit of abstraction whenever he went away, that the king began to be alarmed. He believed all that he saw, and imagined all that he did not see. He particularly remarked that his wife's slippers were blue, and that Zadig's slippers were blue; that his wife's ribbons were yellow, and that Zadig's cap was yellow. Terrible indications these to a prince of such delicate sensibility! Suspicion soon became certainty in his envenomed mind.

All the slaves of kings and queens are so many spies over their hearts. It was soon discovered that Astarte was tender and that Moabdar was jealous. The Envious Man got his wife to send the king her garter, which was like the queen's; and, to make the matter worse, this garter was blue. The monarch thought of nothing now but how to take his revenge. One night he determined to poison the queen, and to have Zadig strangled as soon as it was light. The order was given to a merciless eunuch, the usual executioner of his vengeance. Now there happened to be at the time in the king's chamber a little dwarf, who was dumb but not deaf. He was allowed to wander about when and where he pleased, and, like a domestic animal, was oftentimes a witness of what passed in the strictest privacy. This little mute was much attached to the queen and Zadig, and he heard with no less surprise than horror the order given for their death. But what could he do to prevent this frightful order, which was to be carried out within a few hours? He did not know how to write, but he had learned how to paint, and was particularly skilful in taking likenesses. He spent part of the night in portraying what he wished the queen to understand. His sketch represented in one corner of the picture the king in a furious rage, giving orders to his eunuch; a blue bowstring and a cup on a table, with garters and yellow ribbons; the queen in the middle of the picture, expiring in the arms of her women, and Zadig lying strangled at her feet. A rising sun was represented on the horizon to indicate that this horrible execution was to take place at the earliest glimpse of dawn. As soon as this task was finished he ran to one of Astarte's women, awoke her, and made her understand that she must take the picture that very instant to the queen.

In the middle of the night someone knocked at Zadig's door; he was roused from sleep, and a note from the queen was given him; he doubted whether or not it were a dream, and opened the letter with a trembling hand. What was his surprise, and who could express the consternation and despair with which he was overwhelmed, when he read these words: "Fly, this very moment, or you will be seized and put to death! Fly, Zadig; I command you in the name of our love and of my yellow ribbons. I have done nothing wrong, but I foresee that I am going to die like a criminal."

Zadig, who had scarcely strength enough to speak, sent for Cador, and then, without a word, gave him the letter. Cador forced him to obey its injunction, and to set out immediately for Memphis.

"If you venture to go in search of the queen," said he, "you will only hasten her death; if you speak to the king, that step again will lead to her destruction. Her fate shall be my care; do you follow your own. I will spread the report that you have taken the road to India. I will soon come and find you out, when I will tell you all that shall have passed at Babylon."

Cador, without a moment's delay, had two of the swiftest dromedaries brought to a private postern of the palace, and made Zadig mount one of them; he had to be carried, for he was almost ready to expire. Only one servant accompanied him; and soon Cador, plunged in astonishment and grief, lost sight of his friend.

The illustrious fugitive, when he arrived at the brow of a hill which commanded a view of Babylon, turned his gaze towards the queen's palace, and fainted. He recovered his senses only to shed tears and to wish that he was dead. At last, after having occupied his thoughts awhile with the deplorable fate of the most amiable of women and the best of queens, he returned for a moment to himself, and exclaimed:

"What, then, is human life? O virtue! of what use hast thou been to me? Two women have basely deceived me, and the third, who is innocent and is more beautiful than the others, is about to die! All the good that I have done has always brought upon me a curse, and I have been raised to the height of grandeur only to fall down the most horrible precipice of misfortune. If I had been wicked, like so many others, I should be happy like them."

Overwhelmed with these gloomy reflections, his eyes shrouded with a veil of sorrow, the paleness of death on his countenance, and his soul sunk in the depths of a dark despair, he continued his journey towards Egypt.

CHAPTER IX

The Beaten Woman

Zadig directed his course by the stars. The constellation of Orion and the bright star of Sirius guided him towards the harbour of Canopus. He marvelled at those vast globes of light, which appear only like feeble sparks to our eyes, while the earth, which is in reality nothing more than an imperceptible point in nature, appears to our covetous eyes something grand and noble. He then pictured to himself men as they really are, insects devouring one another on a little atom of clay. This true image seemed to annihilate his misfortunes, by making him realize the insignificance of his own existence and that of Babylon itself. His soul launched forth into the infinitude of space, detached from the operation of the senses, and contemplated the unchangeable order of the universe. But when, afterwards returning to himself and once more looking into his own heart, he thought how Astarte was perhaps already dead for his sake, the universe vanished from his eyes, and he saw nothing in all nature save Astarte dying and Zadig miserable. As he gave himself up to this alternate flow of sublime philosophy and overwhelming grief, he approached the confines of Egypt; and his faithful servant was already in the first village, looking out for a lodging. Zadig was, meanwhile, walking towards the gardens which skirted the village, and saw, not far from the high road, a woman in great distress, who was calling out to heaven and earth for succour, and a man who was following her in a furious rage. He had already reached her before Zadig could do so, and the woman was clasping his knees, while the man overwhelmed her with blows and reproaches. He judged from the Egyptian's violence, and from the repeated prayers for forgiveness which the lady uttered, that he was jealous and she unfaithful; but after he had closely regarded the woman, who was of enchanting beauty, and who, moreover, bore a little resemblance to the unhappy Astarte, he felt moved with compassion towards her, and with horror towards the Egyptian.

"Help me!" she cried to Zadig in a voice choked with sobs; "deliver me out of the hands of this most barbarous man, and save my life!"

Hearing these cries, Zadig ran and threw himself between her and the barbarian; and having some knowledge of the Egyptian tongue, he addressed him in that language, and said:

"If you have any humanity, I entreat you to respect beauty and weakness. How can you ill-treat so cruelly such a masterpiece of nature as lies there at your feet, with no protection but her tears?"

"Ah, ha!" answered the man, more enraged than ever; "then you are another of her lovers! and on you too I must take revenge."

Saying these words, he left the lady, whom he had been holding by the hair with one hand, and, seizing his lance, made an attempt to run the stranger through with it. But he, being cool and composed, easily avoided the thrust of one who was beside himself with rage, and caught hold of the lance near the iron point with which it was armed. The one tried to draw it back, while the other tried to wrench it out of his hand, so that it was broken between the two. The Egyptian drew his sword, Zadig did the same, and they forthwith attacked each other; the former dealing a hundred blows in quick succession, the latter skilfully warding them off. The lady, seated on a piece of turf, readjusted her head-dress, and looked calmly on. The Egyptian was stronger than his antagonist, Zadig was the more dexterous. The latter fought like a man whose arm was guided by his head, the former like a madman who in blind frenzy delivered random strokes. Zadig, attacking him in his turn, disarmed his adversary; and whilst the Egyptian, rendered still more furious, tried to throw himself upon him, the other seized him with a tight grip, and threw him on the ground; then, holding his sword to his breast, he offered to give him his life. The Egyptian, transported with rage, drew his dagger, and therewith wounded Zadig, at the very instant that the conqueror was granting him pardon. Provoked beyond endurance, Zadig plunged his sword into the other's heart. The Egyptian uttered a horrible yell, and died struggling violently. Then Zadig advanced towards the lady, and said in a respectful tone:

"He forced me to kill him; you I have avenged, and delivered out of the hands of the most outrageous man I ever saw. What will you have me do for you now, madam?"

"To die, scoundrel," she replied; "to die! You have killed my lover; I would that I were able to tear out your heart."

"Truly, madam, you had a strange sort of lover in him," returned Zadig; "he was beating you with all his might, and he wanted to have my life because you implored me to help you."

"I wish he was beating me still," answered the lady, giving vent to loud lamentation; "I well deserved it, and gave him good cause for jealousy. Would to heaven that he were beating me and that you were in his place!"

Zadig, more surprised and indignant than he had ever been before in his life, said to her:

"Madam, beautiful as you are, you deserve to have me beat you in my turn for your unreasonable behaviour, but I shall not take the trouble."

So saying, he remounted his camel, and advanced towards the village. He had hardly proceeded a few steps when he turned back at the clatter of four messengers riding post haste from Babylon. One of them, seeing the woman, exclaimed:

"That is the very person! She resembles the description that was given us."

They did not encumber themselves with the dead body, but forthwith caught hold of the lady, who never ceased calling out to Zadig:

"Help me once more, generous stranger! I beg your pardon for having reproached you: help me, and I will be yours till death."

Zadig no longer felt any desire to fight on her behalf.

"Apply to someone else," he answered, "you will not entrap me again."

Moreover he was wounded and bleeding; he had need of help himself; and the sight of the four Babylonians, probably sent by King Moabdar, filled him with uneasiness. So he hastened towards the village, unable to imagine why four messengers from Babylon should come to take this Egyptian woman, but still more astonished at the conduct of the lady.

CHAPTER X

Slavery

As he entered the Egyptian village, he found himself surrounded by the people. Everyone was crying out:

"This is the fellow who carried off the lovely Missouf, and who has just murdered Cletofis!"

"Gentlemen," said he, "may Heaven preserve me from carrying off your lovely Missouf! she is too capricious for me; and with regard to Cletofis, I have not murdered him, I only fought against him in self-defence. He wanted to kill me because I had asked him most humbly to pardon the lovely Missouf, whom he was beating unmercifully. I am a stranger come to seek a refuge in Egypt; and it is not likely that, in coming to claim your protection, I should begin by carrying off a woman and murdering a man."

The Egyptians were at that time just and humane. The people conducted Zadig to the court-house. They began by getting his wound dressed, and then they questioned him and his servant separately, in order to learn the truth. They came to the conclusion that Zadig was not a murderer; but he was found guilty of homicide, and the law condemned him to be a slave. His two camels were sold for the benefit of the village; all the gold that he carried was distributed among the inhabitants; his person was exposed for sale in the market-place, as well as that of his fellow-traveller. An Arab merchant, named Setoc, made the highest bid for him; but the serving-man, as more fit for hard work, was sold at a much higher price than the master. There was no comparison, it was thought, between the two men; so Zadig became a slave of inferior position to his own servant. They were fastened together with a chain, which was passed round their ankles, and in that state they followed the Arab merchant to his house. Zadig, on the way, tried to console his servant, and exhorted him to be patient; and, according to his custom, he made some general reflections on human life.

"I see," he said, "that my unhappy fate has spread its shadow over yours. Hitherto at every turn I have met with strange reverses. I have been condemned to pay a fine for having seen traces of a passing bitch; I thought I was going to be impaled on account of a griffin; I have been sent to execution because I made some complimentary verses on the king; I was on the point of being strangled because the queen had yellow ribbons; and here am I a slave along with you, because a brute of a man chose to beat his mistress. Come, let us not lose courage; all this perhaps will come to an end. It must needs be that Arab merchants should have slaves; and why should not I be one as well as another, since I also am a man? This merchant will not be unmerciful; he must treat his slaves well, if he wishes to make good use of them."

Thus he spoke, but in the depths of his heart he was thinking only of the fate of the queen of Babylon.

Setoc the merchant started, two days afterwards, for Arabia Deserta, with his slaves and his camels. His tribe dwelt near the desert of Horeb, the way to which was long and painful. Setoc, on the journey, took greater care of the servant than of the master, because the former could load the camels much better; and any little distinction that was made between them was in his favour.

A camel died two days before they expected to reach Horeb, and its load was distributed among the men, so that each back had its burden, Zadig's among the rest. Setoc laughed to see how all his slaves were bent almost double as they walked. Zadig took the liberty of explaining to him the reason, and gave him some instruction in the laws of equilibrium. The astonished merchant began to regard him with other eyes. Zadig seeing that he had excited his master's curiosity, increased it by teaching him many things that had a direct bearing on his business, such as the specific gravity of metals and commodities in equal bulk, the properties of several useful animals, and the way in which those might be rendered useful which were not naturally so, until Setoc thought him a sage. He now gave Zadig the preference over his comrade, whom he had before esteemed so highly. He treated him well, and had no reason to repent of it.

Having reached his tribe, the first thing Setoc did was to demand repayment of five hundred ounces of silver from a Jew to whom he had lent them in the presence of two witnesses; but these two witnesses were dead, and the Jew, assured that there was no proof of the debt, appropriated the merchant's money, and thanked God for having given him the opportunity of cheating an Arab. Setoc confided his trouble to Zadig, who was now his adviser in everything.

"In what place was it," asked Zadig, "that you lent these five hundred ounces to the infidel?"

"On a large stone near Mount Horeb," answered the merchant.

"What kind of man is your debtor?" said Zadig.

"A regular rogue," returned Setoc.

"But I mean, is he hasty or deliberate, cautious or imprudent?"

"Of all bad payers," said Setoc, "he is the hastiest man I ever knew."

"Well," pursued Zadig, "allow me to plead your cause before the judge."

In the end he summoned the Jew to take his trial, and thus addressed the judge:

"Pillar of the throne of equity, I come here to claim from this man, in my master's name, repayment of five hundred ounces of silver which he will not restore."

"Have you witnesses?" asked the judge.

"No, they are dead; but there still remains a large stone upon which the money was counted out; and, if it please your lordship to order someone to go and fetch the stone, I hope that it will bear witness to the truth. We will remain here, the Jew and I, until the stone arrives; I will send for it at my master Setoc's expense."

"I am quite willing that that should be done," answered the judge; and then he proceeded to dispatch other business.

At the end of the sitting he said to Zadig:

"Well, your stone is not arrived yet, is it?"

The Jew laughed, and answered:

"Your lordship would have to remain here till tomorrow before the stone could be brought; it is more than six miles away, and it would take fifteen men to move it."

"Now then," exclaimed Zadig, "did I not say well that the stone itself would bear witness? Since this man knows where it is, he acknowledges that upon it the money was counted." The Jew was abashed, and was soon obliged to confess the whole truth. The judge ordered him to be bound to the stone, without eating or drinking, until the five hundred ounces should be restored, and it was not long before they were paid.

After that Zadig the slave was held in high esteem throughout Arabia, and so was the stone.

CHAPTER XI

The Funeral Pile

Setoc was so enchanted with his slave that he made him his intimate friend. He could no more dispense with him than the king of Babylon had done; and Zadig was glad that Setoc had no wife. He found in his master an excellent disposition, with much integrity and good sense; but he was sorry to see that he worshipped the host of heaven (that is to say, the sun, moon, and stars), according to the ancient custom of Arabia. He spoke to him sometimes on the subject with judicious caution. At last he told him that they were material bodies like other things, which were no more worthy of his adoration than a tree or a rock.

"But," said Setoc, "they are immortal beings, from whom we derive all the benefits we enjoy; they animate nature, and regulate the seasons; besides, they are so far from us that one cannot help worshipping them."

"You receive more advantages," answered Zadig, "from the waters of the Red Sea, which bear your merchandise to India. Why may it not be as ancient as the stars? And if you adore what is far away from you, you ought to adore the land of the Gangarides, which lies at the very end of the world."

"No," said Setoc; "the stars are so bright that I cannot refrain from worshipping them."

When the evening was come, Zadig lighted a great number of candles in the tent where he was to sup with Setoc; and, as soon as his patron appeared, he threw himself on his knees before those wax lights, saying:

"Eternal and brilliant luminaries, be ever propitious to me!"

Having offered this prayer, he sat down to table without paying any attention to Setoc.

"What is that you are doing?" asked Setoc in astonishment.

"I am doing what you do," answered Zadig; "I adore these candles, and neglect their master and mine."

Setoc understood the profound meaning of this parable. The wisdom of his slave entered into his soul; he no longer lavished his incense upon created things, but worshipped the Eternal Being who had made them.

There prevailed at that time in Arabia a frightful custom, which came originally from Scythia, and which, having established itself in India through the influence of the Brahmans, threatened to invade all the East. When a married man died, and his favourite wife wished to obtain a reputation for sanctity, she used to burn herself in public on her husband's corpse. A solemn festival was held on such occasions, called *the Funeral Pile of Widowhood*, and that tribe in which there had been the greatest number of women consumed in this way was held in the highest honour. An Arab of Setoc's tribe having died, his widow, named Almona, who was very devout, made known the day and hour when she would cast herself into the fire to the sound of drums and trumpets. Zadig showed Setoc how contrary this horrible custom was to the interests of the human race, for young widows were every day allowed to burn themselves who might have presented children to the State, or at least have brought up those they already had; and he made him agree that so barbarous an institution ought, if possible, to be abolished.

Setoc replied: "It is more than a thousand years since the women acquired the right of burning themselves. Which of us will dare to change a law which time has consecrated? Is there anything more venerable than an ancient abuse?"

"Reason is more ancient," rejoined Zadig. "Do you speak to the chiefs of the tribes, and I will go and find the young widow."

He obtained admission to her presence; and after having insinuated himself into her good graces by commending her beauty, and after having said what a pity it was to commit such charms to the flames, he praised her again on the score of her constancy and courage.

"You must have loved your husband wonderfully?" said he.

53

"I? Oh no, not at all," answered the Arab lady. "I could not bear him, he was so brutal and jealous; but I am firmly resolved to throw myself on his funeral pile."

"Apparently," said Zadig, "there must be some very delicious pleasure in being burned alive."

"Ah! it makes nature shudder to think of it," said the lady; "but I must e'en put up with it. I am a pious person, and I should lose my reputation and be mocked by everybody if I did not burn myself."

Zadig, having brought her to admit that she was burning herself for the sake of other people and out of vanity, spoke to her for a long time in a manner calculated to make her a little in love with life, and even managed to inspire her with some kindly feeling towards himself.

"What would you do now," said he, "if you were not moved by vanity to burn yourself?"

"Alas!" said the lady, "I think that I should ask you to marry me."

Zadig was too much engrossed with thoughts of Astarte to take any notice of this declaration; but he instantly went to the chiefs of the different tribes, told them what had passed, and advised them to make a law by which no widow should be allowed to burn herself until after she had had a private interview with a young man for the space of a whole hour. Since that time no lady has burned herself in Arabia. To Zadig alone was the credit due for having abolished in one day so cruel a custom, and one that had lasted so many ages. Thus he became the benefactor of all Arabia.

CHAPTER XII

The Supper

Setoc, who could not part from the man in whom wisdom dwelt, brought him to the great fair of Bassora, whither the wealthiest merchants of the habitable globe were wont to resort. It was no little consolation to Zadig to see so many men of different countries assembled in the same place. It seemed to him that the universe was one large family which gathered together at Bassora. The second day after their arrival Zadig found himself at table with an Egyptian, an Indian from the banks of the Ganges, an inhabitant of China, a Greek, a Celt, and several other foreigners, who, in their frequent voyages to the Persian Gulf, had learned enough Arabic to make themselves understood. The Egyptian appeared exceedingly angry. "What an abominable country Bassora is!" said he; "I cannot get a loan here of a thousand ounces of gold on the best security in the world."

"How is that?" said Setoc; "on what security was that sum refused you?"

"On the body of my aunt," answered the Egyptian; "she was the worthiest woman in Egypt. She always accompanied me on my journeys, and died on the way hither. I have turned her into one of the finest mummies to be had; and in my own country I could get whatever I wanted by giving her in pledge. It is very strange that no one here will lend me even a thousand ounces of gold on such sound security."

In spite of his indignation, he was just on the point of devouring a capital boiled fowl, when the Indian, taking him by the hand, exclaimed in a doleful voice, "Ah! what are you about to do?"

"To eat this fowl," said the man with the mummy.

"Beware of what you are doing," said the man from the Ganges; "it may be that the soul of the departed has passed into the body of that fowl, and you would not wish to run the risk of eating up your aunt. To cook fowls is plainly an outrage upon nature."

"What do you mean with your nonsense about nature and fowls?" returned the wrathful Egyptian. "We worship an ox, and yet eat beef for all that."

"You worship an ox! Is it possible?" said the man from the Ganges.

"There is nothing more certain," replied the other; "we have done so for a hundred and thirty-five thousand years, and no one among us has any fault to find with it."

"Ah! A hundred and thirty-five thousand years!" said the Indian. "There must be a little exaggeration there; India has only been inhabited eighty thousand years, and we are undoubtedly more ancient than you are; and Brahma had forbidden us to eat oxen before you ever thought of putting them on your altars and on your spits."

"An odd kind of animal, this Brahma of yours, to be compared with Apis!" said the Egyptian. "What fine things now has your Brahma ever done?"

"It was he," the Brahman answered, "who taught men to read and write, and to whom all the world owes the game of chess."

"You are wrong," said a Chaldean who was sitting near him; "it is to the fish Oannes that we owe such great benefits; and it is right to render our homage to him alone. Anybody will tell you that he was a divine being, that he had a golden tail and a handsome human head, and that he used to leave the water to come and preach on land for three hours every day. He had sundry children who were all kings, as everyone knows. I have his likeness at home, to which I pay all due reverence. We may eat as much beef as we please; but there is no doubt that it is a very great sin to cook fish. Moreover, you are, both of you, of too mean and too modern an origin to argue with me about anything. The Egyptian nation counts only one hundred and thirty-five thousand years, and the Indians can boast of no more than eighty thousand, while we have almanacs that go back four thousand centuries. Believe me, renounce your follies, and I will give each of you a beautiful likeness of Oannes."

The Chinaman here put in his word, and said:

"I have a strong respect for the Egyptians, the Chaldeans, the Greeks, the Celts, Brahma, the ox Apis, and the fine fish Oannes, but it may be that Li or Tien,[1] by whichever name one may choose to call him, is well worth any number of oxen and fishes. I will say nothing about my country; it is as large as the land of Egypt, Chaldea, and India all put together. I will enter into no dispute touching antiquity, because it is enough to be happy, and it is a very little matter to be ancient; but if there were any need to speak about almanacs, I could tell you that all Asia consults ours, and that we had very good ones before anything at all was known of arithmetic in Chaldea."

"You are a set of ignoramuses, all of you!" cried the Greek; "is it possible that you do not know that Chaos is the father of all things, and that form and matter have brought the world into the state in which it is?"

This Greek spoke for a long time; but he was at last interrupted by the Celt, who, having drunk deeply whilst the others were disputing, now thought himself wiser than any of them, and affirmed with an oath that there was nothing worth the trouble of talking about except Teutates and the mistletoe that grows on an oak; that, as for himself, he always had some mistletoe in his pocket; that the Scythians, his forefathers, were the only honest people that had ever been in the world; that they had indeed sometimes eaten men, but that no one ought to be prevented by that from having a profound respect for his nation; and finally, that if anyone spoke evil of Teutates, he would teach him how to behave.

Thereupon the quarrel waxed hot, and Setoc saw that in another moment there would be bloodshed at the table, when Zadig, who had kept silence during the whole dispute, at last rose. He addressed himself first to the Celt as the most violent

1 Chinese words signifying respectively *reason* and *heaven*.

of them all; he told him that he was in the right, and asked him for a piece of mistletoe; he commended the Greek for his eloquence, and soothed the general irritation. He said very little to the Chinaman, because he had been the most reasonable of them all. Then he said to the whole party:

"My friends, you were going to quarrel for nothing, for you are all of the same opinion."

When they heard him say that, they all loudly protested.

"Is it not true," he said to the Celt, "that you do not worship this mistletoe, but Him who made the mistletoe and the oak?"

"Assuredly," answered the Celt.

"And you, my Egyptian friend, revere, as it would seem, in a certain ox Him who has given you oxen, is it not so?"

"Yes," said the Egyptian.

"The fish Oannes," continued Zadig, "must give place to Him who made the sea and the fishes."

"Granted," said the Chaldean.

"The Indian," added Zadig, "and the Chinaman recognise, like you, a first principle; I did not understand very well the admirable remarks made by the Greek, but I am sure that he also admits the existence of a Supreme Being, upon whom form and matter depend."

The Greek who was so much admired said that Zadig had seized his meaning very well.

"You are all then of the same opinion," replied Zadig, "and there is nothing left to quarrel over;" at which all the company embraced him.

Setoc, after having sold his merchandise at a high price, brought his friend Zadig back with him to his tribe. On their arrival Zadig learned that he had been tried in his absence, and that he was going to be burned at a slow fire.

CHAPTER XIII

The Assignation

During his journey to Bassora, the priests of the stars had determined to punish Zadig. The precious stones and ornaments of the young widows whom they sent to the funeral pile were their acknowledged perquisite; it was in truth the least they could do to burn Zadig for the ill turn he had done them. Accordingly they accused him of holding erroneous views about the host of heaven; they gave testimony against him on oath that they had heard him say that the stars did not set in the sea. This frightful blasphemy made the judges shudder; they were ready to rend their garments when they heard those impious words, and they would have done so, without a doubt, if Zadig had had the means wherewith to pay them compensation; but dreadfully shocked as they were, they contented themselves with condemning him to be burned at a slow fire.

Setoc, in despair, exerted his influence in vain to save his friend; he was soon obliged to hold his peace. The young widow Almona, who had acquired a strong appetite for life, thanks to Zadig, resolved to rescue him from the stake, the misuse of which he had taught her to recognise. She turned her scheme over and over in her head, without speaking of it to anyone. Zadig was to be executed the next day, she had only that night to save him in. This is how she set about the business, like a charitable and discreet woman. She anointed herself with perfumes; she enhanced her charms by the richest and most seductive attire, and went to ask the chief priest of the stars for a private audience. When she was ushered into the presence of that venerable old man, she addressed him in these terms:

"Eldest son of the Great Bear, brother of the Bull, and cousin of the Great Dog" (such were the pontiff's titles), "I come to confide to you my scruples. I greatly fear that I have committed an enormous sin in not burning myself on my dear husband's funeral pyre. In truth, what had I worth preserving? A body liable to decay, and which is already quite withered." Saying these words, she drew up her long silk sleeves, and displayed her bare arms, of admirable form and dazzling whiteness. "You see," said she, "how little it is worth."

The pontiff thought in his heart that it was worth a great deal. His eyes said so, and his mouth confirmed it; he swore that he had never in his life seen such beautiful arms.

"Alas!" said the widow, "my arms may be a little less deformed than the rest; but you will admit that my neck was unworthy of any consideration," and she let him see the most charming bosom that nature had ever formed. A rosebud on an apple of ivory would have appeared beside it nothing better than madder upon box-wood, and lambs just come up from the washing would have seemed brown and sallow. This neck; her large black eyes, in which a tender fire glowed softly with languishing lustre; her cheeks, enlivened with the loveliest crimson mingled with the whiteness of the purest milk; her nose, which was not at all like the tower of Mount Lebanon; her lips, which were like two settings of coral enclosing the most beautiful pearls in the Arabian sea; all these charms conspired to make the old man fancy himself a youth of twenty summers. With stammering tongue he made a tender declaration; and Almona, seeing how he was smitten, craved pardon for Zadig.

"Alas!" said he, "my lovely lady, though I might grant you his pardon, my indulgence would be of no use, as the order would have to be signed by three others of my colleagues."

"Sign it all the same," said Almona.

"Willingly," said the priest, "on condition that your favours shall be the price of my compliance."

"You do me too much honour," said Almona; "only be pleased to come to my chamber after sunset, when the bright star *Sheat* shall rise above the horizon; you will find me on a rose-coloured sofa, and you shall deal with your servant as you may be able."

Then she went away, carrying with her the signature, and left the old man full of amorous passion and of diffidence as to his powers. He employed the rest of the day in bathing; he drank a liquid compounded of the cinnamon of Ceylon, and the precious spices of Tidor and Ternat, and waited with impatience for the star *Sheat* to appear.

Meanwhile the fair Almona went in search of the second pontiff, who assured her that the sun, the moon, and all the lights of heaven were nothing but faint marsh fires in comparison with her charms. She asked of him the same favour, and he offered to grant it on the same terms. She allowed her scruples to be overcome, and made an appointment with the second pontiff for the rising of the star *Algenib*. Thence she proceeded to the houses of the third and fourth priests, getting from each his signature, and making one star after another the signal for a secret assignation. Then she sent letters to the judges, requesting them to come and see her on a matter of importance. When they appeared, she showed them the four names, and told them at what price the priests had sold Zadig's pardon. Each of the latter arrived at his appointed hour, and was greatly astonished to find his colleagues there, and still more at seeing the judges, before whom they were exposed to open shame. Thus Zadig was saved, and Setoc was so delighted with Almona's cleverness, that he made her his wife.

CHAPTER XIV

The Dance

Setoc was engaged to go on matters of business to the island of Serendib; but the first month of marriage, which is, as everyone knows, the moon of honey, permitted him neither to quit his wife, nor even to imagine that he could ever quit her; so he requested his friend Zadig to make the voyage on his behalf.

"Alas!" said Zadig, "must I put a yet wider distance between the beautiful Astarte and myself? But I must oblige my benefactors." He spoke, he wept, and he set forth on his journey.

He was not long in the island of Serendib before he began to be regarded as an extraordinary man. He became umpire in all disputes between the merchants, the friend of the wise, and the trusted counsellor of that small number of persons who are willing to take advice. The king wished to see and hear him. He soon recognised all Zadig's worth, placed reliance on his wisdom, and made him his friend. The king's intimacy and esteem made Zadig tremble. Night and day he was pierced with anguish at the misfortune which Moabdar's kindness had brought upon him.

"The king is pleased with me," said he; "how shall I escape ruin?"

He could not however decline his majesty's attentions; for it must be confessed that Nabussan, King of Serendib, the son of Nussanab, the son of Nabassan, the son of Sanbusna, was one of the best princes in Asia; when anyone spoke to him, it was difficult not to love him.

This good monarch was continually praised, deceived, and robbed; officials vied with each other in plundering his treasury. The receiver-general of the island of Serendib always set the example, and was faithfully followed by the others. The king knew it, and had time after time changed his treasurer; but he had not been able to change the time-honoured fashion of dividing the royal revenue into two unequal parts, the smaller of which always fell to His Majesty, and the larger to the administrative staff.

King Nabussan confided his difficulty to the wise Zadig: "You who know so many fine things," said he, "can you think of no method of enabling me to find a treasurer who will not rob me?"

"Assuredly," answered Zadig; "I know an infallible way of giving you a man who has clean hands."

The king was charmed, and, embracing him, asked how he was to proceed.

"All you will have to do," said Zadig, "is to cause all who shall present themselves for the dignity of treasurer to dance, and he who dances most lightly will be infallibly the most honest man."

"You are joking," said the king; "truly a droll way of choosing a receiver of my revenues! What! Do you mean to say that the one who cuts the highest capers will prove the most honest and capable financier?"

"I will not answer for his capability," returned Zadig; "but I assure you that he will undoubtedly be the most honest."

Zadig spoke with so much confidence that the king thought he had some supernatural secret for recognising financiers.

"I am not fond of the supernatural," said Zadig; "people and books that deal in prodigies have always been distasteful to me; if Your Majesty will allow me to make the trial I propose, you will be well enough convinced that my secret is the easiest and most simple thing in the world."

Nabussan, King of Serendib, was far more astonished at hearing that this secret was a simple matter, than if it had been presented to him as a miracle.

"Well then," said the king, "do as you shall think proper."

"Give me a free hand," said Zadig, "and you will gain by this experiment more than you think."

The same day he issued a public notice that all who aspired to the post of receiver-in-chief of the revenues of His gracious

Majesty Nabussan, son of Nussanab, were to present themselves in garments of light silk, on the first day of the month of the Crocodile, in the king's ante-chamber. They duly put in an appearance to the number of sixty-four. Fiddlers were posted in an adjoining hall; all was ready for dancing; but the door of the hall was fastened, and it was necessary, in order to enter it, to pass along a little gallery which was pretty dark. An usher was sent to conduct each candidate, one after another, along this passage, in which he was left alone for a few minutes. The king, prompted by Zadig, had spread out all his treasures in this gallery. When all the competitors had reached the hall, his majesty gave orders that they should begin to dance. Never did men dance more heavily and with less grace; they all kept their heads down, their backs bent, and their hands glued to their sides.

"What rogues!" said Zadig, under his breath.

There was only one among them who stepped out freely, with head erect, a steady eye, and outstretched arms, body straight, and legs firm.

"Ah! the honest fellow! the worthy man!" said Zadig.

The king embraced this good dancer, and declared him treasurer; whereas all the others were punished with a fine, and that most justly, for each one of them, during the time that he was in the gallery, had filled his pockets so that he could hardly walk. The king was grieved for the honour of human nature that out of those sixty-four dancers there should have been sixty-three thieves. The dark gallery was henceforth called *the Corridor of Temptation*. In Persia those sixty-three gentlemen would have been impaled; in other countries a court of justice would have been held which would have consumed in legal expenses three times as much as had been stolen; while in yet another kingdom they would have procured a complete acquittal for themselves, and brought the nimble dancer to disgrace; at Serendib they were only condemned to increase the public funds, for Nabussan was very indulgent.

He was also very grateful; he gave to Zadig a sum of money greater than any treasurer had stolen from the king his master. Zadig availed himself of it to send expresses to Babylon, who were to bring him information of Astarte's fate. His voice trembled while giving this order, his blood flowed back towards his heart, a mist covered his eyes, and his soul was ready to take its flight. The messenger departed: Zadig saw him embark. He returned to the king, seeing no one, fancying himself in his own chamber, and pronouncing the name of "love."

"Ah! love," said the king; "that is precisely what is the matter with me; you have rightly divined where my trouble lies. What a great man you are! I hope you will teach me how to recognise a faithful and devoted wife, as you have enabled me to find a disinterested treasurer."

Zadig, having recovered his wits, promised to serve him in love as well as in finance, although the undertaking seemed still more difficult.

CHAPTER XV

Blue Eyes

"My body and my heart—" said the king to Zadig. At these words the Babylonian could not refrain from interrupting His Majesty.

"How glad I am," said he, "that you did not say *my heart and soul*! For one hears nothing else but those words in every conversation at Babylon, and one sees nothing but books devoted to discussions on the heart and soul, written by people who have neither one nor the other. But please, sire, proceed."

Nabussan then continued:

"My body and my heart are predisposed by destiny to love; the former of these two powers has every reason to be satisfied. I have here a hundred women at my disposal, all beautiful, buxom, and obliging, even voluptuously inclined, or pretending to be so when with me. My heart is not nearly so well off. I have found only too often that they lavish all their caresses on the King of Serendib, and care very little for Nabussan. It is not that I think my women unfaithful; but I would fain find a soul to be my own; I would resign for such a treasure the hundred beauties of whose charms I am master. See if, out of these hundred ladies of my harem, you can find me a single one by whom I may feel sure I am loved?"

Zadig answered him as he had done on the subject of the financiers:—

"Sire, leave the matter to me; but allow me first to dispose of what you displayed in the Corridor of Temptation; I will render you a good account of all, and you shall lose nothing by it."

The king gave him unfettered discretion. He chose in Serendib thirty-three little hunchbacks, the ugliest he could find, thirty-three of the most handsome pages, and thirty-three of the most eloquent and most robust bonzes. He left them all at liberty to enter the ladies' private chambers. Each little hunchback had four thousand gold pieces to give them, and the very first day all the hunchbacks were happy. The pages, who had nothing to give away but themselves, failed to achieve a triumph till the end of two or three days. The bonzes had a little more difficulty; but at last thirty-three fair devotees surrendered to them. The king, through the shutter-blinds which admitted a view into each chamber, witnessed all these experiments, and was not a little astonished. Of his hundred women, ninety-nine had succumbed before his eyes. There yet remained one who was quite young and freshly imported, whom His Majesty had never admitted to his arms. One, two, three hunchbacks were successively told off to make her offers which rose to the sum of twenty thousand pieces; she was incorruptible, and could not help laughing at the idea which had entered into these hunchbacks' heads that money could render them less deformed. The two handsomest of the pages were presented to her; she said that she thought the king still more handsome. The most eloquent and afterwards the most intrepid of the bonzes were let loose upon her; she found the first an idle babbler, and would not deign even to form an opinion on the merits of the second.

"The heart is everything," said she; "I will never yield either to the gold of a hunchback, or the personal attractions of a young man, or the cunning enticements of a bonze. I will love no one but Nabussan, son of Nussanab, and will wait till he condescends to love me."

The king was transported with joy, astonishment, and tenderness. He took back all the money that had won the hunchbacks their success, and made a present of it to the fair Falide (for such was the young lady's name). He gave her his heart, and she well deserved it. Never was the flower of youth so brilliant, never were the charms of beauty so enchanting. Historical veracity will not allow me to conceal the fact that she curtsied awkwardly, but she danced like a fairy, sang like a siren, and spoke like one of the graces; she was full of accomplishments and virtues.

Nabussan, loved as he was by her, adored her in his turn. But she had blue eyes, and this was the source of the greatest misfortunes. There was an ancient law which forbade the kings to love one of those women whom the Greeks in later days called βοωπις.. The chief of the bonzes had established this law more than five thousand years before that time, with a view to appropriating the mistress of the first king of the island of Serendib, whom the chief bonze had induced to pass an anathema upon blue eyes as a fundamental article of the constitution. All orders of society came to remonstrate with Nabussan. They publicly declared that the last days of the kingdom had arrived, that iniquity had reached its height, and that all nature was threatened with some untoward accident; that, in a word, Nabussan, son of Nussanab, was in love with two big blue eyes. The hunchbacks, financiers, bonzes, and brunettes, filled the palace with complaints.

The wild tribes that inhabit the north of Serendib took advantage of the general discontent to make an incursion into the territory of the good Nabussan. He demanded subsidies from his subjects; the bonzes, who owned half the revenues of the state, contented themselves with raising their hands to heaven, and refused to put them into their coffers to help the king. They offered up grand prayers to fine music, and left the State a prey to the barbarians.

"O my dear Zadig! Will you rescue me again from this horrible embarrassment?" dolefully exclaimed Nabussan.

"Very willingly," answered Zadig. "You shall have as much money from the bonzes as you wish. Abandon to the enemy the lands on which their mansions are built, and only defend your own."

Nabussan did not fail to follow this advice. The bonzes thereupon came and threw themselves at the king's feet, imploring his assistance. The king answered them in beautiful strains of music, the words to which they were an accompaniment being prayers to Heaven for the preservation of their lands. The bonzes, at last, gave some money, and the king brought the war to a prosperous conclusion. Thus Zadig, by his wise and successful counsel, and by his important services, drew upon himself the irreconcilable hatred of the most powerful men in the State; the bonzes and the brunettes took an oath to ruin him; the financiers and the hunchbacks did not spare him, but did all they could to make him suspected by the excellent Nabussan. "Good offices remain in the ante-chamber when suspicions enter the closet," as Zoroaster has wisely observed. Everyday there were fresh accusations; if the first was repelled, the second might graze the skin, the third wound, and the fourth be fatal.

Zadig, after having advantageously transacted the business of his friend Setoc and sent him his money, thought of nothing now in his alarm but of leaving the island, and resolved to go himself in search of tidings of Astarte.

"For," said he, "if I stay in Serendib, the bonzes will cause me to be impaled. . . . But where can I go? In Egypt I shall be a slave; burnt, in all likelihood, in Arabia; strangled at Babylon. Still I must know what has become of Astarte. . . . Let us be gone, and see for what my sad destiny reserves me."

CHAPTER XVI

The Brigand

On arriving at the frontier which separates Arabia Petræa from Syria, as he was passing near a pretty strong castle, a party of armed Arabs sallied forth. He saw himself surrounded, and the men cried out: "All that you have belongs to us, and your body belongs to our master."

Zadig, by way of answer, drew his sword; his servant, who had plenty of courage, did the same. They routed and slew the Arabs who first laid hands on them; their assailants now numbered twice as many as before, but they were not daunted, and resolved to die fighting. Then were seen two men defending themselves against a multitude. Such a conflict could not last long. The master of the castle, whose name was Arbogad, having seen from a window the prodigies of valour performed by Zadig, conceived such an admiration for him that he hastily descended, and came in person to disperse his men and deliver the two travellers.

"All that passes over my lands is my property," said he, "as well as whatever I find on the lands of other people; but you seem to me such a brave man, that I except you from the general rule."

He made Zadig enter his castle, and bade his people treat him well. In the evening Arbogad desired Zadig to sup with him.

Now the lord of the castle was one of those Arabs who are known as *robbers*; but he sometimes did a good action among a multitude of bad ones. He robbed with fierce rapacity, and gave away freely; he was intrepid in battle, though gentle enough in society; intemperate at table, merry in his cups, and above all, full of frankness. Zadig pleased him greatly, and his animated conversation prolonged the repast. At length Arbogad said to him:

"I advise you to enrol yourself under me; you cannot do better; this calling of mine is not a bad one, and you may one day become what I now am."

"May I ask you," said Zadig, "how long you have practised this noble profession?"

"From my tenderest youth," replied the lord of the castle. "I was the servant of an Arab who was a pretty sharp fellow; I felt my position intolerable; it drove me to despair to see that in all the earth, which belongs equally to all mankind, fortune had reserved no portion for me. I confided my trouble to an old Arab, who said to me: 'My son, do not despair; there was once upon a time a grain of sand which bewailed its fate in being a mere unheeded atom in the desert; but at the end of a few years it became a diamond, and it is now the most beautiful ornament in the King of India's crown.' This story made a great impression on me. I was the grain of sand, and I determined to become a diamond. I began by stealing two horses; I then formed a gang, and put myself in a position to rob small caravans. Thus by degrees I abolished the disproportion which existed at first between myself and other men; I had my share in the good things of this world, and was even recompensed with usury. I was held in high esteem, became a brigand chief, and obtained this castle by violence. The satrap of Syria wished to dispossess me, but I was already too rich to have anything to dread; I gave some money to the satrap, and by this means retained the castle and increased my domains. He even named me treasurer of the tribute which Arabia Petræa paid to the king of kings. I fulfilled my duty well, so far as receiving went, but utterly ignored that of payment. The Grand Desterham of Babylon sent hither in the name of King Moabdar a petty satrap, intending to have me strangled. This man arrived with his orders; I was informed of all, and caused to be strangled in his presence the four persons he had brought with him to apply the bowstring to my neck; after which I asked him what his commission to strangle me might be worth to him. He answered me that his fees might amount to three hundred pieces of gold. I made it clear to him that there was more to be gained with me. I gave him a subordinate post among my brigands, and now he is one of my smartest and wealthiest officers. Take my word for it, you will succeed as well as he. Never has there been a better season for pillage, since Moabdar is slain and all is in confusion at Babylon."

"Moabdar slain!" said Zadig; "and what has become of Queen Astarte?"

"I know nothing about her," replied Arbogad; "all I know is that Moabdar became mad and was killed, that Babylon is one vast slaughter-house, that all the empire is laid waste, that there are fine blows to be struck yet, and that I myself have done wonders in that way."

"But the queen?" said Zadig; "pray tell me, know you nothing of the fate of the queen?"

"I heard something about a prince of Hyrcania," replied he; "she is probably among his concubines, if she has not been killed in the insurrection; but I have more curiosity in the matter of plunder than of news. I have taken a good many women in my raids, but I keep none of them; I sell them at a high price if they are handsome, without inquiring who or what they are, for my customers pay nothing for rank; a queen who was ugly would find no purchaser. Maybe I have sold Queen Astarte, maybe she is dead; it matters very little to me, and I do not think you need be more concerned about her than I am."

As he spoke thus he went on drinking lustily, and mixed up all his ideas so confusedly, that Zadig could extract no information out of him.

He remained confounded, overwhelmed, unable to stir. Arbogad continued to drink, told stories, constantly repeated that he was the happiest of all men, and exhorted Zadig to render himself as happy as he was. At last, becoming more and more drowsy with the fumes of wine, he gradually fell into a tranquil slumber. Zadig passed the night in a state of the most violent agitation.

"What!" said he, "the king become mad! the king killed! I cannot help lamenting him! The empire is dismembered, and this brigand is happy! Alas for fate and fortune! A robber is happy, and the most amiable object that nature ever created has perhaps perished in a frightful manner, or is living in a condition worse than death. O Astarte! what has become of you?"

At break of day he questioned all whom he met in the castle; but everybody was busy, and no one answered him: new conquests had been made during the night, and they were dividing the spoils. All that he could obtain in the confusion that prevailed was permission to depart, of which he availed himself without delay, plunged deeper than ever in painful thoughts.

Zadig walked on restless and agitated, his mind engrossed with the hapless Astarte, with the king of Babylon, with his faithful Cador, with the happy brigand Arbogad, and that capricious woman whom the Babylonians had carried off on the confines of Egypt, in short, with all the disappointments and misfortunes that he had experienced.

CHAPTER XVII

The Fisherman

At a distance of several leagues from Arbogad's castle, he found himself on the brink of a little river, still deploring his destiny, and regarding himself as the very type of misery. There he saw a fisherman lying on the bank, hardly holding in his feeble hand the net which he seemed ready to drop, and lifting his eyes towards heaven.

"I am certainly the most wretched of all men," said the fisherman. "I was, as everybody allowed, the most famous seller of cream cheeses in Babylon, and I have been ruined. I had the prettiest wife that a man could possess, and she has betrayed me. A mean house was all that was left me, and I have seen it plundered and destroyed. Having taken refuge in a hut, I have no resource but fishing, and I cannot catch a single fish. O my net! I will cast you no more into the water, it is myself that I must cast therein."

Saying these words, he rose and advanced in the attitude of a man about to throw himself headlong and put an end to his life.

"What is this?" said Zadig to himself; "there are men then as miserable as I!"

Eagerness to save the fisherman's life rose as promptly as this reflection. He ran towards him, stopped, and questioned him with an air of concern and encouragement. It is said that we are less miserable when we are not alone in our misery. According to Zoroaster this is due, not to malice, but to necessity; we then feel ourselves drawn towards a victim of misfortune as a fellow-sufferer. The joy of a prosperous man would seem to us an insult; but two wretched men are like two weak trees, which, leaning together, mutually strengthen each other against the tempest.

"Why do you give way to your misfortunes?" said Zadig to the fisherman.

"Because," answered he, "I see no way out of them. I was held in the highest estimation in the village of Derlback, near Babylon, and I made, with my wife's help, the best cream cheeses in the empire. Queen Astarte and the famous minister Zadig were passionately fond of them. I had supplied their houses with six hundred cheeses, and went one day into town to be paid, when, on my arrival at Babylon, I learned that the queen and Zadig had disappeared. I hastened to the house of the lord Zadig, whom I had never seen; there I found the police officers of the Grand Desterham, who, furnished with a royal warrant, were sacking his house in a perfectly straightforward and orderly manner. I flew to the queen's kitchens; some of the lords of the dresser told me that she was dead; others said that she was in prison; while others again declared that she had taken flight; but all assured me that I should be paid nothing for my cheeses. I went with my wife to the house of the lord Orcan, who was one of my customers, and we asked him to protect us in our distress. He granted his protection to my wife, and refused it to me. She was whiter than those cream cheeses with which my troubles began, and the gleam of Tyrian purple was not more brilliant than the carnation which animated that whiteness. It was this which made the lord Orcan keep her and drive me away from his house. I wrote to my dear wife the letter of a desperate man. She said to the messenger who brought it:

"'Oh! ah! yes! I know something of the man who writes me this letter. I have heard people speak of him; they say he makes capital cream cheeses; let him send me some, and see that he is paid for them.'

"In my unhappy state I determined to have recourse to justice. I had six ounces of gold left; I had to give two ounces to the lawyer whom I consulted; two to the attorney who undertook my case, and two to the secretary of the first judge. When all this was done, my suit was not yet commenced, and I had already spent more money than my cheeses and my wife were worth. I returned to my village, with the intention of selling my house in order to recover my wife.

"My house was well worth sixty ounces of gold, but people saw that I was poor and forced to sell. The first man to whom I applied offered me thirty ounces for it, the second twenty, and the third ten. I was ready at last to take anything, so blinded was I, when a prince of Hyrcania came to Babylon, and ravaged all the country on his way. My house was first sacked and then burned.

"Having thus lost my money, my wife, and my house, I retired to this part of the country where you see me. I tried to support myself by fishing, but the fishes mock me as much as men do; I take nothing, I am dying of hunger, and had it not been for you, my illustrious consoler, I should have perished in the river."

The fisherman did not tell his story all at once; for every moment Zadig in his agitation would break in with: "What! do you know nothing of what has befallen the queen?" "No, my lord," the fisherman would make reply; "but I know that the queen and Zadig have not paid me for my cream cheeses, that my wife has been taken from me, and that I am in despair."

"I feel confident," said Zadig, "that you will not lose all your money. I have heard people speak of this Zadig; he is an honest man; and if he returns to Babylon, as he hopes to do, he will give you more than he owes you. But as to your wife, who is not so honest, I recommend you not to try to recover her. Take my advice, go to Babylon; I shall be there before you, because I am on horseback, and you are on foot. Apply to the most noble Cador; tell him you have met his friend, and wait for me at his house. Go; perhaps you will not always be unhappy."

"O mighty Ormuzd," continued he, "thou dost make use of me to console this man; of whom wilt thou make use to console me?"

So saying, he gave the fisherman half of all the money he had brought from Arabia, and the fisherman, astonished and delighted, kissed the feet of Cador's friend, and said: "You are an angel sent to save me."

Meanwhile Zadig continued to ask for news, shedding tears as he did so.

"What! my lord," cried the fisherman, "can you then be unhappy, you who bestow bounty?"

"A hundred times more unhappy than you," answered Zadig.

"But how can it be," said the simple fellow, "that he who gives is more to be pitied than him who receives?"

"Because," replied Zadig, "your greatest misfortune was a hungry belly, and because my misery has its seat in the heart."

"Has Orcan taken away your wife?" said the fisherman.

This question recalled all his adventures to Zadig's mind; he repeated the catalogue of his misfortunes, beginning with the queen's bitch, up to the time of his arrival at the castle of the brigand Arbogad.

"Ah!" said he to the fisherman, "Orcan deserves to be punished. But it is generally such people as he who are the favourites of fortune. Be that as it may, go to the house of the lord Cador, and wait for me."

They parted; the fisherman walked on thanking his stars, and Zadig pressed forward still accusing his own.

CHAPTER XVIII

The Cockatrice

Having arrived at a beautiful meadow, he saw there several women searching for something with great diligence. He took the liberty of approaching one of them, and of asking her if he might have the honour of helping them in their search.

"Take good heed not to do that," answered the Syrian damsel; "what we are looking for can only be touched with impunity by women."

"That is very strange," said Zadig; "may I venture to ask you to tell me what it is that only women are allowed to touch?"

"A cockatrice," said she.

"A cockatrice, madam! and for what reason, if you please, are you looking for a cockatrice?"

"It is for our lord and master, Ogul, whose castle you see on the bank of that river, at the end of the meadow. We are his most humble slaves; the lord Ogul is ill, his physician has ordered him to eat a cockatrice stewed in rose-water, and, as it is a very rare animal, and never allows itself to be taken except by women, the lord Ogul has promised to choose for his well-beloved wife, whichever of us shall bring him a cockatrice. Let me prosecute the search, if you please; for you see what it would cost me, if I were anticipated by my companions."

Zadig left this Syrian girl and the others to look for their cockatrice, and continued to walk through the meadow. When he reached the brink of a little stream, he found there another lady lying on the turf, but not in search of anything. Her figure appeared majestic, but her countenance was covered with a veil. She was leaning over the stream; deep sighs escaped from her mouth. She held in her hand a little rod, with which she was tracing characters on the fine sand which lay between the grass and the stream. Zadig had the curiosity to look and see what this woman was writing; he drew near, and saw the letter Z, then an A; he was astonished;

then appeared a D; he started. Never was there surprise to equal his, when he saw the two last letters of his name. He remained some time without moving; then, breaking the silence, he exclaimed in an agitated voice:

"O noble lady! pardon a stranger who is in distress if he ventures to ask you by what astonishing chance I find here the name of Zadig traced by your adorable hand."

At that voice, at those words, the lady raised her veil with a trembling hand, turned her eyes on Zadig, uttered a cry of tenderness, surprise, and joy, and, overcome by all the varied emotions which simultaneously assailed her soul, she fell fainting into his arms. It was Astarte herself, it was the queen of Babylon, it was she whom Zadig adored, and whom he reproached himself for adoring; it was she for whom he had wept so much, and for whom he had so often dreaded the worst stroke of fate. For a moment he was deprived of the use of his senses; then, fixing his gaze on Astarte's eyes, which languidly opened once more with an expression in which confusion was mingled with tenderness, he cried:

"O immortal powers, who preside over the destinies of feeble mortals! Do ye indeed restore to me Astarte? At what a time, in what a place, and in what a condition do I see her again!"

He threw himself on his knees before Astarte, and applied his forehead to the dust of her feet. The queen of Babylon lifted him up, and made him sit beside her on the bank of the stream, while she repeatedly dried her eyes from which tears would soon begin again to flow. Twenty times at least did she take up the thread of the discourse which her sighs interrupted; she questioned him as to what strange chance brought them once more together, and she anticipated his answers by suddenly asking fresh questions. She began to relate her own misfortunes, and then wished to know those of Zadig. At last, both of them having somewhat appeased the tumult of their souls, Zadig told her in a few words how it came to pass that he found himself in that meadow.

"But, O unhappy and honoured queen! how is it that I find you in this remote spot, clad as a slave, and accompanied by other women slaves who are searching for a cockatrice to be stewed in rose-water by a physician's order?"

"Whilst they are looking for their cockatrice" said the fair Astarte, "I will inform you of all that I have suffered, and for how much I have ceased to blame heaven now that I see you again. You know that the king, my husband, took it ill that you were the most amiable of all men; and it was for this reason that he one night took the resolution to have you strangled and me poisoned. You know how heaven permitted my little mute to give me warning of His Sublime Majesty's orders. Hardly had the faithful Cador forced you to obey me and to go away, when he ventured to enter my chamber in the middle of the night by a secret passage. He carried me off, and brought me to the temple of Ormuzd, where his brother, the magian, shut me up in a gigantic statue, the base of which touches the foundations of the temple, while its head reaches to the roof. I was as it were buried there, but waited on by the magian, and in want of none of the necessaries of life. Meanwhile at daybreak His Majesty's apothecary entered my chamber with a draught compounded of henbane, opium, black hellebore, and aconite; and another official went to your apartment with a bowstring of blue silk. Both places were found empty. Cador, the better to deceive him, went to the king, and pretended to accuse us both. He said that you had taken the road to India, and that I had gone towards Memphis; so officers were sent after each of us.

"The messengers who went in search of me did not know me by sight, for I had hardly ever shown my face to any man but yourself, and that in my husband's presence and by his command. They hastened off in pursuit of me, guided by the description that had been given them of my person. A woman of much the same height as myself, and who had, it may be, superior charms, presented herself to their eyes on the borders of Egypt. She was evidently a fugitive and in distress; they had no doubt that this woman was the queen of Babylon, and they brought her to Moabdar. Their mistake at first threw the king into a violent rage; but ere long, taking a nearer look at the woman, he perceived that she was very beautiful, which gave him some consolation. She was called Missouf. I have been told since that the name signifies in the Egyptian tongue *the capricious beauty*. Such in truth she was, but she had as much artfulness as caprice. She pleased Moabdar, and brought him into subjection to such a degree that she made him declare her his wife. Thereupon her character developed itself in all its extravagance; she fearlessly gave herself up to every foolish freak of her imagination. She wished to compel the chief of the magi, who was old and gouty, to dance before her; and when he refused she persecuted him most bitterly. She ordered her master of the horse to make her a jam tart. In vain did the master of the horse represent to her that he was not a pastry cook, he must make the tart; and he was driven from office because it was too much burned. She gave the post of master of the horse to her dwarf, and the place of chancellor to a page. It was thus that she governed Babylon, while all regretted that they had lost me. The king, who had been a tolerably just and reasonable man until the moment when he had determined to poison me and to have you strangled, seemed now to have drowned his virtues in the exorbitant love that he had for the capricious beauty. He came to the temple on the great day of the sacred fire, and I saw him implore the gods on behalf of Missouf, at the feet of the image in which I was confined. I lifted up my voice, and cried aloud to him:

"'The gods reject the prayers of a king who is become a tyrant, who has been minded to put to death a sensible wife to marry a woman of the most extravagant whims.'

"Moabdar was so confounded at these words, that his head became disordered. The oracle that I had delivered, and Missouf's domineering temper, sufficed to deprive him of his senses, and in a few days he became quite mad.

"His madness, which seemed a punishment from heaven,

was the signal for revolt. There was a general insurrection, and all men ran to take up arms. Babylon, so long plunged in effeminate idleness, became the scene of a frightful civil war. I was drawn forth from the cavity of my statue, and placed at the head of one party. Cador hastened to Memphis, to bring you back to Babylon. The prince of Hyrcania, hearing of these fatal dissensions, came back with his army to form a third party in Chaldea. He attacked the king, who fled before him with his wayward Egyptian. Moabdar died pierced with wounds, and Missouf fell into the hands of the conqueror. It was my misfortune to be myself taken prisoner by a party of Hyrcanians, and I was brought before the prince at precisely the same time as they were bringing in Missouf. You will be pleased, no doubt, to hear that the prince thought me more beautiful than the Egyptian; but you will be sorry to learn that he destined me for his harem. He told me very decidedly that as soon as he should have finished a military expedition which he was about to undertake, he would come and keep me company. You may fancy my distress! The tie that bound me to Moabdar was broken, and I might have been Zadig's, if this barbarian had not cast his chains around me. I answered him with all the pride that my rank and my resentment gave me. I had always heard it said that heaven has connected with persons of my condition a greatness of character, which, with a word or a look, can reduce the presumptuous to a humble sense of that deep respect which they have dared to disregard. I spoke like a queen, but found myself treated like a domestic. The Hyrcanian, without deigning to address to me even a single word, told his black eunuch that I was a saucy minx, but that he thought me pretty; so he bade him take care of me, and subject me to the diet of his favourites, that I might recover my complexion, and be rendered more worthy of his favours by the time that he might find it convenient to honour me with them. I told him that I would sooner kill myself; he answered, laughing, that there was no fear of that, and that he was used to such displays of affection; whereupon he left me like a man who has just put a parrot into his aviary. What a state of things for the first queen in all the world, —I will say more, for a heart which was devoted to Zadig!"

At these words he threw himself at her knees, and bathed them with tears. Astarte raised him tenderly, and continued thus:

"I saw myself in the power of a barbarian, and a rival of the crazy woman who was my fellow-prisoner. She told me what had befallen her in Egypt. I conjectured from the description she gave of your person, from the time of the occurrence, from the dromedary on which you were mounted, and from all the circumstances of the case, that it was Zadig who had fought on her behalf. I had no doubt that you were at Memphis, and resolved to betake myself thither.

"'Beautiful Missouf,' said I, 'you are much more pleasing than I am, and will entertain the prince of Hyrcania far better than I can do. Help me to effect my escape; you will then reign alone, and render me happy in ridding yourself of a rival.'

"Missouf arranged with me the means of my flight, and I departed secretly with an Egyptian woman slave.

"I had nearly reached Arabia, when a notorious robber, named Arbogad, carried me off, and sold me to some merchants, who brought me to this castle where the lord Ogul resides. He bought me without knowing who I was. He is a man of pleasure whose only object in life is good cheer, and who is convinced that God has sent him into the world to sit at table. He is excessively fat, and is constantly on the point of suffocation. His physician, in whom he believes little enough when his digestion is all right, exerts a despotic sway over him whenever he has eaten too much. He has persuaded him that he can cure him with a cockatrice stewed in rose-water. The lord Ogul has promised his hand to whichever of his female slaves shall bring him a cockatrice. You see how I leave them to vie with one another in their eagerness to win this honour, for, since heaven has permitted me to see you again, I have less desire than ever to find this cockatrice."

Then Astarte and Zadig gave expression to all that tender feelings long repressed,—all that their love and misfortunes could inspire in hearts most generous and ardent; and the genii who preside over love carried their vows to the orb of Venus.

The women returned to Ogul's castle without having found anything. Zadig, having obtained an introduction, addressed him to this effect:

"May immortal health descend from heaven to guard and keep you all your days! I am a physician, and am come to you in haste on hearing the report of your sickness, and I have brought you a cockatrice stewed in rose-water. I have no matrimonial intentions with regard to you; I only ask for the release of a young female slave from Babylon, who has been several days in your possession, and I consent to remain in bondage in her place, if I have not the happiness of curing the magnificent lord Ogul."

The proposal was accepted. Astarte set out for Babylon with Zadig's servant, having promised to send him a messenger immediately to inform him of all that might have happened. Their parting was as tender as their unexpected recognition. The moment of separation and the moment of meeting again are the two most important epochs of life, as is written in the great book of Zendavesta. Zadig loved the queen as much as he swore he did, and the queen loved Zadig more than she professed to do.

Meanwhile Zadig spoke thus to Ogul:

"My lord, my cockatrice is not to be eaten, all its virtue must enter into you through the pores. I have put it into a little leathern case, well blown out, and covered with a fine skin; you must strike this case of leather as hard as you can, and I must send it back each time; a few days of this treatment will show you what my art can do."

The first day Ogul was quite out of breath, and thought that he should die of fatigue. The second day he was less exhausted, and slept better. In a week's time he had gained all the strength, health, lightness, and good spirits of his most robust years.

"You have played at ball, and you have been temperate," said Zadig; "believe me, there is no such creature in nature as a cockatrice, but with temperance and exercise one is always well, and the art of combining intemperance and health is as chimerical as the philosopher's stone, judicial astrology, and the theology of the magi."

Ogul's former physician, perceiving how dangerous this man was to the cause of medicine, conspired with his private apothecary to despatch Zadig to hunt for cockatrices in the other world. Thus, after having already been punished so often for having done good, he was again nearly perishing for having healed a gluttonous nobleman. He was invited to a grand dinner, and was to have been poisoned during the second course; but whilst they were at the first he received a message from the fair Astarte, at which he left the table, and took his departure. "When one is loved by a beautiful woman," says the great Zoroaster, "one is always extricated out of every scrape."

CHAPTER XIX

The Tournament

The queen had been received at Babylon with the enthusiasm which is always shown for a beautiful princess who has been unfortunate. Babylon at that time seemed more peaceful. The prince of Hyrcania had been killed in a battle; and the victorious Babylonians declared that Astarte should marry the man whom they might elect for monarch. They did not desire that the first position in the world, namely, that of being husband of Astarte and king of Babylon, should depend upon intrigues and cabals. They took an oath to acknowledge as their king the man whom they should find bravest and wisest. Spacious lists, surrounded by an amphitheatre splendidly decorated, were formed at a distance of several leagues from the city. The combatants were to repair thither armed at all points. Each of them had separate quarters behind the amphitheatre, where he was to be neither seen nor visited by anyone. It was necessary to enter the lists four times, and those who should be successful enough to defeat four cavaliers were thereupon to fight against each other, and the one who should finally remain master of the field should be proclaimed victor of the tournament. He was to return four days afterwards with the same arms, and try to solve the riddles which the magi would propound. If he could not solve the riddles, he was not to be king, and it would be necessary to begin the jousts over again, until a knight should be found victorious in both sorts of contest; for they wished to have a king braver and wiser than any other man. The queen, during all this time, was to be strictly guarded; she was only allowed to be present at the games covered with a veil, and she was not permitted to speak to any of the competitors, in order to avoid either favouritism or injustice.

This was the intelligence that Astarte sent her lover, hoping that for her sake he would display greater valour and wisdom than anyone else. So he took his departure, entreating Venus to fortify his courage and enlighten his mind. He arrived on the banks of the Euphrates the evening before the great day, and caused his device to be inscribed among those of the combatants, concealing his countenance and his name, as the law required. Then he went to take repose in the lodging that was assigned him by lot. His friend Cador, who had returned to Babylon, after having vainly searched for him in Egypt, despatched to his quarters a complete suit of armour which was the queen's present. He also sent him, on her behalf, the finest steed in Persia. Zadig recognised the hand of Astarte in these gifts; his courage and his love gained thereby new energy and new hopes.

On the morrow, the queen having taken her place under a jewelled canopy, and the amphitheatre being filled with ladies and persons of every rank in Babylon, the combatants appeared in the arena. Each of them came and laid his device at the feet of the grand magian. The devices were drawn by lot, and Zadig's happened to be the last. The first who advanced was a very rich lord named Itobad, exceedingly vain, but with little courage, skill, or judgment. His servants had persuaded him that such a man as he ought to be king; and he had answered them: "Such a man as I ought to reign." So they had armed him from head to foot. He had golden armour enamelled with green, a green plume, and a lance decked with green ribbons. It was evident at once, from the manner in which Itobad managed his horse, that it was not for *such a man as he* that heaven reserved the sceptre of Babylon. The first knight who tilted against him unhorsed him; the second upset him so that he lay on his horse's crupper with both his legs in the air and arms extended. Itobad recovered his seat, but in such an ungainly fashion that all the spectators began to laugh. The third did not condescend to use his lance, but after making a pass at him, took him by the right leg, turned him half round, and let him drop on the sand. The squires of the tourney ran up to him laughing, and replaced him on his saddle. The fourth combatant seized him by the left leg, and made him fall on the other side. He was accompanied with loud jeers to his quarters, where he was to pass the night according to the law of the games; and he said as he limped along with difficulty: "What an experience for such a man as I!"

The other knights acquitted themselves better. There were some who defeated two antagonists one after the other, a few went as far as three, but the prince Otame was the only one who conquered four. At last Zadig tilted in his turn; he unseated four cavaliers in succession in the most graceful manner possible. It then remained to be seen whether Otame or Zadig would be the victor. The arms of the former were blue and gold, with a plume of the same colour, while those of Zadig were white. The sympathies of all were divided between the knight in blue and the knight in white. The queen, whose heart was throbbing violently, put up prayers to heaven that the white might be the winning colour.

The two champions made passes and wheeled round with such agility, they delivered such dexterous thrusts, and sat so firmly on their saddles, that all the spectators, except the queen, wished that there might be two kings in Babylon. At last, their chargers being exhausted, and their lances broken, Zadig had recourse to this stratagem: he steps behind the blue prince, leaps upon the crupper of his horse, seizes him by the waist, hurls him down, takes his place in the saddle, and prances round Otame, as he lies stretched upon the ground. All the amphitheatre shouts: "Victory to the white cavalier!" Otame rises, indignant at his disgrace, and draws his sword; Zadig springs off the horse's back, sabre in hand. Then, lo and behold! both of them on foot in the arena begin a new conflict, in which strength and agility by turns prevail. The plumes of their helmets, the rivets of their arm-pieces, the links of their armour, fly far afield under a thousand rapid blows. With point and edge they thrust and cut, to right and left, now on the head, and now on the chest; they retreat, they advance, they measure swords, they come to close quarters, they wrestle, they twine like serpents, they attack each other like lions; sparks are sent forth every moment from their clashing swords. At last Zadig, recovering his coolness for an instant, stops, makes a feint, and then rushes upon Otame, brings him to the ground, and disarms him, when the vanquished prince exclaims: "O white cavalier! you it is who should reign over Babylon."

The queen's joy was at its climax. The cavalier in blue and the cavalier in white were conducted each to his own lodging, as well as all the others, in due accordance with the law. Mutes came to attend them and to bring them food. It may be easily guessed that the queen's little mute was the one who waited on Zadig. Then they were left to sleep alone until the morning of the next day, when the conqueror was to bring his device to the grand magian to be compared with the roll, and to make himself known.

In spite of his love Zadig slept soundly enough, so tired was he. Itobad, who lay near him, did not sleep a wink. He rose in the night, entered Zadig's quarters, took away his white arms and his device, and left his own green armour in their place. As soon as it was daylight, he went up boldly to the grand magian, and announced that such a man as he was victor. This was unexpected, but his success was proclaimed while Zadig was still asleep. Astarte, surprised, and with despair at her heart, returned to Babylon. The whole amphitheatre was already almost empty when Zadig awoke; he looked for his arms, and found only the green armour. He was obliged to put it on, having nothing else near him. Astonished and indignant, he armed himself in a rage, and stepped forth in that guise.

All the people who were left in the amphitheatre and arena greeted him with jeers. They pressed round him, and insulted him to his face. Never did man endure such bitter mortification. He lost patience, and with his drawn sword dispersed the mob which dared to molest him; but he knew not what course to adopt. He could not see the queen, nor could he lay claim to the white armour which she had sent him, without compromising her; so that, while she was plunged in grief, he was tortured with rage and perplexity. He walked along the banks of the Euphrates, convinced that his star had marked him out for inevitable misery, reviewing in his mind all the misfortunes he had suffered, since his experience of the woman who hated one-eyed men up to this present loss of his armour.

"See what comes," said he, "of awaking too late; if I had slept less, I should now be king of Babylon and husband of Astarte. Knowledge, conduct, and courage have never served to bring me anything but trouble."

At last, murmurs against Providence escaped him, and he was tempted to believe that the world was governed by a cruel destiny, which oppressed the good, and brought prosperity to cavaliers in green. One of his worst grievances was to be obliged to wear that green armour which drew such ridicule upon him; and he sold it to a passing merchant at a low price, taking in exchange from the merchant a gown and a nightcap. In this garb he paced beside the Euphrates, filled with despair, and secretly accusing Providence for always persecuting him.

CHAPTER XX

The Hermit

While walking thus, Zadig met a hermit, whose white and venerable beard descended to his girdle. He held in his hand a book which he was reading attentively. Zadig stopped, and made him a profound obeisance. The hermit returned his salutation with an air so noble and attractive, that Zadig had the curiosity to enter into conversation with him. He asked him what book he was reading.

"It is the book of destiny," said the hermit; "do you desire to read aught therein?"

He placed the book in Zadig's hands, but he, learned as he was in several languages, could not decipher a single character in the book. This increased his curiosity yet more.

"You seem to me much vexed," said the good father.

"Alas! and with only too much reason!" answered Zadig.

"If you will allow me to accompany you," rejoined the old man, "perhaps I may be of service to you; I have sometimes poured consolation into the souls of the unhappy."

The hermit's aspect, his beard, and his book, inspired Zadig with respect. He found in conversing with him the light of a superior mind. The hermit spoke of destiny, of justice, of morality, of the chief good, of human frailty, of virtue, and of vice, with an eloquence so lively and touching, that Zadig felt himself drawn towards him by an irresistible charm. He earnestly besought him not to leave him, until they should return to Babylon.

"I myself ask the same favour of you," said the old man; "swear to me by Ormuzd that you will not part from me for some days to come, whatever I may do."

Zadig swore not to do so, and they set out together.

The two travellers arrived that evening at a magnificent castle, where the hermit craved hospitality for himself and for the young man who accompanied him. The porter, who might have been taken for a distinguished nobleman, introduced them with a sort of disdainful politeness. They were presented to one of the principal domestics, who showed them the master's splendid apartments. They were admitted to the lower end of his table, without being honoured even with a look from the lord of the castle; but they were served like the others, with elegance and profusion. A golden bowl studded with emeralds and rubies was afterwards brought them, wherein to wash their hands. For the night they were consigned to fine sleeping apartments, and in the morning a servant brought each of them a piece of gold, after which they were courteously dismissed.

"The master of the house," said Zadig, when they were again on their way, "seems to me to be a generous man, but a little too proud; he practises a noble hospitality."

As he said these words, he perceived that a very wide sort of pocket which the hermit was wearing appeared stretched and stuffed out, and he caught sight of the golden bowl adorned with precious stones, which the hermit had stolen. He did not at first venture to take any notice of it, but he experienced a strange surprise.

Towards midday, the hermit presented himself at the door of a very small house, inhabited by a very rich miser, of whom he begged hospitable entertainment for a few hours. An old servant, meanly clad, received them roughly, and conducted the hermit and Zadig to the stable, where some rotten olives, mouldy bread, and sour beer were given them. The hermit ate and drank with as contented an air as on the evening before; then, turning to the old servant who was watching them both to see that they stole nothing, and who kept urging them to go, he gave him the two pieces of gold which he had received that morning, and thanked him for all his attentions.

"Pray," added he, "let me speak a word to your master."

The astonished servant introduced the two strangers.

"Magnificent lord," said the hermit, "I cannot refrain from offering you my most humble thanks for the noble manner in which you have treated us; deign to accept this golden bowl as a slight token of my gratitude."

The miser almost fell backward from his seat, but the hermit, not giving him time to recover from his sudden surprise, departed with his young companion as quickly as possible.

"Father," said Zadig, "what is all this that I see? You do not seem to me to resemble other men in anything that you do; you steal a bowl adorned with precious stones from a nobleman who entertained you sumptuously, and you give it to a miser who treats you with indignity."

"My son," replied the old man, "that pompous person, who entertains strangers only out of vanity, and to excite admiration of his riches, will learn a needful lesson, while the miser will be taught to practise hospitality; be astonished at nothing, and follow me."

Zadig was still uncertain whether he had to do with a man more foolish or more wise than all other men; but the hermit spoke with a tone of such superiority, that Zadig, bound besides by his oath, felt constrained to follow him.

In the evening they arrived at a house built in a pleasing but simple style, where nothing betokened either prodigality or avarice. The master was a philosopher who, retired from the world, pursued in peace the study of wisdom and virtue, and who, nevertheless, felt life no tedious burden. It had pleased him to build this retreat, into which he welcomed strangers with a generosity which was free from ostentation. He went himself to meet the travellers, and ushered them into a comfortable apartment, where he first left them to repose awhile. Some time afterwards he came in person to invite them to a clean and well-cooked meal, during which he spoke with great good sense about the latest revolutions in Babylon. He seemed sincerely attached to the queen, and expressed a wish that Zadig had appeared in the lists as a competitor for the crown.

"But mankind," added he, "do not deserve to have a king like Zadig."

The latter blushed, and felt his disappointment return with double force. In the course of conversation it was generally agreed that matters in this world do not always fall out as the wisest men would wish. The hermit maintained throughout that we are ignorant of the ways of Providence, and that men are wrong in judging of the whole by the very small part which alone they are able to perceive.

They spoke of the passions. "Ah! how fatal they are!" said Zadig.

"They are the winds that swell the sails of the vessel," replied the hermit; "they sometimes sink the vessel, but it could not make way without them. The bile makes men choleric and sick, but without the bile they could not live. Everything here below has its danger, and yet everything is necessary."

Then they spoke of pleasure, and the hermit proved that it is a gift of the Deity.

"For," said he, "man can give himself neither sensation nor idea, he receives them all; pain and pleasure come to him from without like his very existence."

Zadig marvelled how a man who had acted so extravagantly could argue so well. At length, after a discourse as profitable as it was agreeable, their host conducted the two travellers back to their apartment, blessing heaven for having sent him two men so virtuous and so wise; and he offered them money in a frank and easy manner that could give no offence. The hermit, however, refused it, and told him that he must now take leave of him, as he purposed departing for Babylon before morning. Their parting was affectionate, Zadig especially felt full of esteem and love for so amiable a man.

When the hermit and he were alone in their chamber, they passed a long time in praising their host. The old man at daybreak awoke his comrade.

"We must start," said he, "while all the household is asleep. I wish to leave this man a token of my regard and affection."

Saying these words, he seized a light, and set fire to the house. Zadig uttered a cry of horror, and would fain have prevented him from committing so dreadful a deed, but the hermit dragged him away by superior force, and the house was soon in flames. The hermit, who was now at a safe distance with his companion, calmly watched it burning.

"Thank God!" said he; "there goes the house of my dear host, destroyed from basement to roof! Happy man!"

At these words Zadig was tempted at once to burst out laughing, to overwhelm the reverend father with reproaches, to beat him, and to fly from him; but he did none of these things; still overawed by the hermit's dominating influence, he followed him in spite of himself to their last quarters for the night.

It was at the house of a charitable and virtuous widow, who had a nephew fourteen years of age, full of engaging qualities, and her only hope. She did the honours of her house as well as she could, and on the morrow she bade her nephew conduct the travellers as far as a bridge which, having broken down a short time before, was now dangerous to cross. The lad walked before them with alacrity. When they were on the bridge, the hermit said to the youth:

"Come, I must prove my gratitude to your aunt."

Then he seized him by the hair, and threw him into the river. The boy sank, rose for a moment above the water, and was then swallowed up by the torrent.

"O monster! Most wicked of all mankind!" exclaimed Zadig.

"You promised to be more patient," said the hermit, interrupting him. "Know that under the ruins of that house to which Providence set fire, the master has found an immense treasure; and that this youth, whose neck Providence has twisted, would have murdered his aunt within a year, and yourself within two."

"Savage, who told you so?" cried Zadig; "and though you may have read this event in your book of destiny, are you allowed to drown a child who has done you no harm?"

While the Babylonian was speaking, he perceived that the old man had no longer a beard, and that his countenance assumed the features of youth. The habit of a hermit disappeared; four beautiful wings covered a form majestic and glittering with light.

"O messenger from heaven! Divine angel!" cried Zadig, falling on his knees; "art thou then descended from the empyrean to teach a feeble mortal to submit to the eternal decrees?"

"Mankind," said the angel Jesrad, "judge of everything when knowing nothing; of all men you were the one who most deserved to be enlightened."

Zadig asked if he might have permission to speak.

"I distrust myself," said he, "but may I venture to ask thee to resolve my doubt? Would it not have been better to have corrected this youth, and to have rendered him virtuous, than to drown him?"

Jesrad answered: "If he had been virtuous, and had continued to live, it would have been his destiny to be murdered himself, together with the wife he was to marry, and the son whom she was to bear."

"What!" said Zadig, "is it inevitable then that there should be crimes and misfortunes? The misfortunes too, fall upon the good!"

"The wicked," answered Jesrad, "are always unhappy; they serve to try a small number of righteous men scattered over the earth, and there is no evil from which some good does not spring."

"But," said Zadig, "what if there were only good, and no evil at all?"

"Then," answered Jesrad, "this earth would be another world, the chain of events would be ordered by wisdom of another kind; and this order, which would be perfect, can only exist in the eternal abode of the Supreme Being, which evil cannot approach. He has created millions of worlds, not one of which can resemble another. This boundless variety is an attribute of His boundless power. There are not two leaves of a tree upon this earth, nor two globes in the infinite fields of heaven, which are alike, and everything that you see on this little atom where you have been born must fill its own place, and exist in its own fixed time, according to the immutable decrees of Him who embraces all. Men think that this child who has just perished fell into the water by accident, that it was by accident likewise that that house was burned; but there is no such thing as accident; all that takes place is either a trial, or a punishment, or a reward, or a providential dispensation. Remember that fisherman who deemed himself the most miserable of men. Ormuzd sent you to change his destiny. Feeble mortal, cease to dispute against that which it is your duty to adore."

"But," said Zadig—

As the word was on his lips, the angel was already winging his way towards the tenth sphere. Zadig on his knees adored Providence, and was resigned. The angel cried to him from on high:

"Take your way towards Babylon."

CHAPTER XXI

The Riddles

Zadig, in a state of bewilderment, and like a man at whose side the lightning has fallen, walked on at random. He entered Babylon on the day when those who had contended in the lists were already assembled in the grand vestibule of the palace to solve the riddles, and to answer the questions of the grand magian. All the knights were there, except him of the green armour. As soon as Zadig appeared in the city, the people gathered round him; they could not satisfy their eyes with the sight of him, their mouths with blessing him, or their hearts with wishing him to be king. The Envious Man saw him pass, trembled, and turned aside, while the people escorted him to the place of assembly. The queen, to whom his arrival was announced, became a prey to the agitation of fear and hope; she was devoured with uneasiness, and could not comprehend why Zadig was unarmed, and how it came to pass that Itobad wore the white armour. A confused murmur arose at the sight of Zadig. All were surprised and delighted to see him again; but only the knights who had taken part in the tournament were permitted to appear in the assembly.

"I have fought like the others," said he; "but another here wears my armour, and, while I must wait to have the honour of proving it, I ask leave to present myself in order to explain the riddles."

The question was put to the vote; his reputation for integrity was still so deeply impressed on the minds of all, that there was no hesitation about admitting him.

The grand magian first proposed this question:

"What, of all things in the world, is alike the longest and the shortest, the quickest and the slowest, the most minutely divided and the most widely extended, the most neglected and the most regretted, without which nothing can be done, which devours everything that is little, and confers life on everything that is great?"

Itobad was to speak first; he answered that such a man as he understood nothing about riddles, that it was enough for him to have conquered by the might of his arm. Some said that the answer to the riddle was fortune; according to others it was the earth, and according to others again light. Zadig said that it was time:

"Nothing is longer," added he, "since it is the measure of eternity; nothing is shorter, since it fails to accomplish our projects. There is nothing slower to one who waits, nothing quicker to one who enjoys. It extends to infinity in greatness, it is infinitely divisible in minuteness. All men neglect it, all regret its loss. Nothing is done without it. It buries in oblivion all that is unworthy of being handed down to posterity; and it confers immortality upon all things that are great."

The assembly agreed that Zadig's answer was the right one.

The next question was:

"What is it which we receive without acknowledgment, which we enjoy without knowing how, which we bestow on others when we know nothing about it, and which we lose without perceiving the loss?"

Everybody had his own explanation. Zadig alone guessed that it was life, and explained all the other riddles with the same readiness. Itobad said on each occasion that nothing was easier, and that he would have come to the same conclusion with equal facility, if he had cared to give himself the trouble. Questions were afterwards propounded on justice, the chief good, and the art of government. Zadig's replies were pronounced the soundest.

"What a pity," it was said, "that one whose judgment is so good should be so bad a knight!"

"Illustrious lords," said Zadig, "I have had the honour of conquering in the lists. It is to me that the white armour belongs. The lord Itobad possessed himself of it while I slept; he thought, apparently, that it would become him better than the green. I am ready to prove upon his person forthwith before you all, in this garb and armed only with my sword, against all this fine white armour which he has stolen from me, that it was I who had the honour of vanquishing brave Otame."

Itobad accepted the challenge with the greatest confidence. He felt no doubt that, armed as he was with helmet, breastplate, and brassarts, he would soon see the last of a champion arrayed in a nightcap and a dressing gown. Zadig drew his sword, and saluted the queen, who gazed on him with the deepest emotion of mingled joy and alarm. Itobad unsheathed his weapon without saluting anyone. He advanced upon Zadig like a man who had nothing to fear, and made ready to cleave his head open. Zadig adroitly parried the stroke, opposing the strongest part of his sword to the weakest part of that of his adversary, in such a way that Itobad's blade was broken. Then Zadig, seizing his enemy round the waist, hurled him to the ground, and, holding the point of his sword where the breastplate ended, said:

"Submit to be disarmed, or I take your life."

Itobad, who was always surprised at any disgrace which befell such a man as he, suffered Zadig to do what he pleased, who peaceably relieved him of his splendid helmet, his superb breastplate, his fine brassarts, and his glittering thigh-pieces, put them on himself again, and ran in this array to throw himself at Astarte's knees.

Cador had no difficulty in proving that the armour belonged to Zadig. He was acknowledged king by unanimous consent, and most of all by Astarte, who tasted, after so many adversities, the delight of seeing her lover regarded by all the world as worthy of being her husband. Itobad went away to hear himself called his lordship in his own house. Zadig was made king, and he was happy. What the angel Jesrad had said to him was present to his mind, and he even remembered the grain of sand which became a diamond. The queen and he together adored Providence. Zadig left the beautiful and capricious Missouf to range the world at will. He sent in search of the brigand Arbogad, gave him an honourable post in his army, and promised to promote him to the highest rank, if he behaved himself like a true warrior, but threatened to have him hanged, if he followed the trade of a robber.

Setoc was summoned from the heart of Arabia, together with the fair Almona, and set at the head of the commerce of Babylon. Cador was loved and honoured, receiving an appointment such as his services deserved; he was the king's friend, and Zadig was then the only monarch upon earth who had one. The little mute was not forgotten. A fine house was given to the fisherman, while Orcan was condemned to pay him a large sum, and to give him back his wife; but the fisherman, now grown wise, took the money only.

The fair Semira was inconsolable for having believed that Zadig would be blind of an eye; and Azora never ceased lamenting that she had wished to cut off his nose. He soothed their sorrow with presents. The Envious Man died of rage and shame. The empire enjoyed peace, glory, and abundance; that age was the best which the earth had known, for it was ruled by justice and by love. All men blessed Zadig, and Zadig blessed heaven.

[The manuscript containing Zadig's history ends here. We know that he experienced many other adventures which have been faithfully recorded. Interpreters of oriental tongues are requested, if they should meet with any such records, to make them public.]

CANDIDE

OR
OPTIMISM

Translated from the German of Dr. Ralph,
with the additional matter found in the doctor's pocket,
after his death at Minden, in the year of grace 1759

CHAPTER I

How Candide was Brought Up in a Fine Castle, and how he was Driven Out of the Same

Once upon a time there lived in the castle of the noble Baron of Thundertentrunk, in Westphalia, a young lad to whom nature had given the most pleasing manners. His countenance expressed his soul. He had a pretty correct judgment, together with the utmost simplicity of mind; and it was for that reason, I suppose, that he bore the name of Candide. The old servants of the house suspected that he was the son of the noble Baron's sister and of a worthy gentleman in the neighbourhood, whom the young lady would never marry, because he could show no more than three score and eleven quarterings, the rest of his family tree having perished through the ravages of time.

The Baron was one of the most powerful nobles of Westphalia, for his castle had a gate as well as windows, and his great hall was even adorned with tapestry. All the dogs in his stable-yard formed at need a pack of hounds, and his grooms acted as whippers in; the vicar of the village was his grand almoner. Everybody called him "my lord," and laughed at all his good stories.

My lady the Baroness, who weighed about three hundred and fifty pounds and thereby commanded the greatest consideration, did the honours of the house with a dignity which raised its reputation still higher. Her daughter Cunegund, aged seventeen years, was of a fresh and ruddy complexion, plump, and appetising. The Baron's son appeared in all respects worthy of his sire. The tutor Pangloss was the oracle of the house, and little Candide listened to his lessons with all the ready faith natural to his age and disposition.

Pangloss used to teach the science of metaphysico-theologo-cosmologo-noodleology. He demonstrated to admiration that there is no effect without a cause, and that, in this best of all possible worlds, the castle of my lord Baron was the most magnificent of castles, and my lady the best of all possible baronesses.

"It has been proved," said he, "that things cannot be otherwise than they are; for, everything being made for a certain end, the end for which everything is made is necessarily the best end. Observe how noses were made to carry spectacles, and spectacles we have accordingly. Our legs are clearly intended for shoes and stockings, so we have them. Stone has been formed to be hewn and dressed for building castles, so my lord has a very fine one, for it is meet that the greatest baron in the province should have the best accommodation. Pigs were made to be eaten, and we eat pork all the year round. Consequently those who have asserted that all is well have said what is silly; they should have said of everything that is, that it is the best that could possibly be."

Candide listened attentively, and innocently believed all that he heard; for he thought Miss Cunegund extremely beautiful, though he never had the boldness to tell her so. He felt convinced that, next to the happiness of being born Baron of Thundertentrunk, the second degree of happiness was to be Miss Cunegund, the third to see her every day, and the fourth to hear Professor Pangloss, the greatest philosopher in the province, and therefore in all the world.

One day Miss Cunegund, whilst taking a walk near the castle, in the little wood which was called the park, saw through the bushes Dr. Pangloss giving a lesson in experimental physics to her mother's chambermaid, a little brunette, very pretty and very willing to learn. As Miss Cunegund had a great taste for science, she watched with breathless interest the repeated experiments that were carried on under her eyes; she clearly perceived that the doctor had sufficient reason for all he did; she saw the connection between causes and effects, and returned home much agitated, though very thoughtful, and filled with a yearning after scientific pursuits, for sharing in which she wished that young Candide might find sufficient reason in her, and that she might find the same in him.

She met Candide as she was on her way back to the castle, and blushed; the youth blushed likewise. She bade him good morning, in a voice that struggled for utterance; and Candide answered her without well knowing what he was saying. Next day, as the company were leaving the table after dinner, Cunegund and Candide found themselves behind a screen. Cunegund let fall her handkerchief; Candide picked it up; she innocently took hold of his hand, and the young man, as innocently, kissed hers with an ardour, a tenderness, and a grace quite peculiar; their lips came in contact, their eyes sparkled, their knees trembled, and their hands began to wander. His lordship the Baron of Thundertentrunk happened to pass by the screen, and, seeing that particular instance of cause and effect, drove Candide out of the castle with vigorous kicks on his rear. Cunegund swooned away, but, as soon as she recovered, my lady the Baroness boxed her ears, and all was confusion and consternation in that most magnificent and most charming of all possible castles.

CHAPTER II

What Befell Candide among the Bulgarians

Candide, driven out of his terrestrial paradise, walked on for a long time without knowing whither, weeping, lifting up his eyes to heaven, and often turning them towards that most magnificent of castles, which contained the most beautiful of all barons' daughters. He laid himself down supperless in the midst of the fields, between two ridges, and the snow began to fall upon him in thick flakes. Next morning, Candide, benumbed with cold, dragged himself to the nearest town, which bore the name of Waldberghofdikdorf, without a coin in his pocket, and dying of hunger and fatigue. He stopped in melancholy mood at a tavern door. Two men dressed in blue noticed him.

"Comrade," said one of them, "there is a fine young fellow, and just of the right size."

They stepped forward, and very politely invited Candide to dine with them.

"Gentlemen," says he with engaging modesty, "you do me much honour, but I have no money to pay my reckoning."

"Oh! sir," says one of the men in blue, "persons of your figure and merit never pay anything; are you not five feet five inches tall?"

"Yes, gentlemen, that is my height," says he with his best bow.

"Come, sir, pray take a seat; we will not only pay your score, but we will never allow such a man as you to want money. What are men made for but to help one another?"

"You are right," says Candide; "that is what Dr. Pangloss always told me, and I see clearly that all is for the best."

They beg him to accept a few crowns; he takes them, and is about to tender his note of hand for the amount, but they will not hear of it; and so they sit down to table.

"Are you not warmly attached—"

"Oh, yes," exclaims Candide, "I am warmly attached to Miss Cunegund."

"Excuse me," says one of the gentlemen, "but what we want to know is whether you are not warmly attached to the king of the Bulgarians?"

"Not in the least," says he, "for I have never seen him."

"You don't say so! He is the most charming of monarchs, and we must drink his health."

"With the greatest pleasure, gentlemen." And he drinks accordingly.

"Enough," say they; "lo, now you are the prop, the pillar, the defender, and the hero of the Bulgarians; your fortune is made, and your glory assured."

They forthwith clap fetters on his feet, and conduct him to the headquarters of their regiment. There he is made to wheel to the right, and wheel to the left, to draw his ramrod, and to return it, to present, to fire, and to march at the double; and he gets thirty strokes of a stick for his pains. On the following day he goes through his exercises not quite so badly, and receives only twenty strokes; while on the next after that he escapes with ten, and is regarded as a prodigy by his comrades.

Candide, astonished to find himself a hero, could not very well make out how it came to pass. One fine spring day he took it into his head to go out for a walk, and followed his nose straight on, supposing that it was the privilege of the human species as well as of the brute creation to make use of their legs at their own will and pleasure. He had not proceeded two leagues, when, lo and behold, four other heroes, each of them six feet high, caught him up, bound him, and led him off to prison. He was brought before a court-martial, and asked whether he would prefer to be flogged thirty-six times by the whole regiment, or to receive at once a dozen balls in his brain. It was of no use for him to protest that the will is free, and that he wished neither the one nor the other; he found himself obliged to make a choice, and he determined, in virtue of the divine gift called *freedom*, to run the gauntlet thirty-six times. He tried it twice, and, the regiment consisting of two thousand men, this meant for him four thousand blows, which pretty well laid bare his muscles and nerves from the nape of the neck to the end of the spine. As they were going to give him a third course, Candide, unable to bear any more, entreated them to have the kindness to knock him on the head and finish him. This favour was granted, his eyes were bandaged, and he was made to kneel down. The king of the Bulgarians, happening to pass by that moment, made inquiry into the culprit's offence; and, as he was a man of discernment, and gathered, from all that Candide told him, that he was a young metaphysician and quite ignorant of the ways of the world, the king graciously vouchsafed him his pardon with a clemency that will be praised by all the papers and appreciated by posterity. A clever surgeon cured Candide's back in three weeks with the ointments prescribed by Dioscorides; and he had already a little fresh skin and was fit to march, when the king of the Bulgarians gave battle to the king of the Avarians.

CHAPTER III

How Candide made his Escape from the Midst of the Bulgarians, and what Became of him

Never was seen a spectacle so fine, so smart, so splendid, so well arrayed as the two armies. Trumpets, fifes, hautboys, drums, and cannon made such harmony as never had its match in hell itself. Cannon balls swept off in the first instance nearly six thousand men on each side; then musket bullets removed from this best of all possible worlds about nine or ten thousand worthless fellows that tainted its surface. The bayonet was also the suffecent reason for the death of some thousands of men. The total may have amounted to thirty thousand souls. Candide, who trembled as any other philosopher would have done, hid himself as well as he could during this heroic butchery. At last, while both kings were causing a *Te Deum* to be sung, each in his own camp, he made up his mind to go and reason upon causes and effects somewhere else. He passed over heaps of the dead and dying, and reached first of all a neighbouring village; he found it laid in ashes. It was an Abarian village, which the Bulgarians had burned in accordance with the laws of nations. Here old men, covered with wounds, looked helplessly on, while their wives were dying with their throats cut, and still holding their infants to their blood-stained breasts; there young girls, ripped open after having satisfied the natural wants of several heroes, were breathing forth their last sighs; while others again, half roasted, cried out for someone to put them out of their agony. Brains were scattered over the ground, and legs and arms cut off lay beside them.

Candide fled as quickly as he could into another village; it belonged to the Bulgarians, and the Abarian heroes had treated it after the same fashion. Candide, making his way continually over quivering limbs or smoking ruins, found himself at last beyond the theatre of war, with some scanty provisions in his haversack, and never for a moment forgetful of Miss Cunegund. His provisions failed him by the time he arrived in Holland; but having heard it said that everybody was rich in that country, and that the people were good Christians, he felt no doubt that he would meet with as generous treatment as he had experienced in the castle of my lord Baron, before he was kicked out of it on account of Miss Cunegund's bright eyes.

He asked alms of several grave-looking personages, all of whom answered his appeal with threats that if he continued to follow that trade, they would have him shut up in a house of correction and taught how to make an honest livelihood.

He next accosted a man who had just been speaking for a whole hour together on the subject of charity before a large audience. The orator looked at him through the corner of his eye, and asked:

"What brings you here? Are you for the good cause?"

"There is no effect without a cause," was Candide's modest reply; "all things are linked together by a necessary chain of events, and arranged for the best. It could not but be that I should be banished from Miss Cunegund's presence, that I should have to run the gauntlet as I have done, that I should be forced to beg my bread until such time as I can earn it; all this could not have been otherwise."

"My friend," said the orator, "do you believe that the Pope is Antichrist?"

"I never yet heard him called so," answered Candide; "but whether he be Antichrist or not, I am in want of bread."

"You do not deserve to eat any," said the other; "go, rascal, go, wretch, and never in all your life, come near me again."

The orator's wife, putting her head out of a window and perceiving a man who doubted whether the Pope was Antichrist, emptied a chamber-pot over his head—Heavens! To what excesses will not a zeal for religion carry the ladies!

A man who had never been christened, a kind-hearted Anabaptist, whose name was James, witnessed this cruel and ignominious treatment of one of his brethren, a featherless biped, who had a soul; he took him home with him, he wiped him down, gave him some bread and beer, made him a present of two florins, and even proposed to teach him the art of weaving those fabrics of Persia which are manufactured in Holland. Candide almost threw himself on his knees before him, and exclaimed:

"Dr. Pangloss was right when he told me that everything is for the best in this world, for I am infinitely more affected by your extreme generosity than by the heartlessness of the gentleman in the black cloak, and of the lady his wife."

On the morrow, as he was out walking, he met a beggar all covered with sores, with lack-lustre eyes, the tip of his nose eaten away, his mouth twisted to one side, and teeth as black as charcoal. His voice was hoarse, he was tormented with a violent cough, and at each effort he made to spit a tooth dropped out.

CHAPTER IV

How Candide Met his Old Master in Philosophy, Dr. Pangloss, and what Came of it

Candide, more moved with compassion even than with disgust, bestowed upon this frightful beggar the two florins which he had received from his honest friend James the Anabaptist. The spectre stared fixedly at him, then shed tears, and finally leaped upon his neck. Candide drew back in alarm.

"Alas!" said the one wretch to the other, "do you no longer recognize your dear Pangloss?"

"What do I hear? Is it you, my dear master?-you in this horrible state! What misfortune then has befallen you? How is it that you are no longer in the finest of all castles? What is become of Miss Cunegund, the pearl of young maidens, the very masterpiece of nature?"

"I cannot utter a word more," said Pangloss.

Candide immediately led him into the Anabaptist's stable, where he made him eat a morsel of bread; and when Pangloss was somewhat restored, he asked:

"Well! what have you to tell me of Cunegund?"

"She is dead," answered the other.

Candide fainted away on hearing these tidings; his friend recalled him to his senses with a little stale vinegar which he happened to find in the stable. Candide once more opened his eyes.

"Cunegund is dead! Alas, thou best of all possible worlds! Where art thou now?-But of what illness did she die? Was it from grief at having seen me kicked with such violence out of her father's magnificent castle?"

"No," said Pangloss; "she was ripped up by Bulgarian soldiers, after having been outraged to the last possible degree; they broke my lord Baron's skull for trying to defend her; my lady the Baroness was cut to pieces; my poor young pupil was treated as barbarously as his sister; and as for the castle, not

114

one stone remains upon another, not a shed is left, not a sheep, not a duck, not a single tree. But we have been well avenged, for the Abarians have done as much on a neighbouring estate that belonged to a Bulgarian nobleman."

On hearing this narrative Candide fainted again; but when he came to himself and had said all that it was proper to say, he inquired into the cause and effect, and the sufficient reason which had brought poor Pangloss to such a deplorable plight.

"Alas!" said the other, "it was love; love, the consoler of the human race, the preserver of the universe, the soul of all sentient beings,-the tender passion of love!"

"Ah me!" said Candide, "I too have known what love is, that sovereign of the heart, that soul of our soul; I have derived no advantage from it but one sweet kiss, and twenty kicks on the rump. But how has a cause so pleasing been able to produce in you effect so hideous?"

Pangloss replied in these terms:

"O my dear Candide! you knew Paquette, the pretty girl who waited on our august Baroness; I tasted in her arms the pleasures of paradise, and they have produced these torments of hell with which you see me consumed: she was infected with this malady herself, and perhaps she has died of it. She caught it from a very learned friar who had traced it to its source, for he had received it from an old countess, on whom it had been bestowed by a cavalry officer, who himself owed it to a marchioness, who had it from a page, to whom it had been imparted by a Jesuit, who, when a novice, had received it in a direct line from one of the companions of Christopher Columbus. As for me, I shall give it to nobody, for I am at the point of death."

"O Pangloss!" exclaimed Candide, "what a singular genealogy! Was it not the devil who originated it?"

"By no means," answered the great man; "it was a thing that could not be dispensed with, a necessary ingredient in this best of all possible worlds; for if Columbus had not, in an island off the coast of America, caught this disease, which poisons the springs of generation, often prevents it altogether, and is clearly repugnant to the great object of nature, we should have had neither chocolate nor cochineal. Furthermore, it must be noted that up to the present day, in our hemisphere, this malady, like our controversies, is strictly confined to ourselves. The Turks, Indians, Persians, Chinese, Siamese, and Japanese are not yet acquainted with it; but there is sufficient reason why they should become acquainted with it in their turn before many centuries are over. Meanwhile it has made marvellous progress among us, especially in those huge armies composed of gallant and well-trained hirelings, which decide the destinies of kingdoms; for it is pretty certain that whenever thirty thousand men stand up in battle array against an army of equal numbers, some twenty thousand are more or less infected on either side."

"Wonderful indeed!" said Candide; "but you must be cured."

"And how can that be done?" said Pangloss; "I am penniless, my friend; and in all this wide world one cannot get oneself bled, nor have an injection administered, without paying a fee or getting someone else to pay for us."

This last observation decided Candide; he went and threw himself at the feet of his charitable Anabaptist James, and drew such an affecting picture of the state to which his friend was reduced, that the good man did not hesitate to receive Dr. Pangloss into his house, and he had him cured at his own expense; in which process Pangloss lost only one eye and an ear. As he wrote a clear hand, and knew arithmetic perfectly, James the Anabaptist made him his accountant. At the end of two months, being obliged to go to Lisbon on matters of business, he took his two philosophers on board with him, and on the voyage Pangloss explained to him how everything was so ordered that it could not be better. But James was not of this opinion.

"Men," said he, "must have corrupted their nature a little, for they were not born wolves, yet wolves they have become. God never gave them cannons, and twenty-four pound shot, and

116

bayonets; but they have made these things for their mutual destruction. I might adduce the misery caused by bankruptcies, and the justice of the law which takes possession of the bankrupt's property so as to deprive the creditors of it."

"All that was indispensable," answered the one-eyed philosopher; "private misfortunes promote the public good, so that the more private misfortunes there are, the better it is for the world."

While he was arguing in this manner, the sky grew dark, the wind blew from all points of the compass, and the ship was attacked by a most frightful storm, within sight of the harbour of Lisbon.

CHAPTER V

A Storm, a Shipwreck, an Earthquake, and all that happened to Dr. Pangloss, Candide, and James the Anabaptist

Half of the passengers, exhausted almost to death by those inconceivable tortures which the rolling of a vessel communicates to the nerves and all the humours of the body tossed about in opposite directions, had not even the energy to feel alarmed at the danger to which they were exposed; whilst the other half gave vent to piteous cries and prayers. The sails were torn to rags, the masts were shattered, the ship was leaking. All who were able were hard at work, but no one heard what another said, and no orders were given. The Anabaptist was on deck, lending a little help at the ropes, when a savage sailor dealt him a rude buffet which stretched him on the planks; but, with the force of the blow that he gave him, the sailor was thrown forward so violently that he fell overboard head foremost. He remained suspended in midair, caught by a piece of a broken mast. The kind-hearted James ran to his rescue, and assisted him to climb back, but, overbalancing himself in the effort, he was himself precipitated into the sea before the sailor's eyes, who allowed him to perish without deigning so much as to look at him. Candide hastened to the spot, and saw his benefactor rise to the surface for a moment, and then disappear for ever. He was inclined to cast himself into the sea after him, but the philosopher Pangloss prevented his doing so, proving to him that the roadstead of Lisbon had been made expressly that the Anabaptist might be drowned there. While he was engaged in demonstrating this proposition on *a priori* grounds, the vessel was broken up, and all on board perished with the exception of Pangloss, Candide, and the brutal mariner who had caused the excellent Anabaptist to be drowned; the rascal swam safely to shore, whither Pangloss and Candide were carried on a plank.

When they had recovered a little strength, they walked towards Lisbon; they had still some money, with which they hoped to save themselves from starvation, after having escaped the fury of the tempest.

Hardly had they entered the city, bewailing the death of their benefactor, when they felt the earth tremble under their feet, the sea rose in the harbour as if it were boiling, and dashed to pieces the ships that were at anchor. Clouds of fiery ashes filled the streets and public places, the houses tottered and fell, overturned from roof to basement, the very foundations being broken up; thirty thousand inhabitants of all ages and of both sexes were crushed beneath the ruins. The sailor whistled, and said with an oath:

"There will be something to be picked up here."

"What can be the sufficient reason of this phenomenon?" said Pangloss.

"This is surely the last day!" exclaimed Candide.

The sailor immediately rushed among the ruins, facing death itself in the search for money, found some, took possession of it, got drunk on it, and, having slept himself sober, purchased the favours of the first willing wench he met amidst the wreck of fallen houses, surrounded by the dying and the dead. Pangloss, however, pulled him by the sleeve, saying:

"My friend, this is not right, you are wanting in respect to the universal reason, and choose your time badly."

"Blood and thunder!" returned the other, "I am a sailor, and was born at Batavia; I have trampled four times on the crucifix in as many voyages to Japan; you have found a fine subject for your universal reason!"

Some fragments of falling masonry had wounded Candide, and he was lying prostrate in the street, covered with a heap of rubbish. He said to Pangloss:

"Oh! get me a little wine and oil; I am dying."

"This earthquake is no new thing," answered Pangloss; "the city of Lima in America experienced similar shocks last year; the same causes, the same effects; there is doubtless a vein of sulphur underground all the way from Lima to Lisbon."

"Nothing is more probable," returned Candide; "but, for God's sake, a little oil and wine!"

"Probable, say you!" replied the philosopher; "I maintain that there is positive proof of it."

Hereupon Candide lost consciousness, and Pangloss brought him a little water from a fountain that was near.

On the morrow, in crawling over the ruins, they discovered some provisions, and therewith recruited their strength a little, and then, like others, began to busy themselves in relieving the injured inhabitants who had escaped death. Some citizens, to whom they had brought succour, gave them as good a dinner as they could supply under such disastrous circumstances; it is true that the meal was a sad one, and that the company watered their bread with their tears, but Pangloss did his best to console them by the assurance that things could not have happened otherwise:

"For," said he, "nothing could have been better, for if there is a volcano under Lisbon, it could not be elsewhere, for it is impossible that things should not be where they are, for all is well."

A little fellow dressed in black, a familiar of the Inquisition, who was seated at his side, politely took up the conversation, and said:

"It would seem that the gentleman does not believe in original sin, for, if all is as good as can be, there can have been neither a fall of man nor divine punishment."

"I most humbly beg your Excellency's pardon," answered Pangloss still more politely, "for the fall of man and the consequent curse necessarily entered into the scheme of the best of all possible worlds."

"Then, sir, you do not believe in free will?" asked the familiar.

"Excuse me, your Excellency," said Pangloss; "free will is compatible with absolute necessity, for it was necessary that we should be free; for, in fact, the will being determined—"

Pangloss was in the middle of his sentence, when the familiar gave a significant nod to his stout serving-man, who was helping him to a cup of the wine of Oporto, commonly called port.

CHAPTER VI

*How a Fine Auto-da-fé was Held to Prevent Earthquakes, and
how Candide was Flogged on the Breech*

After the earthquake, which had destroyed three-quarters of
Lisbon, the wise men of the country had found no means more
effectual for obviating total ruin than that of giving the people
a fine *auto-da-fé;* it was decided by the university of Coimbra
that the spectacle of a few people roasted at a slow fire, with
grand ceremonies, is an infallible specific for preventing
earthquakes. They had therefore seized a native of Biscay, who
had been convicted of marrying a fellow god-parent, and two
Portuguese, who in eating a fowl had rejected the bacon.

After dinner was over, messengers arrived to bind Dr.
Pangloss and his pupil Candide, the one for having spoken as
he had done, and the other for having heard him with an air of
approbation; they were led away separately to apartments
which were exceedingly cool and airy, where they were never
incommoded with the sun. A week or so afterwards each of
them was dressed in a *sanbenito*, and their heads were
adorned with paper mitres; on Candide's mitre and *sanbenito*
were painted flames directed downwards, and devils which
had neither tails nor claws; but the devils that Pangloss
displayed had both, and the flames were upright.

Thus arrayed they marched in procession and heard a very
touching sermon, followed by a fine anthem delivered in a
solemn drone. While the singing went on, Candide was
flagellated in time to the music, the Biscayan and the two men
who would not eat bacon were burned, and Pangloss was
hanged, though that was unusual. The same day there was a
fresh earthquake, accompanied by a frightful noise.

Candide horrified, perplexed, and confounded, trembling all
over, and covered with blood, said to himself:

"If this is the best of all possible worlds, I wonder what the
others are like! It would not much matter if I had only been

flogged, I met with the same treatment among the Bulgarians, but, O my dear Pangloss, greatest of philosophers, why was I obliged to see you hanged, without knowing the reason? O my dear Anabaptist, noblest of men, where was the necessity of your being drowned within sight of land? O Miss Cunegund, pearl of young maidens, was it necessary that you should have been ripped open?"

He was returning, hardly able to support himself, after having been preached at, and scourged, and absolved, and blessed, when an old woman approached him, and said:

"Take courage, my son, and follow me."

CHAPTER VII

*How an Old Woman Took Care of Candide, and how he
Recovered the Object of his Affections*

Candide did not by any means take courage, but he followed
the old woman into a half-demolished house; she gave him a
pot of ointment to apply to his sores, and after showing him a
clean little bed, near which was a complete suit of clothes, she
left him some food and drink.

"Eat, drink, and sleep," said she, "and may our Lady of
Atocha, Saint Anthony of Padua, and Saint James of Compostella watch over you! I will come back tomorrow."

Candide, astonished as he was at all that he had seen, at all
that he had suffered, and most of all at the charity of this old
dame, attempted to kiss her hand.

"The hand you should kiss is not mine," said she; "I will come
back tomorrow. Rub yourself with the ointment, eat, and go to
sleep."

In spite of so many misfortunes, Candide ate and fell asleep.
Next morning the old woman brought him some breakfast,
examined his back, and rubbed it herself with another kind of
ointment; afterwards she brought him dinner, and returned
in the evening with his supper. On the following day she
repeated the same ceremonies.

"Who are you?" Candide kept saying to her; "and who has
inspired you with so much kindness? How can I show my
gratitude?"

The good woman never gave any reply. When she came back
that evening, she brought him no supper, but told him to come
with her and not say a word. She held him by the arm, and
walked with him about a quarter of a mile into the country, till
they arrived at a lonely house surrounded by gardens and
canals. The old woman tapped at a little door, and, when it was
opened, conducted Candide by a private staircase into a gilded
chamber; then leaving him on a richly brocaded sofa, she shut

the door, and departed. Candide thought he must be in a trance, and began to look upon all his past life as a dismal nightmare, and upon the present moment as a dream of a more agreeable character.

The old dame soon reappeared, supporting with difficulty another woman's trembling form. The latter was tall and stately, glittering with jewels, and with a veil over her face.

"Take off that veil," said the old woman to Candide.

The young man draws near; with timid hand he lifts the veil. What a moment of surprise! He fancies that he sees Miss Cunegund; he saw her in reality, for it was she herself. Strength fails him, he cannot utter a word, he falls at her feet, and Cunegund falls on the sofa. The old crone doses them with cordials, they recover their senses, they converse together; their words are at first broken and incoherent, cross questions and crooked answers, mingled with sighs, tears, and exclamations. The old woman advises them to make less noise, and leaves them to themselves.

"Ah! Is it indeed yourself?" said Candide; "you are still alive! I find you once more, here in Portugal! Then you were never ravished after all? You were not ripped open, then, as the philosopher Pangloss assured me?"

"Yes, I was," said the lovely Cunegund; "but death does not always result from either of those accidents."

"But your father and mother—were they killed?"

"It is but too true," said Cunegund, weeping.

"And your brother?"

"My brother was killed as well."

"And why are you in Portugal? And how did you know that I was here? And by what strange chance have you succeeded in bringing me into this house?"

"I will tell you everything," replied the lady; "but you must first inform me of all that has happened to yourself since you gave me that innocent kiss, for which you were kicked out of doors."

Candide very respectfully obeyed her, and, though he was bewildered, though his voice was weak and stammering, and his hinder parts were still a little sore, he related in the most artless manner all that he had gone through since the moment of their parting. Cunegund raised her eyes to heaven; she shed tears when she heard of the death of the kind Anabaptist and of Pangloss; after which she spoke as follows to Candide, who was careful not to lose a single word, and seemed as if he would fain devour her with his eyes.

CHAPTER VIII

Cunegund's Story

"I was in my bed and fast asleep, when it pleased heaven to send the Bulgarians into our magnificent castle of Thunder-tentrunk; they murdered my father and my brother, and hacked my mother to pieces. A big Bulgarian, six feet high, seeing that I had lost consciousness at this dreadful spectacle, began to ravish me. That brought me round; I recovered my senses, I screamed, I struggled, I bit, I scratched, and tried to tear the big Bulgarian's eyes out, not knowing that all that was happening in my father's castle was the usual thing under the circumstances. The brutal fellow stabbed me with a knife in my left side, and I still bear the mark of the wound."

"Alas! How I long to see it!" said Candide simply.

"You shall do so," said Cunegund; "but let me proceed."

"Pray proceed," said Candide.

So she took up the thread of her story.

"A Bulgarian captain now came in, and saw me all covered with blood, while the soldier never troubled himself to stir. The captain, enraged at this want of respect shown towards himself, killed the brute as he lay upon me. Then he had my wound dressed, and took me as a prisoner of war to his own quarters. There I washed the few shirts that he possessed, and cooked his meals for him; he thought me exceedingly pretty,—excuse my saying so,—nor can I deny that he was a very well-made man, and that his skin was smooth and white; but he had little wit or philosophy,—it was easy to see that he had not been educated by Dr. Pangloss. At the end of three months, having lost all his money and grown tired of me, he sold me to a Jew named Don Issachar, who traded in Holland and Portugal, and was passionately fond of the fair sex. This Jew was greatly taken with my charms, but he could not conquer my modesty; I repulsed his overtures better than those of the Bulgarian soldier. An honourable lady may be violated once in a way, but her virtue is thereby strengthened. The Jew, in order to tame me to submission, carried me off to this country house in which you now find me. Till then I had supposed that there was nothing on earth so magnificent as the castle of Thundertentrunk, but I have been undeceived.

"The Grand Inquisitor noticed me one day at mass; he ogled me a good deal, and sent me a message that he had something of a private nature to communicate to me. I was conducted to his palace, and I told him of my home and parentage; he represented to me how far beneath my rank it was to belong to an Israelite. A proposal was made on his behalf to Don Issachar that he should give me up to His Reverence. Don Issachar, who is the court banker, and a man of credit, would do nothing of the sort. The Inquisitor threatened him with an *auto-da-fé*. At last my Jew, under intimidation, concluded a bargain by which the house and I should be shared by both in common; that the Jew should have Monday, Wednesday, and the Sabbath to himself, and that the Inquisitor should have the other days of the week. This arrangement has lasted six months; but not without quarrels, for a dispute has often arisen as to whether the night between Saturday and Sunday belonged to the old or the new law. For my part, I have hitherto successfully resisted both of them; and I believe that it is for that reason each of them loves me still.

"At length, to avert the scourge of earthquakes, and to frighten Don Issachar, it pleased His Reverence the Inquisitor to celebrate an *auto-da-fé*, to which he did me the honour to invite me. I had a capital seat, and the ladies were served with refreshments between the mass and the executions. I was, indeed, seized with horror when I saw those two Jews burned, and that poor simple Biscayan who had married his fellow god-parent; but what was my astonishment, my terror, and my distress, when I beheld in a *sanbenito*, with a mitre on his head, a form which resembled that of Pangloss! I rubbed my eyes, I gazed attentively, I saw him hanged, and I fainted at the sight. Scarcely had I recovered my senses, when I saw you stripped naked; that put the crowning touch to my horror, consternation, grief, and despair. Let me tell you that your skin is even more perfectly white and rosy than that of my Bulgarian captain. That spectacle sharpened the anguish that pierced my soul and utterly consumed me. I screamed aloud, and would fain have said: 'Stop, savages!' but my voice failed me, nor would my cries have been of any use. After you had been soundly whipped, I said to myself:

"'How can it have happened that the amiable Candide and the wise Pangloss should turn up here in Lisbon, one to receive a hundred lashes, and the other to be hanged by order of His Reverence the Inquisitor, whose sweetheart I am? How cruelly did Pangloss deceive me when he said that everything goes on in the best possible way!'

"Agitated and distracted, at one moment beside myself with indignation, and at the next feeling too weak to live, I had my head full of all I had seen and suffered,—the massacre of my father, mother, and brother, the insults to which that vile Bulgarian soldier had subjected me, the wound that he had given me with his knife, my captivity, my apprenticeship in cookery, my Bulgarian captain, my ugly Don Issachar, my abominable Inquisitor, the hanging of Dr. Pangloss, the grand *miserere* droned out while you were being whipped, and, above all, the kiss I had given you behind a screen the day I saw you, as I thought, for the last time. I praised God for having brought you back to me after so many trials. I recommended you to the care of this old servant, and told her to bring you hither as soon as she could. She has faithfully executed her commission, and I have tasted the inexpressible pleasure of seeing you again, of hearing you, and speaking to you. But you must be famishing, and I am pretty hungry myself; let us begin supper."

So down they sat together at table; and after supper, they placed themselves once more on that splendid sofa which I have already mentioned, and there they were when one of the masters of the house in the person of Don Issachar, arrived. It was the Sabbath day, and he came to enjoy his rights, and to declare his tender attachment.

CHAPTER IX

*What Befell Cunegund, Candide, the Grand Inquisitor, and
the Jew*

This Issachar was the most irascible Hebrew that had ever
been seen since the Babylonian captivity.

"What is this?" said he; "bitch of a Galilean, was not my lord
Inquisitor enough, but this rascal must also have his share of
what belongs to me?"

So saying, he drew a long dagger, with which he was always
provided, and, not imagining that his adversary was armed, he
threw himself upon Candide. But our worthy Westphalian had
received a fine sword from the old woman along with the suit
of clothes; he drew this weapon, though his manners were as a
rule extremely gentle, and stretched the Israelite stark dead
upon the floor at the feet of the fair Cunegund.

"Holy Virgin!" she exclaimed. "What will become of us? A
man slain in my house! If the officers of justice come, we are
lost."

"If Pangloss had not been hanged," said Candide, "he would
have given us some good advice in this extremity, for he was a
great philosopher. Failing him, let us consult the old woman."

She had a large stock of prudence, and was beginning to give
her advice, when another little door was opened. It was an
hour after midnight, so Sunday had begun, a day that belonged
to His Reverence the Inquisitor. He entered, and saw the lately
castigated Candide, sword in hand, a dead body stretched
upon the ground, Cunegund scared out of her senses, and the
old woman calmly giving her advice.

This is what passed that moment through Candide's mind,
and thus it was he reasoned with himself:

"If this holy man calls for help, he will undoubtedly have me
burned, and he may possibly do as much for Cunegund; he has
already had me whipped unmercifully; he is my rival; I have
just fleshed my sword; there is no time to hesitate."

This train of thought was rapid and concise, and, without giving the Inquisitor time to recover from his surprise, Candide ran his sword right through the other's body, and hurled him beside the Jew.

"What! another of them!" exclaimed Cunegund; "there is no longer any possibility of pardon; we are excommunicated; our last hour is come! Whatever can have possessed you, who are of so mild a disposition, to kill within a couple of minutes a Jew and a dignitary of the Church?"

"My beautiful young lady," answered Candide, "when a man is under the influence of love and jealousy, and has been whipped by the Inquisition, he is no longer like himself."

The old woman then put in her word, and said:

"There are three Andalusian steeds in the stable, with saddles and bridles; let the brave Candide get them ready; you, my lady, have moidores and diamonds; let us mount without delay,— though I have only one side to sit on,—and go to Cadiz. It is the finest weather in the world, and travelling is very enjoyable during the coolness of the night."

Candide immediately saddled the three horses, and Cunegund, the old woman, and he, rode thirty miles without drawing rein. When they were already far away, the holy *Hermandad* arrived upon the scene; they buried His Reverence in a magnificent church, and cast Issachar's corpse into the common sewer.

Candide, Cunegund, and their old attendant had now reached the little town of Aracena, amidst the Sierra Morena mountains, and this was the conversation that they held together at an inn there.

CHAPTER

Tells in what a State of Distress Candide, Cunegund, and the Old Woman Arrived at Cadiz, and of their Subsequent Embarkation

"Who can have robbed me of my pistoles and my jewels?" said Cunegund weeping. "How shall we live? What are we to do? Where can I find Inquisitors and Jews to give me any more?"

"Alas!" said the old woman, "I strongly suspect a reverend Franciscan friar, who lodged last night at the same inn with us at Badajoz—Heaven preserve me from forming a rash judgment!—but he came into our chamber twice, and left the place long before we did."

"Ah!" sighed Candide; "the excellent Pangloss used often to assure me that the good things of this world are the common property of all men, and that each of us has an equal right to them. According to those principles, this friar ought certainly to have left us wherewithal to finish our journey. Have you then nothing at all remaining, my fair Cunegund?"

"Not a maravedi," said she.

"What course must we adopt?" said Candide.

"Let us sell one of the horses," suggested the old woman; "I will ride on a pillion behind the young lady,—though I can only sit upon one side,—and so we shall get to Cadiz after all."

There happened to be in the same hostelry a prior of the Benedictine order, who purchased the horse very cheaply. Candide, Cunegund, and the old woman passed through Lucena, Chillas, and Lebrija, and arrived at last at Cadiz. There they found a fleet being fitted out, and troops mustered, in order to bring to their senses the reverend Jesuit fathers of Paraguay, who were accused of stirring up a revolt among the natives against the kings of Spain and Portugal, near the city of San Sacramento. Candide, having seen some service with the Bulgarians, went through his exercises before the general of the little expedition with so much grace, quickness, skill, spirit, and agility, that he gave him the command of a company of infantry. So now, being made a captain, he embarks with Miss Cunegund, the old woman, two men servants, and the two Andalusian horses which had belonged to the Grand Inquisitor of Portugal.

During the passage they had many discussions upon the philosophy of poor Pangloss.

"We are going into another world," said Candide; "it is there no doubt that everything is right; for it must be confessed that we have had cause to complain a little of what happens in our own, whether with respect to physical or moral evils."

"I love you with all my heart," said Cunegund; "but I am still shocked and terrified at what I have seen and undergone."

"All will now go well," replied Candide; "the sea of this new world is already better than those of Europe; it is calmer, and the winds are more regular. Assuredly it is the new one which is the best of all possible worlds."

"God grant it!" sighed Cunegund; "but I have been so horribly unhappy in the old one, that my heart is almost shut against hope."

"You murmur," interposed the old woman, "and yet, alas! you have experienced no such misfortunes as mine."

Cunegund nearly laughed in her face, for she thought it very droll of this good dame to pretend to be more unhappy than herself.

"Ah! my good woman," said she, "unless you have been outraged by two Bulgarians, received two wounds from a knife in your belly, had two castles demolished, had two mothers and two fathers murdered before your eyes, and seen two lovers of yours flogged at an *auto-da-fé*, I do not see how you can claim the palm in misfortune over me; to all this add that I was born a baroness, with seventy-two quarterings, and yet I have been reduced to the position of a cook."

"My young lady," answered the old woman, "you do not know my birth and lineage; and if I were to show you what is behind, you would not speak as you do, but would suspend your judgment."

This mysterious language created extreme curiosity in the minds of Cunegund and of Candide, and the old woman then addressed them in the following terms.

CHAPTER XI

The Old Woman's Story

"My eyes have not always been bleared and rimmed with red, my nose has not always touched my chin, nor was I always a servant. I am the daughter of Pope Urban X. and of the Princess of Palestrina.[1] Until the age of fourteen years I was brought up in a palace, to which the castles of all your German barons would not have been fit for stables; and a single one of my dresses cost more than all the magnificence of Westphalia. I grew in beauty, accomplishments, and talents, surrounded by pleasure, hope, and admiration. I had already power to inspire love; my bust was fully formed, and what a bust!—white, firm, and shaped like that of the Venus de Medici. And what eyes! what eyelids! what dark eyebrows! what flames shot forth from either pupil, and eclipsed the brightness of the stars!—as the poets of our part of the country used to tell me. The women who dressed and undressed me used to fall into raptures as they looked upon me in front and behind; and all the men would fain have been in their place.

"I was betrothed to the Prince of Massa-Carrara. Such a prince! As handsome as myself, a compound of sweetness and grace, beaming with wit, and burning with passion. I loved him as one loves for the first time,-with idolatry, with transport. Preparations were made for our wedding with unheard of pomp and magnificence; there were incessant banquets, tournaments, and comic operas; all Italy made sonnets in my praise, not one of which was even passable. I had almost attained the summit of my happiness, when an old marchioness, who had been my prince's mistress, invited him to drink chocolate at her house. He died in less than two hours afterwards in frightful convulsions; but that was a mere trifle to

1 Voltaire has here the following note: "Observe the author's extreme discretion, for there has not up to the present time been any pope named Urban X. He is afraid of attributing illegitimate offspring to an actual pope. What circumspection! what delicacy of conscience!"

what followed. My mother, in despair, though far less afflicted than I was, determined to retire for some time from so fatal a place. She had a very fine estate near Gaeta, for which we embarked in a native galley which was gilded like the high altar of St. Peter's at Rome. Suddenly a Sallee rover bore down upon us, and attacked us. Our men defended themselves like soldiers of the Pope; they all fell upon their knees, throwing down their arms, and begging the Corsair to grant them absolution *in articulo mortis*.

"They were immediately stripped as naked as apes, nor did they spare my mother, nor our maids of honour, nor myself. It is marvellous with what alacrity these gentry undress people; but what surprised me more was the way in which they pryed into every nook and cranny of our persons. This ceremony seemed to me a very strange one; for thus it is that we are apt to judge of everything new when we have never been out of our own land. I soon found out that the object of this proceeding was to discover if we had any diamonds hidden about us; it is a custom established from time immemorial among the refined races which scour the sea. I have been informed that those religious gentlemen, the Knights of Malta, never fail to act in this way whenever they take Turkish prisoners of either sex, it is a rule of the law of nations from which they never depart.

"I need not tell you how hard it was for a young princess to be brought to Morocco as a slave along with her mother; you may imagine, too, all we had to suffer in the pirate ship. My mother was still very handsome; our maids of honour and our mere waiting-women had more charms than were to be found in all Africa. As for me, I was simply enchanting,—beauty and grace personified; moreover I was a virgin,—but I did not remain so long. That flower which had been reserved for the handsome Prince of Massa-Carrara was snatched from me by the Corsair captain, an abominable negro, who thought he was thereby doing me a great honour. Certainly Her Highness the Princess of Palestrina and I must have had strong constitutions to withstand all we went through until our arrival at Morocco! But let us pass on; these are matters of such common occurrence that they are not worth the trouble of mentioning.

"Morocco was deluged with blood when we arrived. Of the fifty sons of the Emperor Muley Ismäel each had his adherents, a state of things which resulted in fifty civil wars, of blacks against blacks, of blacks against tawnies, of tawnies against tawnies, of mulattoes against mulattoes; it was continual carnage throughout the whole extent of the empire.

"Scarcely had we landed before some negroes belonging to a faction opposed to that of my Corsair presented themselves to rob him of his booty. Next to the gold and diamonds we were the most precious part of his cargo. I was then witness of a conflict such as you never see in the colder climates of Europe. The blood of northern nations is not so in flammable; they do not carry their rage for the fair sex to the degree that is common in Africa. It would seem as if you Europeans had nothing stronger than milk in your veins; but it is vitriol, it is liquid fire that flows in the veins of the inhabitants of Mount Atlas and the adjoining countries. They fought with the fury of the lions, tigers, and serpents of their native land, to decide which of them should have us. A Moor seized my mother by the right arm, my captain's lieutenant held her fast by the left; a Moorish soldier took her by one leg, while one of our pirates was holding her by the other. There was hardly one of our maids but found herself in a moment drawn in opposite directions by four soldiers. My captain kept me hidden behind him; scimitar in hand, he killed all who ventured to oppose his rage. At last I saw all our Italian women and my mother torn, hacked, and massacred by the monsters who disputed for their possession. My captive companions, those who had taken us prisoners, soldiers, sailors, blacks, tawnies, whites, mulattoes, and last of all my captain, all were slain, and I alone was left dying on a heap of dead. Scenes like this take place, we know, over a space of more than three hundred leagues, without causing anyone to neglect the five prayers a day which Mohammed has enjoined.

"I freed myself with great difficulty from the heap of bleeding carcasses, and dragged myself under a large orange-tree on the bank of a stream hard by, where I sank down overcome with fright, fatigue, horror, despair, and hunger. Soon afterwards my overstrained senses gave way to unconsciousness, which had more of the nature of a swoon than of peaceful repose. I was still in that state of weakness and insensibility, hovering between life and death, when I felt myself pressed down by something that moved above me; I opened my eyes, and saw a white man of prepossessing appearance, who was sighing and muttering between his teeth: "*O che sciagura d'essere senza coglioni!*'

CHAPTER XII

The Story of the Old Woman's Misfortunes Continued

"Astonished and delighted at hearing the language of my native land, and no less surprised at the words which the man uttered, I told him that there were greater misfortunes than that of which he complained. I gave him a brief account of the horrors I had undergone, and I then fell back again in a swoon. He carried me into a neighbouring house, had me put to bed, caused some food to be given me, waited on me, soothed me with words of consolation and compliment, telling me that he had never seen anything so beautiful as myself, and that he had never felt so much regret as then for what no one could ever restore to him.

"'I was born at Naples,' said he, 'where two or three thousand children are treated like capons every year; some of them die in consequence, others acquire a voice finer than a woman's, and others again come to be rulers of States. The operation in my case was very successful, and I have been leader of the choir in the chapel of Her Highness the Princess of Palestrina.'

"'My mother!' I exclaimed.

"'Your mother?' cried he, bursting into tears. 'Why, you must be that young princess whom I instructed till she was six years of age, and who even then gave promise of being as lovely as you now are.'

"'The very same; my mother is lying four or five hundred steps from where we are, cut into quarters, and covered by a heap of dead bodies.'

"I then related to him all that had happened to me, and he, in his turn, gave me an account of his adventures, and informed me that he had been sent to the King of Morocco by a Christian power in order to conclude a treaty with that monarch, engaging to furnish him with gunpowder, cannon, and ships to help him in exterminating the commerce of other Christians.

"'My mission is fulfilled,' said this obliging eunuch; 'I am about to embark at Ceuta, and will take you back with me to Italy. *Ma che sciagura d'essere senza coglioni!*'

"I thanked him with tears of grateful emotion; but, instead of taking me to Italy, he brought me to Algiers, and sold me to the Dey of that province. Hardly had the sale been effected, when the plague which has made the round of Africa, Asia, and Europe, broke out with fury at Algiers. You have witnessed earthquakes, my young lady, but have you ever had the plague?"

"Never," replied the Baroness.

"If you had had it," continued the old woman, "you would acknowledge that an earthquake is nothing to it. It is exceedingly common in Africa, and it attacked me. Picture to yourself the situation of the daughter of a Pope, only fifteen years of age, who in the space of three months had been subjected to poverty and slavery, had been violated nearly every day, had seen her mother cut into quarters, had experienced all the horrors of war and famine, and was now dying of the plague at Algiers! I did not die of it, however; but my eunuch and the Dey, and almost the whole seraglio of Algiers, perished.

"When the first ravages of that frightful pestilence were over, the Dey's slaves were put up for sale. A merchant bought me, and took me to Tunis; there I was sold to another merchant, who sold me again at Tripoli; from Tripoli I was passed on to Alexandria, from Alexandria to Smyrna, and from Smyrna to Constantinople. At last I became the property of an Aga of the janissaries, who was ere long commanded to go and defend the town of Azov against the Russians who were besieging it.

"The Aga, who was a man greatly devoted to our sex, took all his harem with him, and lodged us in a little fort on the Sea of Azov, with two black eunuchs and twenty soldiers to guard us. A prodigious number of Russians were slain, but they soon made us an adequate return; Azov was given up to fire and sword, and neither sex nor age was spared. Our little fort alone held out, and the enemy determined to starve us into submission. The twenty janissaries had sworn that they would never surrender; the extremities of hunger to which they were now reduced constrained them, for fear of breaking their oath, to eat our two eunuchs. At the end of a few days more they resolved to devour the women.

"We had with us a very pious and compassionate *Imam*, who delivered a very fine discourse, in which he urged them not to kill us outright.

"'Only cut off,' said he, 'a rump steak from each of these ladies, you will find it excellent fare; if, in the course of a few days, it should be necessary to return, you will then be able to get a second supply; heaven will be pleased with you for acting so charitably, and send you succour.'

"He had a great deal of eloquence, and persuaded them to follow his advice. We were subjected to that horrible operation, and the Imam applied to our wounds the same healing balm which is used in the case of boys who have been circumcised; but we nearly lost our lives.

"The janissaries had no sooner finished the meal with which we had furnished them, than the Russians arrived in flat-bottomed boats, and not a janissary escaped. The Russians paid no attention to the state in which we were, but, French surgeons being found everywhere, a very clever one took us in hand and cured us; and I shall remember all my life what proposals he made me after my wounds were well closed. Moreover he told us all to cheer up, and assured us that such things had happened at a good many sieges, and that it was quite in accordance with the laws of war.

"As soon as my companions were able to walk they were sent to Moscow; while I fell into the possession of a *boyard*, who made me work in his garden, and used to give me twenty lashes a day. But at the end of two years, my master having been broken on the wheel with thirty other *boyards* for some plot against the court, I took advantage of the event, and made my escape. I traversed the whole of Russia; I was for a long time a servant at a tavern at Riga, afterwards at Rostock, Wismar, Leipsick, Cassel, Utrecht, Leyden, the Hague, and Rotterdam; I have grown old in the midst of misery and contempt, having only half of what I once had behind, and never being able to forget that my father was a pope. A hundred times have I determined to kill myself, but I always found I was still too fond of life. That ridiculous weakness may he considered one of our most unfortunate propensities, for can there be anything more absurd than to wish to carry for ever a burden which we are always desiring to throw upon the ground; to have a horror of existence, and yet to cling to it; in other words, to cherish the serpent which devours us, until it has eaten our very heart?

"I have seen in the various countries through which it has been my fortune to travel, as well as at the taverns where I have been a servant, a prodigious number of persons who abhorred their existence, but I have not known more than twelve who of their own accord put an end to their misery,—three negroes, four Englishmen, four from Geneva, and one German professor named Robeck. At last I came to be a servant in the house of the Jew, Don Issachar, who placed me about your person, my sweet young lady, and I have become attached to your fortunes, and been more interested in your adventures than in my own. I should never even have spoken to you of my misfortunes, if you had not given me a little provocation, and if it were not the custom on board a ship to tell stories to relieve the tediousness of the voyage. So you see, Miss, I have had experience and know the world; amuse yourself now by getting every passenger to tell you his history, and if a single one of them be found who has not often cursed his life, who has not often said to himself that he was the most wretched of all men, I give you leave to throw me headforemost into the sea."

CHAPTER XIII

How Candide was Obliged to Part from the Fair Cunegund and the Old Woman

The fair Cunegund, having heard the old woman's story, made her all the polite acknowledgments that were due to a person of her rank and merit. She welcomed her proposal and engaged all the passengers, one after another, to relate their adventures; after which Candide and she had to confess that the old lady was in the right.

"It is a great pity," said Candide, "that the wise Pangloss was hanged contrary to the usual practice at an *auto-da-fé*, for he would have made some admirable remarks on the physical and moral evils which cover land and sea, and I should feel that I have arguments strong enough to embolden me to offer some objections in a respectful manner."

As the passengers were relating their adventures the ship made way, and they landed at last at Buenos Ayres. Cunegund, Captain Candide, and the old woman proceeded to the house of the Governor don Fernando d'Ibaraa y Figueora y Mascarenas y Lampourdos y Souza. This gentleman had a pride suitable to a man who bore so many names. To those who addressed him he spoke with the most magnificent disdain, holding his nose so high in the air, and raising his voice so unmercifully, assuming a tone so imposing, and affecting so pompous a gait, that all who paid him their humble salutations felt inclined to kick him. He loved the ladies to distraction, and when Cunegund appeared before him, he thought he had never seen a lovelier sight. The first thing he did was to inquire if she were the captain's wife. The air with which he asked this question alarmed Candide; he dared not say that she was his wife, for in point of fact that was not the case; he dared not assert that she was his sister, for she was not that either; and, however fashionable this convenient falsehood may have been with the ancients, and however useful it might be found in modern times, his soul was too pure to tamper with the truth.

"Miss Cunegund," said he, "is to do me the honour of marrying me, and we beg your Excellency to condescend so far as to countenance our nuptials."

Don Fernando d'Ibaraa y Figueora y Mascarenas y Lampourdos y Souza twirled his moustache with a bitter smile, and ordered Captain Candide to go and inspect his company. Candide obeyed, and the Governor was left alone with Miss Cunegund. He made a declaration of his passion, protesting that he was ready to marry her the next day, in the face of the Church or otherwise, just as it might best please her charming self. Cunegund requested to be allowed a quarter of an hour to collect her thoughts, to consult the old woman, and to make her decision.

The old woman said to Cunegund:

"My dear young lady, you have seventy-two quarterings on your coat of arms, and not a farthing in your pocket; it rests only with yourself to become the wife of the most distinguished personage in South America, whose moustache is simply superb. Is it for you to pride yourself upon a fidelity which is proof against every assault? You have been ravished by the Bulgarians; a Jew and an Inquisitor have shared your good graces. Misfortunes confer new rights, and I must confess, that were I in your place, I should have no scruple in marrying His Excellency, and making the fortune of Captain Candide."

Whilst the old lady was speaking with all the prudence which age and experience bestow, they saw a little vessel enter the harbour; on board were an *alcalde* and *alguazils*. What had happened was as follows.

The old woman had rightly suspected that it was the grey friar with the long sleeves who stole Cunegund's money and jewels in the city of Badajoz, when she was on her hasty flight with Candide. This Franciscan wished to sell some of the precious stones to a jeweller, but the tradesman recognised them as having belonged to the Grand Inquisitor. The friar, before he was hanged, confessed that he had stolen them, described the persons in whose possession they had been, and pointed out the direction in which they had gone, the flight of Cunegund and Candide being already known. They were followed to Cadiz, and a vessel sent after them without loss of time. This was the ship now in harbour at Buenos Ayres. The report was spread that an *alcalde* was about to land with his officers, and that they were in pursuit of the murderers of the Grand Inquisitor. The old woman, with her usual foresight, saw in an instant what was to be done.

"You cannot fly," she said to Cunegund, "and you have nothing to fear; it was not you who killed His Reverence. Besides, the Governor, being in love with you, will not allow you to be ill-treated. Stay where you are."

Then she instantly hastened to Candide.

"Fly," she said, "or in an hour's time you will be burned alive."

There was not a moment to be lost; but how was he to tear himself away from Cunegund, and whither was he to fly for refuge?

CHAPTER XIV

How Candide and Cacambo were Received among the Jesuits of Paraguay

Candide had brought with him from Cadiz a serving-man belonging to a class plentiful enough on the coast of Spain and in the colonies. He was one-quarter Spanish, having been born of a mulatto mother in Tucuman. He had been by turns choir-boy, sexton, sailor, monk, porter, soldier, and lackey. His name was Cacambo, and he was strongly attached to his master, because his master was very good-natured. He saddled the two Andalusian horses as quickly as he could.

"Come, my master, let us follow the old woman's advice, and be off, without taking a look behind us as we gallop away."

Candide shed tears as he exclaimed:

"O my dear Cunegund! must I forsake you just at the time when His Excellency the Governor was about to countenance our nuptials? After having come with me so far, what, Cunegund, will become of you?"

"She will do the best she can," said Cacambo. "Women never find much trouble in disposing of themselves; heaven takes good care of that—let us be off."

"Whither do you propose to take me? In what direction are we going? What shall we do without Cunegund?" asked Candide.

"By St. James of Compostella!" said Cacambo, "you were going to fight against the Jesuits, let us go and help them instead. I know the roads pretty well, and will guide you into their territories; they will be delighted to have a captain expert in the Bulgarian drill, and you will make a prodigious fortune. When luck goes against us in one place, we may be better off in another. It is no small pleasure to see and do new things."

"You have been in Paraguay already then?" said Candide.

"Yes, indeed," answered Cacambo; "I was a scout in the College of Asuncion, and know all about the government of the *padres* as well as I know the streets of Cadiz, and an admirable thing it is. Their territory is already more than three hundred leagues across, and it is divided into thirty provinces. The *padres* have everything there, and the people nothing-it is the very masterpiece of reason and justice. For my part, I have never seen anything so divine as the *padres*, who here make war on the King of Spain and the King of Portugal, whilst in Europe they act as their father confessors; here they kill Spaniards, and in Madrid they teach them the way to heaven. This behaviour charms me-let us proceed. You are destined to be the happiest of all men. How pleased the *padres* will be when they know that a captain who is acquainted with the Bulgarian drill is coming to help them!"

As soon as they reached the first outpost, Cacambo told the advanced guard that a captain requested an audience of His Reverence the Commandant. Information was conveyed to the main guard, and a Paraguayan officer hastened to prostrate himself at the feet of the Commandant, and to deliver the message. Candide and Cacambo were in the first place disarmed, and their two Andalusian horses seized. Then the strangers were led forward between two files of soldiers, at the further end of which stood the Commandant, with his three-cornered cap on his head, his gown tucked up, a sword at his side, and a half-pike in his hand. He made a sign, and immediately four-and-twenty soldiers surrounded the two new-comers. A sergeant told them that they must wait, that the Commandant could not speak with them, and that the Reverend Father Provincial did not allow any Spaniard to open his mouth except in his own presence, or to stay longer than three hours in the country.

"And where is the Reverend Father Provincial?" asked Cacambo.

"He is at parade, after having said mass," answered the sergeant, "and you cannot kiss his spurs for three hours."

"But," said Cacambo, "my master, the captain, who is famished like myself, is no Spaniard; he is a German. Can we

148

not have some breakfast while we wait for His Reverence?"

The sergeant immediately went off to report this speech to the Commandant.

"God be praised!" said that personage; "since he is a German, I can speak to him. Let him be brought to my arbour."

So Candide was straightway conducted into a green bower, adorned with a very handsome marble colonnade of green and gold, with trellis-work, behind which were confined parrots, humming-birds of all sorts and sizes, guinea-fowl, and all the rarest of the feathered tribe. An excellent breakfast was provided in vessels of gold, and whilst the Paraguayans were eating Indian corn out of wooden bowls, in the open field, exposed to the fierce heat of the sun, the Reverend Father Commandant entered his leafy arbour.

He was a very handsome young man, his face well filled out, of a fair and fresh-coloured complexion, with high arched eyebrows, bright eyes, ruddy ears and ruby lips; his air was proud, but with a pride which was neither that of a Spaniard nor of a Jesuit. The arms of which they had been deprived were given back to Candide and Cacambo, as well as their two Andalusian horses; and Cacambo fed them with oats near the arbour, without taking his eyes off them for fear of a surprise.

Candide first kissed the hem of the Commandant's gown, and then they seated themselves at table.

"You are German, it seems?" said the Jesuit in that language.

"Yes, reverend father," replied Candide.

As they uttered these words, they looked at each other with extreme astonishment and an emotion which they could not control.

"And to what part of Germany do you belong?" asked the Jesuit.

"To the dirty province of Westphalia," said Candide; "I was born in the castle of Thundertentrunk."

"O heavens! is it possible!" exclaimed the Commandant.

"What a miracle!" exclaimed Candide.

"Can it be you?" said the Commandant.

"This is quite impossible!" said Candide.

They both started back, then threw themselves into each other's arms, and shed torrents of tears.

"What! Can it indeed be yourself, reverend father? Are you the brother of the beauteous Cunegund? you who were killed by the Bulgarians! you, the son of my lord Baron! you, a Jesuit in Paraguay! It must be confessed that this world is a strange place. O Pangloss! Pangloss! how pleased you would be, if you had not been hanged!"

The Commandant ordered the negro slaves to retire, as well as the Paraguayans who were pouring out wine for them into goblets of rock crystal. He thanked God and Saint Ignatius a thousand times; he pressed Candide to his heart, and their faces were bathed in tears.

"You would be still more amazed, more affected, more transported," said Candide, "were I to tell you that your sister, Miss Cunegund, whom you believed to have been ripped open, is well and hearty."

"Where?"

"In your neighbourhood, in the house of His Excellency the Governor of Buenos Ayres; and I myself came to South America to fight against you."

Each word that they uttered during a long conversation contributed to pile wonder upon wonder. Their whole soul seemed to hover over their lips, to listen at their ears, and to sparkle in their eyes. As they were Germans, they sat at table a considerable time, while they waited for the Reverend Father Provincial; and the Commandant spoke as follows to his dear Candide.

CHAPTER XV

How Candide Killed the Brother of his Beloved Cunegund

"I shall never cease to remember all my life long the terrible day on which I saw my father and mother killed, and my sister ravished. When the Bulgarians were gone, that charming sister of mine was nowhere to be found, but my father and mother, together with myself, two female servants, and three little boys with their throats cut, were laid in a cart and taken for burial to a chapel of the Jesuits, at a distance of two leagues from my ancestral home. A Jesuit sprinkled us with holy water, which was horribly salt, and some drops of it went into my eyes; the good father noticed that my eyelids slightly quivered; he placed his hand on my heart, and felt it beat; my life was saved, and at the end of three weeks I was as well as ever. You know, my dear Candide, that I was exceedingly good-looking, and I became still more so; accordingly the Reverend Father Croust, Superior of the House, conceived the most tender affection for me. He gave me the dress of a novice, and some time afterwards I was sent to Rome. The Father General had need of young German Jesuits to serve as recruits in Paraguay, where the native chieftains admit as few Spanish Jesuits as they can; they like other Europeans better, for they expect to find them more submissive to their authority. I was judged fit by the Reverend Father General to go and work in that vineyard. A Pole, a Tyrolese, and I set sail together. On my arrival I was honoured with the sub-diaconate and a lieutenancy; I am now a colonel and a priest. We shall give the troops of the King of Spain a vigorous reception; I warrant you they will be excommunicated and soundly thrashed. Providence sends you hither to support us. But is it indeed true that my dear sister Cunegund is in this neighbourhood, and living at the house of the Governor of Buenos Ayres?"

Candide solemnly assured him that nothing was more certain, and their tears began to flow afresh.

The Baron seemed as if he would never be weary of embracing Candide; he called him his brother and his preserver.

"Perhaps," said he, "we may be able, my dear Candide, to enter the town together as conquerors, and recover my sister Cunegund."

"That is my dearest wish," said Candide, "for I intended to marry her, and I still hope to do so."

"Insolent fellow!" exclaimed the Baron; "can you have the impudence to think of marrying my sister, who has no less than seventy-two quarterings of nobility? I count it intolerable effrontery in you to dare to speak to me of a project so presumptuous!"

Candide, astonished at hearing such language, replied thus:

"Reverend Father, all the quarterings in the world matter not a straw; I rescued your sister from the arms of a Jew and of an Inquisitor; she is under very considerable obligations to me, and is minded to be my wife. Dr. Pangloss always told me that all mankind are equal, and, you may depend upon it, I will marry her."

"That remains to be seen, you scoundrel," said the Jesuit Baron of Thundertentrunk, and so saying he gave him a heavy blow on the face with the flat of his sword.

Candide instantly drew his own, and buried it up to the hilt in the body of the Jesuit Baron; but, as he pulled out the reeking weapon, he burst into tears, and exclaimed:

"Good God! I have slain my quondam master and friend, my prospective brother-in-law! I am the best-hearted man in the world, yet, lo and behold, I have already killed three men, and amongst those three two of them are priests."

Cacambo, who had been keeping watch at the door of the arbour, ran up to his master, who said to him:

"Nothing now remains for us to do but to sell our lives as dearly as possible. People, no doubt, will soon visit this arbour; since die we must, let it be with arms in our hands."

Cacambo, who had often been in similar predicaments, did

not lose presence of mind; he took the Jesuit's gown which the Baron wore, and put it upon Candide, gave him the dead man's square cap, and made him mount on horseback. All this was done in the twinkling of an eye.

"Let us gallop away, master; everybody will take you for a Jesuit going to give some orders, and we shall have passed the frontiers before they can run after us."

He was already in full flight as he uttered these words, and cried out in Spanish:

"Make way! make way for the Reverend Father the Colonel!"

CHAPTER XVI

What Happened to the Two Travellers in Connection with Two Girls, Two Monkeys, and the Savages Called Oreillons

Candide and his servant were beyond the barriers before anyone in the camp yet knew of the death of the German Jesuit.

The provident Cacambo had taken care to fill his haversack with bread, chocolate, ham, fruit, and some flasks of wine. Riding their Andalusian horses, they penetrated into an unknown country where they found no track. At last a beautiful meadow land, intersected by rivulets, was spread out before them, where our two travellers allowed their steeds to graze. Cacambo urged his master to eat, and himself set him the example.

"How can you expect me to eat ham, when I have slain the son of my lord Baron, and find myself condemned never to see the fair Cunegund again all my days? What is the good of prolonging this wretched life, which I must drag on far from her in remorse and despair? And what will the *Trévoux Gazette* say?"

As he asked these questions, he never ceased eating. The sun was now setting, when the two wanderers heard some faint cries, uttered apparently by women. They were uncertain whether they were the cries of sorrow or of joy; but they rose hurriedly, with that feeling of uneasiness and alarm which every sound inspires in a strange country. The clamour proceeded from two girls in nature's garb who were running at full speed along the side of the meadow, while a couple of monkeys were closely pursuing them and biting their buttocks. Candide was moved with pity at the sight; he had learned to shoot so well when he was with the Bulgarians, that he could hit a nut on a hazel bush without touching a leaf. He seized his double-barrelled Spanish musket, fired, and killed both the monkeys.

"Thank God, my dear Cacambo! I have delivered these two poor creatures from a great danger; if I committed a sin in killing an Inquisitor and a Jesuit, I have made ample amends by saving the lives of two young women. Perhaps they are damsels of high degree, and this adventure may procure us considerable advantage in this country."

He was going to continue, but his tongue was paralysed on his seeing the two girls embrace the monkeys most tenderly, burst into tears over their dead bodies, and fill the air with cries of bitter lamentation.

"I was not prepared for such a display of kind good-nature," said he at last to Cacambo, who replied:

"That is a pretty piece of work of yours, master; you have killed these two young ladies' lovers."

"Their lovers! Can it be possible? You are jesting with me, Cacambo; how can I believe you?"

"My dear master," answered Cacambo, "you are always astonished at everything. Why should you find it so strange that there are some countries were monkeys are in high favour with the ladies? They are a fourth part human, just as I am by a fourth part a Spaniard."

"Ah!" rejoined Candide, "I remember hearing Dr. Pangloss say that in ancient times such things had happened, and that those mixtures had produced goat-footed Pans, fauns, and satyrs, and that divers distinguished men of antiquity had seen some of them; but I took all such stories for fables."

"You should be convinced now that they are true; you see how these creatures are treated by persons who have received no proper education. All that I am afraid of is that these ladies will do us some serious mischief."

These weighty reflections induced Candide to leave the meadow, and retire into the depths of an adjoining wood. There he and Cacambo had supper, and both of them, after cursing the Portuguese Inquisitor, the Governor of Buenos Ayres, and the Baron, went to sleep on a couch of moss. When they awoke, they found themselves unable to stir, the reason of which was that during the night the Oreillons, who inhabit that country, and to whom the two damsels had denounced them, had tied them down with ropes made of the bark of a tree. They were surrounded by about fifty of the tribe, stark naked, and armed with bows and arrows, clubs, and stone hatchets; some were boiling water in a huge cauldron, others were preparing spits, and all were shouting:

"A Jesuit! He is a Jesuit! We shall have our revenge, and first-rate fare. Let us eat up the Jesuit! let us eat up the Jesuit!"

"I told you plainly, my dear master," said Cacambo dolefully, "that these two girls would play us some nasty trick."

Candide, catching sight of the cauldron and the spits, exclaimed:

"We are certainly going to be roasted or boiled. Ah! What would Dr. Pangloss say, if he saw what human nature is like in its unsophisticated simplicity? All is right,—be it so; but I must confess that it is right hard to have lost Miss Cunegund, and to be stuck on a spit by Indians."

Cacambo, who never lost his presence of mind, said to the disconsolate Candide:

"Do not despair; I understand a little of the jargon of this tribe, and will speak to them."

"Be sure that you impress upon them," said Candide, "the horrible inhumanity of cooking their fellow-men, and how little it is in accordance with Christianity."

"Gentlemen," said Cacambo, "you are intending, I think, to eat up a Jesuit today,—is it not so? And such a proceeding is quite right; nothing is more just than to treat one's enemies in that way. In fact the voice of nature teaches us to kill our neighbour, and that is what people are doing all over the earth. If we do not avail ourselves of the right of eating them as well, that is because we have other means of furnishing our feasts; but you have not the same recources as we have, and assuredly it is far better to eat one's enemies than to abandon the fruit of our victories to ravens and crows. But, gentlemen, you would not wish to eat up your friends. You fancy that you are about to

156

spit a Jesuit, whereas it is your defender and the foe of your foes that you are on the point of roasting. As for me, I was born in your own country, and the gentleman you see before you is my master. So far from being a Jesuit, he has just killed one of them, whose spoils he is wearing; that is how your mistake arose. To ascertain the truth of what I tell you, take his gown, convey it to the first outpost of the Jesuits' territory, and inquire whether my master has not killed a Jesuit officer. It will not require much time; you will still be able to eat us up, if you find that I have lied to you. But if I have told you the truth, you are too well acquainted with the principles of public justice, morality, and law, not to grant us acquittal."

The Oreillons thought this proposal very reasonable, and they deputed two of their leading men to go without delay and make inquiry into the facts. The two delegates discharged their commission like men of sense, and soon returned with good tidings. The Oreillons thereupon released their two prisoners, treated them with every sort of civility, offered them their daughters, gave them refreshment, and escorted them back to the confines of their State, crying out with animation:

"He is no Jesuit! He is no Jesuit!"

Candide never grew weary of wondering at the cause of his deliverance.

"What a people!" said he; "what men and manners to be sure! If I had not had the good fortune to drive my sword right into the body of Miss Cunegund's brother, I should have been killed and eaten without mercy. But, after all, there is a great deal of goodness in unsophisticated nature, since these people, instead of eating me up, have paid me a thousand attentions, as soon as they knew that I was not a Jesuit."

CHAPTER XVII

Arrival of Candide and his Servant in the Land of El Dorado,
and what they Saw there

When they reached the frontier of the Oreillons Cacambo said
to Candide:

"You see that this hemisphere is no better than the other;
take my advice, and let us return to Europe by the quickest way
we can."

"How are we to return?" said Candide; "and whither shall we
go? If I seek my own country, the Bulgarians and Abarians
massacre everybody there; if I go back to Portugal, I shall be
burned at the stake; and if we remain in this country, we run
the risk every moment of being stuck on a spit. But how can I
make up my mind to leave a part of the world which contains
Miss Cunegund?"

"Let us turn our steps towards Cayenne," proposed Cacambo;
"we shall find French people there, for they travel all over the
world; they will perhaps help us. It may be that Heaven will
have pity upon us."

It was no easy task for them to make their way to Cayenne;
they had a general knowledge of the direction in which they
must go, but mountains, rivers, precipices, robbers, and savages
were everywhere formidable obstacles to their progress. Their
horses died of fatigue, their provisions were consumed, they
had no food for a whole month, except wild fruits, till they
found themselves at last near a little river bordered by coconut
trees, which served to sustain both life and hope.

Cacambo, whose advice was always as judicious as that of
the old woman had been, said to Candide:

"We can hold out no longer, we have gone far enough on
foot. I see an empty canoe on the bank; let us fill it with coco-
nuts, get into the little bark and drift with the stream; a river
always leads to some inhabited place. If we meet with nothing
agreeable, we shall at least meet with something new."

"Let us go," said Candide, "and commit ourselves to Providence."

They rowed along for many leagues between banks, in some places gay with flowers, and in others arid wastes; at one time level, and at another steep. The river grew ever wider and wider, but at last it disappeared under an archway of frowning rocks which rose high into the sky. The two travellers were bold enough to trust themselves to the agitated water beneath this arch. The river, contracted in this part of its course, carried them along swiftly and with terrific uproar. At the end of four-and-twenty hours they saw daylight once more; but their canoe was shattered against the jagged reefs, and they were obliged to creep from rock to rock for a whole league, until at length they found an extensive prospect all around, with inaccessible mountains on the horizon. The land was cultivated as much for pleasure as for necessity; the useful was everywhere mixed with the agreeable; the roads were covered, or rather adorned, with carriages, the form and material of which were alike splendid, wherein were seated men and women of singular beauty, and which were drawn along rapidly by large red sheep, surpassing in speed the finest horses of Andalusia, Tetuan, and Miknas.

"Here," said Candide, "is a country, after all we have gone through, which is better than Westphalia."

He landed with Cacambo near the first village to which they came, at the entrance of which some children, clad in gold brocade, but all in tatters, were playing at quoits. Our two inhabitants of the other world amused themselves with looking on; the quoits were pretty large round objects, yellow, red, and green, which shone with remarkable brilliance. The travellers were seized with a desire to pick up some of them, and found that they were gold, emeralds, and rubies, the smallest of which would have formed the chief ornament of the throne of the Great Mogul.

"Doubtless," said Cacambo, "these children who are playing here are the sons of the king of the country."

The village schoolmaster appeared at that moment to call them into school again.

"That," said Candide, "must be the tutor of the royal family."

The ragged little urchins immediately stopped their game, leaving their quoits on the ground, with all their other playthings. Candide picked them up, and running to the tutor, humbly presented them to him, giving him to understand by signs that their royal highnesses had forgotten their gold and precious stones. The village pedagogue with a smile threw them on the ground, regarded Candide for a moment from head to foot with considerable surprise, and then walked on.

The travellers did not fail to gather up the gold, the rubies, and the emeralds.

"Where are we?" exclaimed Candide. "The children of the kings of this country must be very well brought up, when they are taught to despise gold and precious stones."

Cacambo was as much astonished as Candide.

At length they reached the first house in the village itself, which was built as a palace would be in Europe. A great crowd was thronging the door, and a still larger number were inside; most exquisite strains of music were heard, and a tempting smell proceeded from the kitchen. Cacambo went up to the door, and heard those within speaking in the language of Peru; it was his mother tongue, for everybody knows that Cacambo was born in Tucuman, at a village where no other language was known.

"I will act as your interpreter," said he to Candide; "let us enter; this is evidently an inn."

Immediately two waiters and two servant-maids belonging to the tavern, dressed in cloth of gold, and having their hair fastened with gold-embroidered ribbons, invited them to join the ordinary. There were set on the table four different kinds of soup, each garnished with a brace of parrots, a boiled condor which weighed two hundred pounds, two roasted monkeys of a delicate flavour, three hundred of the larger sized humming-birds in one dish and six hundred of the smaller in another,

160

exquisite ragouts, and delicious pastry; all were served up in dishes made of a kind of rock crystal. The waiters and waitresses handed round a variety of cordials made out of the juice of the sugar-cane.

The guests were for the most part shopkeepers and waggoners, but all were exceedingly polite, asking Cacambo a few questions with the most respectful discretion, and answering his own inquiries in a perfectly satisfactory manner.

When the meal was done, both Candide and Cacambo thought they were paying handsomely for their share by laying on the table two or three of the large pieces of gold which they had picked up, but the host and hostess burst out laughing, and held their sides for a good while before they could recover their gravity.

"Gentlemen," said the innkeeper at last, "it is very evident that you are strangers, and we are not in the habit of seeing such; you must forgive us if we could not help laughing when you offered us for payment the stones which are found upon our high roads. Doubtless you have none of the money of the country, but it is not necessary for you to have any in order to dine here. All the inns established for the convenience of trade are supported by government. You have fared meanly here, because this is a poor village, but everywhere else you will meet with the entertainment due to your merits."

Cacambo interpreted to Candide all that the landlord had said, and Candide heard it with the same wonder and bewilderment as his friend Cacambo betrayed in reporting it.

"What land can this be," they said to each other, "which is unknown to all the rest of the world, and where human nature is altogether different from ours? This is in all probability the land where everything goes on well, for there must infallibly be one of that sort somewhere. And whatever Dr. Pangloss might choose to say about it, I often perceived that things went on badly enough in Westphalia."

CHAPTER XVIII

What the Travellers Saw in the Land of El Dorado

Cacambo expressed all his curiosity to the landlord, and the latter said:

"I am very ignorant, and I find it all the better for me that I am so; but we have in our village an old gentleman, retired from Court, who is the most learned man in the kingdom, and the most ready to impart information."

Therewith he conducted Cacambo to the old man's house. Candide only played second fiddle, and accompanied his servant. They entered a house that was very unpretending, for the front door was only silver, and the panels of the rooms were merely gold, but worked with so much taste that the most sumptuous wainscoting could not have eclipsed them. The entrance hall, indeed, was incrusted with nothing more valuable than rubies and emeralds; but the order in which everything was disposed made ample amends for such extreme simplicity.

The old gentleman received the two strangers on a sofa covered with the feathers of humming-birds, and ordered cordials to be handed to them in diamond goblets, after which he proceeded to satisfy their curiosity as follows:

"I am a hundred three score and twelve years old, and I have heard from my deceased father, who was the King's equerry, of the astonishing revolutions that took place in Peru, of which he had been an eye-witness. The kingdom where we are is the ancient home of the Incas, which they very imprudently quitted to go and subdue another part of the world, being in the end themselves destroyed by the Spaniards.

"The princes of their house who stayed behind in their native country showed themselves wiser; with the consent of the people they forbade any inhabitant ever to leave our little kingdom, and that law is what has preserved to us our innocence and our happiness. The Spaniards acquired a vague knowledge of this country, and have called it El Dorado, while an Englishman, named Sir Walter Raleigh, actually came within reach of it a hundred years ago; but we are hemmed in by inaccessible rocks and precipices. We have always hitherto been protected from the greed of European nations, which have an incomprehensible rage for the stones and dirt of our land, and would, in order to possess them, slay us all to the very last man."

The conversation that followed was a long one, and turned on the form of government, the manners of the people, their women, their public shows, and the state of the arts among them. At last Candide, who always had a taste for metaphysics, inquired through Cacambo if there was any religion in their country.

The old man blushed a little at being asked such a question.

"Pray, can you doubt it?" said he. "Do you take us for wretches incapable of gratitude?"

Cacambo respectfully inquired what was the religion of El Dorado. The old man blushed again.

"Can there be two religions?" said he. "We hold what I suppose is the religion of all the world; we worship God from morning till night."

"Do you worship only one God?" pursued Cacambo, who always served as the interpreter of Candide's doubts.

"Clearly," replied the old gentleman, "there are not two, nor three, nor four Gods. I must confess that I think the people of your world ask very singular questions."

Candide still continued to interrogate the courteous old man; he wanted to know how prayers were offered to God in El Dorado.

"We do not pray to Him at all," said the devout and venerable sage; "we have nothing to ask Him to give us. He has already bestowed upon us all we need, and we thank Him continually."

Candide had the curiosity to wish to see some of their priests, and he bade Cacambo ask where they were to be found. The good old man said with a smile:

"My friends, we are all of us priests; the King and all the heads of families solemnly sing hymns of thanksgiving every morning, and five or six thousand musicians accompany them."

"What! Have you no monks among you, who teach, and wrangle, and govern, and intrigue, and have people burned who do not agree with their opinions?"

"We should have to lose our senses first," said the old man; "we are all of the same way of thinking here, and we do not understand what you mean by your monks."

Candide remained wrapt in astonishment during this talk, and said to himself:

"This is very different from Westphalia, and my lord Baron's castle; if our friend Pangloss had seen El Dorado, he would no longer have maintained that Thundertentrunk was the best castle on the surface of the earth. Assuredly one ought to travel."

After this long conversation the kind old gentleman ordered a coach and six sheep to be got ready, and lent the services of a dozen of his domestics to escort the two travellers to Court.

"Excuse me," said he, "if my age deprives me of the honour of accompanying you. The King will receive you in a manner which will leave you no reason to complain, and you will, I have no doubt, pardon any customs of the country which may happen to displease you."

Candide and Cacambo entered the carriage, the six sheep flew along, and in less than four hours they reached the King's palace, which was situated at the further end of the capital. The portico was two hundred and twenty feet high, and one hundred feet in width; it is impossible to describe the material of which it was built, but it may very well be imagined how infinitely superior it must have been to the stones and gravel which we call gold and precious stones.

A score of beautiful girls who were on guard received Candide and Cacambo as they alighted from the coach, conducted them to the bath, and arrayed them in robes woven of the down of humming-birds; afterwards the high officers of the Court, male and female, ushered them into the presence of His Majesty between two lines, each of which consisted of a thousand musicians, according to the usual custom. When they drew near the throne-room, Cacambo asked a grand officer what posture they would have to adopt in paying their respects to His Majesty,—whether they should simply kneel, or prostrate themselves on the ground at full length; whether they were to put their hands on their heads or behind their backs; whether it was usual to lick the dust off the floor; in short, what was the ceremony to be observed on such an occasion.

"The custom," said the high official, "is to embrace the King and kiss him on both cheeks."

Candide and Cacambo accordingly threw their arms round His Majesty's neck, who received them most graciously, and politely invited them to sup with him.

In the meantime they were taken to see the town,—the public buildings, that seemed to touch the clouds; the market-places, beautified with a thousand columns; the fountains of pure water, the fountains of rose water, and those from which the juice of sugar-canes flowed constantly through the great squares, paved with a kind of precious stone which diffused an odour like that of cinnamon and cloves. Candide asked permission to see the Courts of Justice, or Parliament House; he was told that there were none, and that they never had any law-suits. He inquired if there were any prisons, and was answered in the negative. What surprised him yet more, and gave him most pleasure, was the Palace of Science, in which he saw a gallery two thousand feet long, all full of mathematical and philosophical instruments.

After they had spent the whole afternoon in inspecting hardly the thousandth part of the town, they were conducted back to the King. Candide sat down to table with His Majesty, his servant Cacambo, and several ladies. Never was there better fare, never was more wit displayed at any supper-party than was shown by His Majesty. Cacambo interpreted the King's witticisms to Candide, and, in spite of passing through the medium of translation, they lost none of their point. Of all the things that filled Candide with surprise this did not astonish him least.

They passed a month in this haven of refuge, and Candide never ceased saying to Cacambo:

"To tell you the truth once more, my friend, the castle where I was born bears no comparison with the country where we are now; but after all Miss Cunegund is not here, and you, no doubt, have some sweetheart in Europe. If we stay here we shall be no better than others around us, whereas if we return to our own world with only a dozen sheep laden with the stones of El Dorado, we shall be richer than any king, or all put together; we shall no longer have to dread Inquisitors, and we shall be easily able to recover Miss Cunegund."

This speech pleased Cacambo; people love so much to roam about, to make themselves important in the eyes of their countrymen, and to parade all that they have seen on their travels, that these two happy fellows determined to be so no longer, and to ask His Majesty for leave to depart.

"You are doing a foolish thing," the Sovereign said to them; "I am well aware that my country is insignificant, but when one is tolerably well off anywhere, there one had best remain. I have assuredly no right to detain strangers, that would be an act of tyranny in accordance neither with our customs nor our laws. All men are free; depart when you will, but the way out is exceedingly difficult. It is impossible to reascend the rapid river on which you reached us by a miracle, and which runs under rocky tunnels. The mountains which surround my whole kingdom are ten thousand feet high, and as steep as if they were walls; each of them occupies a space of more than ten leagues across, and there is no descent from them except by precipices. However, since you are quite resolved to go, I will give orders to the managers of my machinery department to construct an engine which may be capable of carrying you over without inconvenience. After you have been conducted to the other side of the mountains, no one will be able to accompany you any further, for my subjects have made a vow never to pass beyond their rocky inclosure, and they are too wise to break their vow. Ask of me anything else you please."

"We only ask Your Majesty," said Cacambo, "for a few sheep laden with provisions, and the stones and clay of the country."

The King answered with a smile:

"I cannot comprehend the taste which your people of Europe have for our yellow clay; but take away as much of it as you like, and great good may it do you!"

He immediately ordered his engineers to make a machine by which these two extraordinary men might be hoisted out of the kingdom. Three thousand skilful mechanicians set to work upon it; it was ready at the end of a fortnight, and did not cost more than twenty millions of pounds sterling, in the money of the country. Candide and Cacambo were placed on the machine, together with two large red sheep saddled and bridled for them to mount when they should have crossed the mountains, twenty pack sheep laden with victuals, thirty which carried presents consisting of the rarest curiosities of the country, and fifty loaded with gold, diamonds, and other precious stones. The King tenderly embraced the two wanderers on bidding them farewell.

It was a fine sight to see them start, so ingenious was the manner in which they were made to rise into the air, and their sheep with them, as high as the mountains. The mechanicians took leave of them after having placed them in safety, and Candide had now no other desire or object than to go and present his sheep to Miss Cunegund.

"We have," said he, "wherewithal to pay the Governor of Buenos Ayres, if Miss Cunegund may be redeemed. Let us travel toward Cayenne, and there embark, and we shall soon see what kingdom it will be in our power to purchase."

CHAPTER XIX

What Befell the Two Travellers at Surinam, and how Candide Became Acquainted with Martin

Our two travellers found their first day's journey tolerably agreeable. They were encouraged by the idea of seeing themselves the possessors of greater treasures than Europe, Asia, and Africa could unite to furnish, and Candide, in a transport of delight, carved Cunegund's name upon the trees. On the second day two of their sheep sank into a quagmire and were swallowed up, together with their loads; two others died of exhaustion some days afterwards; then seven or eight perished of hunger in passing through a desert tract; and at the end of a few days more others fell down precipices. At last, after a march of a hundred days, they had only two sheep left. Candide said to Cacambo:

"You see, my friend, how perishable are the riches of this world; there is nothing solid but virtue and the happiness of seeing Miss Cunegund again."

"I cannot deny it," said Cacambo; "but we still have two sheep left us, with treasures greater than the King of Spain will ever have; and I see plainly in the distance a town which I take to be Surinam, belonging to the Dutch. We are at the end of our troubles and at the beginning of our happiness."

As they drew near the town they came across a negro stretched at full length upon the ground, and only half clothed, that is to say, with nothing on but a pair of blue cotton drawers; this poor fellow had lost his left leg and his right hand.

"Good Heavens!" said Candide to him in Dutch; "what are you doing there, my friend, in that horrible state?"

"I am waiting for my master, Mr. Vanderdendur, the famous merchant," replied the negro.

"Was it Mr. Vanderdendur who treated you like this?" asked Candide.

"Yes, sir," answered the negro; "but that is nothing unusual. We have a pair of cotton drawers given us for our only dress twice a year. When we work at the sugar-refineries, and the mill catches one of our fingers, they cut off the hand; when we try to run away, they cut off a leg; both the one fate and the other has happened to me. This is the cost at which you eat sugar in Europe. And yet when my mother sold me for ten patacoons on the Guinea Coast, she said to me: 'My dear child, bless our fetishes, worship them constantly, they will make you live happily; you have the honour of becoming the slave of our lords, the white men, and you thereby make the fortune of your father and mother.' Alas! I know not whether I have made their fortune, but certainly they have not made mine! The dogs, monkeys, and parrots are a thousand times less wretched than we are. The Dutch fetishes who have converted me tell me every Sunday that we are all the children of Adam, blacks and whites alike. I am no genealogist; but, if those preachers say what is true, we are all second cousins. In that case you must admit that relations could not be treated in a more horrible way."

"O Pangloss!" cried Candide, "you never conceived the possibility of such abominations; it is all over with your Optimism, I shall be obliged to renounce it after all."

"What is Optimism?" asked Cacambo.

"Alas!" replied Candide; "it is the mania for maintaining that all is right when everything is wrong;" and he could not help shedding tears, as he looked at the poor negro. It was in this frame of mind that he entered Surinam.

The first inquiry they made was whether there were any vessel in port which could be sent to Buenos Ayres. The person whom they addressed happened to be a Spanish skipper, who offered to strike an honest bargain with them, appointing a tavern at which to meet them; and thither went Candide and the faithful Cacambo, with their two sheep, to wait for him.

Candide, who wore his heart upon his lips, related all his adventures to the Spaniard, and confessed that he wanted to carry off Miss Cunegund.

"Then I shall take good care not to give you a passage to

Buenos Ayres," said the skipper; "I should be ruined, and so would you; the fair Cunegund is my lord Governor's favourite mistress."

This piece of news fell like a thunderbolt on Candide, and he wept for a long time. At last he drew Cacambo aside, and said to him:

"Look here, my dear friend, this is what you must do. We have, each of us, in our pockets, about five or six millions of diamonds; you are cleverer than I am, go to Buenos Ayres, and get possession of Miss Cunegund. If the Governor raises any difficulty, give him a million; if he still holds out, double it. You have not killed an Inquisitor, and no one will suspect you. I will fit out another ship, sail to Venice, and await you there; it is a free country, where one has nothing to fear from Bulgarians, or Abarians, or Jews, or Inquisitors."

Cacambo approved of this wise resolution. Though he was in despair at parting from so good a master, who had become his intimate friend, yet the pleasure of doing him a service overcame the pain of leaving him. As they embraced each other with tears, Candide charged him not to forget the good old dame. Cacambo took his departure the same day; he was a very honest fellow, this Cacambo.

Candide remained some time longer at Surinam, waiting till another skipper would take him to Italy, together with the couple of sheep that were left him. He hired domestics, and bought all that was required for a long voyage. At last Mr. Vanderdendur, who was the master of a large vessel, came to call upon him.

"How much do you want," he asked this man, "for taking me straight to Venice,—me, my people, my baggage, and the two sheep which you see here?"

The skipper consented to take ten thousand piastres, and Candide closed with the offer without hesitation.

"Oh, ho!" said the crafty Vanderdendur to himself, "this stranger gives ten thousand piastres all at once! He must be very rich!"

Then, returning a moment later, he intimated that he could not yet set sail for less than twenty thousand.

"Ah! well, you shall have them," said Candide.

"Bless my soul!" said the trader softly to himself; "this fellow gives away twenty thousand piastres as easily as ten thousand."

He came back again, and said that he could not possibly take him to Venice for less than thirty thousand piastres.

"You shall have thirty thousand, then," answered Candide.

"Hullo!" said the Dutchman to himself once more; "thirty thousand piastres are nothing to this fellow here; no doubt his two sheep carry immense treasures. However, I will not press him for any more, but make him in the first place pay down the thirty thousand piastres, and then we shall see what is to be done next."

Candide sold two little diamonds, the smaller one of which was worth more than all the money that the skipper asked. He paid him beforehand. The two sheep were taken on board, and Candide followed in a small boat to join the vessel at anchor in the roads. The skipper seizes his opportunity, spreads sail, and leaves his moorings before a favourable wind. Candide, dismayed and dumbfounded, soon lost sight of the ship.

"Alas!" he exclaimed, "this is a piece of knavery worthy of the old world."

He returned to shore, overwhelmed with sorrow, for in one moment he had lost wealth enough to make the fortune of twenty monarchs.

He betook himself to the house of the Dutch magistrate, and, being somewhat agitated, knocked violently at the door. When he was admitted, he raised his voice a little higher than was quite becoming, as he described the manner in which he had been cheated. The magistrate began by making him pay ten thousand piastres for having made so much noise; then he heard him out patiently, promised to examine his case as soon as the merchant should return, and ordered Candide to pay ten thousand piastres more as the price of the audience.

This proceeding added the finishing stroke to Candide's

despair; he had indeed experienced misfortunes a thousand times more painful; but the cool behaviour alike of the magistate and of the captain by whom he had been robbed stirred up his bile, and plunged him in the blackest melancholy. The wickedness of men presented itself to his mind in all its hideousness, and he harboured none but the most gloomy thoughts. At length, a French vessel being on the point of sailing for Bordeaux, as he had no longer any sheep laden with diamonds to put on board, he engaged a cabin at a fair rate, and gave it out in the town that he was willing to pay for the passage and food of any honest man who would accompany him on the voyage, and would give him two thousand piastres besides, provided that this man was the most disgusted with his condition and the most unfortunate in the whole province.

Thereupon such a crowd of applicants presented themselves that a fleet would not have been able to contain them. Candide, wishing to choose among those who were likely to suit him, picked out twenty persons who seemed to him of a sociable disposition, all of whom claimed to deserve the preference. He collected them together at his inn and gave them a supper, on condition that each of them should take an oath to relate his own history faithfully, promising to select that one who should appear to him in the most pitiable case and the most justly discontented with his lot, and to give each of the others something by way of consolation.

The meeting lasted till four o'clock in the morning. Candide, as he listened to all their adventures, recalled what the old woman had said to him on the voyage to Buenos Ayres, and the wager she had laid that there was no one on board the vessel to whom serious misfortunes had not happened. Every story that was related made him think, too, of Pangloss.

"The learned doctor would be sadly puzzled," said he, "to make good his system. I wish he were here. Assuredly, if all goes on well anywhere, it is in El Dorado, and nowhere else on earth."

At last he decided in favour of a poor scholar who had toiled ten years for the booksellers at Amsterdam, being convinced that there was no trade in the world with which one could have greater reason to be disgusted.

The scholar, who was moreover a worthy man, had been robbed by his wife, beaten by his son, and deserted by his daughter, who had run away with a Portuguese. He had just been deprived of a petty employment, on which he depended for a livelihood; and the preachers of Surinam persecuted him, because they took him for a Socinian. It must be owned that the other competitors were, to say the least, as unfortunate as he, but Candide hoped that the society of this learned man would relieve the monotony of the voyage. All his defeated rivals thought that Candide did them great injustice; but he appeased their wrath by presenting each of them with a hundred piastres.

CHAPTER XX

What Happened to Candide and Martin whilst at Sea

The old scholar then, whose name was Martin, embarked with Candide for Bordeaux. Both of them had seen and suffered much, and, even if the vessel had been bound for Japan past the Cape of Good Hope, they would have had plenty of material for discussing the topic of physical and moral evil during the whole voyage.

Candide, however, had a great advantage over Martin, for he still hoped to see Miss Cunegund again, whereas Martin had nothing whatever to hope for; Candide, moreover, had gold and diamonds, and, though he had lost a hundred large red sheep, laden with the greatest treasures on earth, though he could never banish from his mind the painful remembrance of the Dutch skipper and his trickery, still, when he thought of what he had left in his pockets, and whenever he spoke of Cunegund, especially after a good meal, he was inclined to agree with the views of Pangloss.

"And you now, Mr. Martin," said he to the man of letters, "what is your opinion touching moral and physical evil?"

"Sir," replied Martin, "our clergy have accused me of being a Socinian, but the fact of the matter is that I am a Manichean."

"You are jesting with me," said Candide; "there are no Manicheans in the world nowadays."

"There is myself, at any rate," said Martin; "I do not know how to help it, for I cannot think otherwise."

"You must have the devil inside you," said Candide.

"He mixes himself up so much with the affairs of this world," answered Martin, "that I should not wonder if he were inside my body as well as everywhere else; and I confess that on casting my eyes over this globe, or I should rather say this globule, it seems to me that God has given it over to some malignant being,—El Dorado always excepted. I have scarcely seen a single town which did not desire the destruction of its nearest neighbour, scarcely a family which did not wish to exterminate some other. Everywhere the weak curse the strong before whom they crawl, and are themselves treated like sheep,—bought and sold for their wool and for their flesh. A million assassins enrolled in regiments, marching from one end of Europe to the other, commit, under discipline, licensed murder and robbery to gain their daily bread, since no profession is held in higher honour; and even in those cities which appear to enjoy peace, and where the arts flourish, the inhabitants are more harassed by envy, anxiety, and alarm than by all the plagues to which a besieged city is exposed. Secret vexations are ever harder to bear than public calamities. In a word, I have seen and experienced so many of them myself, that I am a Manichean."

"And yet there is surely some good in life," said Candide.

"It may be so," replied Martin, "but I am not acquainted with any."

Whilst they were in the midst of this dispute, the report of cannon was heard, and the noise of firing grew louder every moment. Each of them seized his spy-glass, and perceived two ships engaged at close quarters about three miles off. The wind brought them both so near the French vessel, that all on board had the pleasure of witnessing the conflict at their ease. At last one of the two ships discharged at the other a broadside so low and well directed, that it sent it to the bottom. Candide and Martin distinctly perceived at least a hundred men on the deck of the sinking craft, who lifted up their hands to heaven, and uttered fearful cries; in a moment they were swallowed up, ship and all.

"See," said Martin, "that is how men treat one another."

"Truly," said Candide, "there is something diabolical in this affair."

As he was speaking, he caught sight of a strange object, of a bright red colour, swimming near their vessel. The long boat was lowered to see what it might be. It proved to be one of his sheep, and Candide felt more joyful at recovering this sheep than he had been afflicted at losing a hundred of them, all laden with big diamonds from El Dorado.

The French captain soon perceived that the commander of the victorious vessel was a Spaniard, and learned that the captain of the vessel which had been sunk was a Dutch pirate; in fact he was no other than the man who had robbed Candide. The immense treasures which the rascal had seized were buried with him in the sea, only a single sheep being saved.

"You see," said Candide to Martin, "that crime is sometimes punished; that rogue of a Dutch skipper has met with the fate which he deserved."

"Yes," answered Martin, "but was it necessary that the passengers who were on board his vessel should perish also? God has punished this scoundrel, the devil has drowned the others."

Meanwhile the French and Spanish vessels continued on their course, and Candide continued his conversations with Martin. They disputed for a whole fortnight together, and, at the end of that time, they were no nearer an agreement than at first; but for all that, they talked away, interchanged ideas, and administered mutual consolation. Candide caressed his sheep:

"Since I have found you again," said he, "it may well come to pass that I shall find Miss Cunegund again also."

CHAPTER XXI

The Discussion that took Place between Candide and Martin as they Approached the coast of France

At length the French coast came into view.

"Have you ever been in France, Mr. Martin?" asked Candide.

"Yes," said Martin, "I have passed through several provinces; there are some where half the inhabitants are crazy, some where they are too sharp, others where they are for the most part as stupid as they are good-natured, others again where they affect to be witty, and in all alike the main occupation is love, the next in importance slander, and the third talking nonsense."

"But, Mr. Martin, have you seen Paris?"

"Oh yes, I have seen Paris, and a strange medley it is of all those classes I have mentioned. It is a confused chaos, in which everyone is in search of pleasure, and hardly anyone finds it, at least so far as I have observed. I did not stay there long. On my arrival I was robbed of all I possessed by pickpockets at the fair of St. Germains. I was taken for a thief myself, and spent a week in prison. Afterwards I got employment as a corrector of the press, so as to earn enough to take me back to Holland on foot. I made acquaintance with the rabble who write, the rabble who deal in plots and conspiracies, and the rabble who go into convulsions. They say there are some people of the highest polish in that city. I am quite willing to believe it."

"For my part," said Candide, "I feel no curiosity to visit France; you may easily suppose that after having spent a month in El Dorado, I no longer concern myself about seeing anything on earth except Miss Cunegund. I am going to await her arrival at Venice, and shall pass through France in order to reach Italy. You will bear me company, will you not?"

"Most willingly," said Martin. "I have heard it said that Venice is not a good place of residence for any but Venetian noblemen, but that strangers are nevertheless received very

177

well there, when they have plenty of money. You have some of that commodity, though I have none, so I will follow you anywhere you like."

"By the bye," said Candide, "are you of opinion that the earth was originally all sea, as that big book assures us which belongs to the captain of our vessel?"

"I know nothing at all about it," said Martin, "any more than I do about all the idle dreams that have been retailed to us for ever so long."

"For what purpose was the world made, do you suppose?" asked Candide.

"To drive us wild," answered Martin.

"Are you not very much astonished," continued Candide, "at the affection shown by those two girls, in the country of the Oreillons, for the two monkeys, about which I told you?"

"Not in the least," said Martin; "I do not see anything particularly strange in that passion. I have seen so many extraordinary things, that nothing seems extraordinary to me now."

"Do you believe," said Candide, "that mankind have always murdered each other as they do at the present day? Have they always been liars, cheats, traitors, ungrateful wretches, and robbers; weak, fickle, lazy, and envious; gluttons and drunkards; avaricious, ambitious, and bloodthirsty; slanderers, libertines, fanatics, hypocrites, and fools?"

"Do you believe," responded Martin, "that hawks have always devoured pigeons, whenever they met with them?"

"Yes, no doubt," said Candide.

"Well," said Martin, "if hawks have always had the same nature, why will you have it that men have changed theirs?"

"Oh!" exclaimed Candide, "there is a great deal of difference between the two cases; for free will—" And arguing thus, they arrived at Bordeaux.

CHAPTER XXII

What Befell Candide and Martin in France

Candide stayed at Bordeaux only so long as was necessary to sell a few of the stones from El Dorado, and to provide himself with a good post-chaise which would seat two persons; for he could no longer do without his philosopher Martin. He found it hard enough to part from his sheep, which he left at the Academy of Science at Bordeaux. This learned body proposed as the prize subject for the year to find out why the wool of this sheep was red; and the prize was awarded to a professor from the north, who demonstrated by A *plus* B *minus* C divided by Z, that the sheep could not be of any other colour than red, and was bound to die of the rot.

Meanwhile all the travellers whom Candide encountered in the various inns on the road told him that they were on their way to Paris. This general eagerness at last inspired even him with a longing to see that capital; it would not take him much out of the direct route to Venice.

He entered Paris by the suburb of Saint Marceau, and fancied he was in one of the meanest villages of Westphalia.

Scarcely had Candide reached his quarters, when he was seized with a slight indisposition, brought on by fatigue. As he was wearing on his finger an enormous diamond, and an uncommonly heavy strong box had been seen among his effects, he immediately found a couple of physicians at his elbows, without having been sent for, together with a few devoted friends who never quitted him for a moment, and two pious ladies who warmed his broth for him. Said Martin:

"I remember that I too fell ill here at Paris on my first visit; I was very poor; moreover I had neither friends, nor pious ladies, nor physicians,—and I recovered."

Candide's disorder, however, in consequence of his being dosed and bled unmercifully, became serious. A priest attached to a church in the neighbourhood came with an insinuating manner, and asked him for a bill payable to bearer to be repaid in the other world. Candide would have nothing to do with him. The pious ladies assured him that it was the latest fashion. Candide replied that he did not pretend to be a man of fashion. Martin wanted to throw the fellow out of the window. The clergyman swore that Candide should not have Christian burial. Martin swore that he would bury the clergyman, if he continued to pester them. The quarrel waxed warm, till Martin took him by the shoulders, and roughly turned him out of the house, a proceeding that caused a great scandal, and resulted in an action-at-law.

At length Candide began to grow better; and during his convalescence he entertained some very good company to supper. They played high. Candide was much astonished that he never found any aces in his hand; Martin was not surprised at it.

Among those who did the honours of the town there was a little abbé from Périgord, one of those obliging people, always on the alert, always ready to do one a service, never abashed, fawning and accommodating, who lie in wait for strangers, gratify their ears with the latest scandal, and offer to provide them with pleasures at all prices. This gentleman took Candide and Martin first of all to the principal theatre, where a new tragedy was being acted. Candide found himself seated among some men of wit, but that did not prevent him from shedding tears at scenes which were admirably performed. One of the critics at his side said to him during an interval between the acts:

"You are quite wrong in weeping; that actress plays very badly, the man who acts with her plays still worse, the piece is even worse than the performers; the author does not know a word of Arabic, yet the scene is laid in Arabia, and, moreover, he is a man who does not believe in innate ideas; I will show you tomorrow a score of pamphlets that have been written against him."

"Sir," said Candide, to the Abbé, "how many dramas have you in France?"

"Five or six thousand," was his reply.

"That is a large number," said Candide; "and how many of those are really good?"

"Fifteen or sixteen," answered the other.

"That is a large number," said Martin.

Candide was much delighted with an actress who took the part of Queen Elizabeth in a tolerably dull tragedy which is sometimes put upon the boards.

"This actress," said he to Martin, "pleases me much; she has a slight resemblance to Miss Cunegund, and I should be very glad to pay her my compliments."

The Périgord Abbé offered to introduce him to her at her own house. Candide, brought up as he had been in Germany, asked what were the proper formalities to be observed, and how queens of England were treated in France.

"That depends upon circumstances," said the Abbé; "in the country we take them to a tavern; at Paris we pay them every respect when they are good-looking, and throw them into the common sewer when they are dead."

"What! Queens thrown into a sewer!" exclaimed Candide.

"Yes, indeed," said Martin, "the gentleman is right; I was at Paris when Mademoiselle Monime made her exit, as one may say, from this world into the next; she was refused what these people call *the honours of sepulture*, that is to say, the privilege of rotting with all the beggars of the district in some dismal graveyard; she was buried all alone by her company at the corner of the *rue de Bourgogne*, a treatment which might well cause her acute pain, for her mind was ever noble and generous."

"That was exceedingly impolite," said Candide.

"What could you expect?" said Martin; "it is the way these people here are constituted. Imagine all possible contradictions and incompatibilities; you will see them all in the government, in the courts of justice, in the churches, and in the public spectacles of this most ridiculous nation."

"Is it true that people are always laughing in Paris?" asked Candide.

"Yes," said the Abbé, "but it is with rage in their hearts; for their bitterest complaints are uttered in bursts of laughter; they even smile blandly when they commit the most detestable actions."

"Who was that fellow, as fat as a pig," said Candide, "who spoke so disparagingly to me of the play which affected me so much, and of the actors who afforded me so much pleasure?"

"He is an ill-natured scribbler," answered the Abbé, "who earns his living by abusing all the last new books and plays; he hates anyone who is successful, just as eunuchs hate those who are more capable than themselves; he is one of those literary vipers who batten on slime and poison; in a word, he is a pamphleteer."

"And what do you mean by a pamphleteer?" asked Candide.

"A penny-a-liner," said the Abbé, "a Fréron."

It was thus that Candide, Martin, and the Périgord Abbé conversed at the head of the staircase, as they watched the audience trooping out of the theatre.

"Although I am very anxious to see Miss Cunegund again," said Candide, "I should nevertheless like to sup with Mademoiselle Clairon, for she seemed to me an admirable actress."

Now the Abbé was not a man who could venture to visit Mademoiselle Clairon, who was very select in the company she kept. So he said:

"She is engaged this evening, but let me have the honour of taking you to the house of a lady of high position, where you may become as well acquainted with Paris as if you had lived here four or five years."

Candide, whose disposition was not deficient in curiosity, allowed himself to be conducted to the lady's house, which was at the further end of the surburb of Saint Honoré. There he found a party playing at faro; a dozen punters sat with melancholy air, each of them holding a small hand of cards, which, with corners turned down, registered their bad luck. Profound silence reigned, pallor sat on the faces of the punters, uneasiness on that of the banker; and the lady of the house, seated near that inexorable functionary, took notice, with lynx-like eyes, of all doubling of the stakes, and all the other hazardous ventures with which each player turned down his cards; she made them turn them up with rigorous but polite insistence, and never showed any displeasure for fear of losing her customers. The lady called herself the Marchioness of Parolignac. Her daughter, some fifteen years of age, was one of the punters, and intimated to her mother by a wink any cheating on the part of those poor creatures who might thus try to repair the severities of fortune. When the Périgord Abbé entered with Candide and Martin, no one rose to salute them, nor took any notice of them, all were so deeply engrossed with their cards.

"My lady, the Baroness of Thundertentrunk, was more civil," said Candide.

The Abbé, however, whispered a word or two into the lady's ear, and, half rising from her seat, she favoured Candide with a gracious smile, and Martin with a dignified inclination of the head. She bade an attendant bring Candide a chair, and he was included in the next deal. Before the end of the second round he had lost fifty thousand francs, after which they had a very merry supper, and everyone was astonished that Candide bore his ill luck so lightly; the lackeys said among themselves in their own phraseology:

"He must be some *milord Anglais!*"

The supper, as suppers are wont to be at Paris, was begun in solemn silence, then came a confused babble of words, jokes followed more or less insipid, fictitious news, illogical arguments, with a spice of politics and a large infusion of scandal; the last new books also were passed under review,

"Have you seen," said the Abbé of Périgord, "the romance written by Dr. Gauchat, the eminent divine?"

"Yes," answered one of the guests; "but I could not finish it. We have a swarm of impertinent writers nowadays, but all the rest put together do not come within measurable distance of your eminent divine, Dr. Gauchat. I have been so surfeited with the endless succession of worthless books with which we are flooded, that I am reduced to punting at faro as a distraction."

"And what do you think of Archdeacon Trublet's miscellanies?" said the Abbé.

"Ah!" exclaimed the Marchioness of Parolignac; "what a dreadful bore he is! What pains he takes to tell you what everybody knows! How laboriously he discusses what is not worth even a passing remark! How inaptly he appropriates the wit of others! How he spoils whatever he pilfers! I am perfectly sick of him! But he shall disgust me no more; it is quite enough to read two or three pages of the archdeacon."

There was sitting at table a man of taste and learning, who supported what the Marchioness had said. The conversation then turned on the drama, and the lady asked how it was that there were some tragedies which had a short run when acted, but which would not bear reading. The man of taste explained very well how a play might have some points of interest, and yet be destitute of almost any real merit. He convinced them in a few words that it is not enough to introduce one or two of those situations which are found in all romances and never fail to charm the spectators; that it is necessary to be original without being eccentric, often sublime but always natural; to know the human heart and how to express its feelings; to be a true poet without any personage in the piece appearing in that character; to have perfect mastery over language, so as to speak it with purity and unfailing harmony, but without any sacrifice of sense to sound.

"Unless an author," added he, "observes all these rules, he may compose one or two tragedies applauded on the stage, but he will never be ranked among classical writers. There are very few good tragedies; some are idylls in dialogue, well written and in faultless rhyme; and there are political disquisitions that send one to sleep, or amplifications that irritate and disgust; others again are the ravings of a lunatic, in a barbarous idiom, with disjointed sentences, long apostrophes to the gods,—because that is easier than to talk to men,—maxims of false morality, and bombastic commonplaces."

184

Candide listened to these remarks with great attention, and conceived a high opinion of the speaker; and as the Marchioness had been careful to seat him beside herself, he took the liberty of whispering into her ear an inquiry as to who that man might be who spoke so well.

"He is a scholar," said the lady, "whom, though he does not play at cards, the Abbé brings in here sometimes to supper; he has a thorough knowledge of books and plays; he has written a tragedy himself, which was hissed off the boards, and a book which has never been seen outside his publisher's shop, except a copy that he sent with a dedication to me."

"What a great man!" said Candide, "he is a second Pangloss."

Then turning towards him he said:

"Sir, you are doubtless of opinion that all is for the best in the physical and in the moral world, and that nothing could be otherwise than it is?"

"I, sir?" replied the man of letters; "that is certainly not my opinion: I find that everything goes contrary with us; that nobody knows his proper rank, nor what are its requirements, neither what he is doing, nor what he ought to do, and except supper time, which passes pleasantly enough and with every appearance of harmony, all the rest of the day is taken up with senseless quarrels,—Jansenists against Molinists, lawyers against Churchmen, men of letters against men of letters, courtiers against courtiers, farmers of the revenue against the people, wives against husbands, kinsfolk against kinsfolk,—it is all a state of perpetual warfare."

Candide replied:

"I have seen a worse state of affairs than that; but a sage, who has since had the misfortune to be hanged, taught me that all is admirably arranged; these things are but shadows in a beautiful picture."

"Your friend who was hanged," said Martin, "must have been mocking the world's misery; the shadows of which you speak are horrible blots."

"It is men who make the blots," said Candide, "and they

cannot act otherwise than they do."

"It is no fault of theirs, then," said Martin.

The greater part of the punters, who did not comprehend a word of all this, went on drinking, while Martin entered upon a discussion with the man of letters, and Candide related some of his adventures to the lady of the house.

After supper the Marchioness invited Candide into her closet, and made him sit on a sofa.

"Well," said she, "and are you still then as desperately in love with Miss Cunegund of Thundertentrunk as ever?"

"Yes, madam," said Candide.

The Marchioness responded with a tender smile:

"You answer me like a young man of Westphalia; a Frenchman would have said: 'It is true that I once loved Miss Cunegund, but, seeing you, madam, I fear I can love her no longer.'"

"Pardon me! madam," said Candide, "I will return you what answer you will."

"Your passion for her," said the Marchioness, "began, as I understand, by your picking up her handkerchief; I should like you to pick up my garter."

"With the greatest pleasure," said Candide, and suited the action to the word.

"But I wish you to tie it on again," added the lady; and Candide restored it to its place.

"Look, my friend," said she, "although you are a stranger, and I sometimes make my Parisian admirers languish for me as long as a fortnight, yet I surrender to you the first night I see you, because it is only right and proper to do the honours of one's country to a young man from Westphalia."

The fair enchantress, having caught sight of two enormous diamonds on the young stranger's hands, praised them so sincerely, that from Candide's fingers they passed on to those of the Marchioness.

As Candide returned home with his friend the Périgord Abbé, he felt some remorse at having been guilty of infidelity to Miss Cunegund. The Abbé sympathised with his uneasiness. He had come in for only a small share in the fifty thousand francs which Candide had lost at play, and in the value of the two brilliants, which may be said to have been half given, half extorted; and his purpose was to make as much profit as he could out of the advantages afforded him by his acquaintance with Candide. He talked much to him of Cunegund, and Candide told him that he would earnestly entreat pardon from the fair one for his faithlessness, when he should see her at Venice.

The Abbé was more profuse than ever in his polite attentions, and took a tender interest in all that Candide said, or did, or wanted to do.

"You have then, sir," said he, "an appointment at Venice?"

"Yes, my good sir," said Candide; "it is absolutely necessary that I should go and find Miss Cunegund."

Then, unable to resist the pleasure of speaking about the object of his affection, he related, as he had so often done before, some of his adventures with that illustrious Westphalian damsel.

"I imagine," said the Abbé, "that Miss Cunegund has plenty of native wit, and writes delightful letters."

"I have never received one," said Candide; "for, as you may suppose, just after having been kicked out of the castle for making love to her, I had no opportunity of writing, and soon afterwards I heard that she was dead; then I found her again, lost her once more, and lastly I have despatched an express messenger to her at a place two thousand four hundred leagues from this, whose answer I am now awaiting."

The Abbé listened attentively, and seemed somewhat absorbed in thought. He soon took leave of his two companions, after having embraced them tenderly. On awaking next morning Candide found a letter expressed in the following terms:

"My honoured sir and most dear lover, I have been laid up with illness for more than a week in this city, where I learn that you also are staying. I would fly to your arms, if only I could move. I heard of your journey hither when I was at Bordeaux, where I left the faithful Cacambo and the old woman, who are to follow me shortly. The Governor of Buenos Ayres has taken everything from me except your heart, which I still retain. Come; your presence will either restore me to life, or else make me die of gladness."

While this charming, this unhoped for letter transported Candide with unutterable joy, the illness of his beloved Cunegund overwhelmed him with grief. Divided between these two conflicting feelings, he took with him his gold and his diamonds, and drove with Martin to the house where Miss Cunegund was lodging. He entered, trembling with emotion; his heart beat fast, and his voice was choked with sobs. He would fain have drawn aside the bed-curtains, and had a light brought in; but the female in attendance told him to be careful not to do so, for the light would certainly kill her, and she closed the curtain again immediately.

"My dear Cunegund," said Candide, weeping, "tell me how you are? If you may not see me, at least speak to me."

"She cannot speak," said the attendant.

The lady hereupon put a plump hand out of bed, which Candide bathed with tears for a long time, and afterwards filled with diamonds, leaving a purse full of gold on the arm-chair.

In the midst of his distracting grief an officer of police with some of his men arrived, accompanied by the Périgord Abbé.

"There," said the latter, "are the two suspected foreigners!"

He had them forthwith arrested, and the officer ordered his brave fellows to drag them off to prison.

"This is not the way in which travellers are treated in El Dorado," said Candide.

"I am more of a Manichean now than ever," said Martin.

"But whither, sir, are you conducting us?" asked Candide.

"To the black hole of a dungeon," replied the officer.

Martin, on recovering his coolness, decided that the lady who pretended to be Cunegund was a cheat, that the Périgord

Abbé was a knave, who had lost no time in abusing Candide's simplicity, and that the police officer was another of the same kidney, of whom it would be easy to get rid.

Rather than expose himself to judicial proceedings, Candide, enlightened by his companion's counsel, and eager moreover to see once more the real Cunegund, offered the sergeant three small diamonds, worth about three thousand pistoles apiece.

"Oh! sir," said the man of the ivory-headed staff, "had you committed all the crimes that can be imagined, you would yet be the most honest man in the world for me. Three diamonds! each of them worth three thousand pistoles! Sir, I would gladly die to defend you, instead of carrying you off to prison. All foreigners are subject to arrest, but leave the matter in my hands; I have a brother at Dieppe in Normandy; I will conduct you thither, and, if you happen to have a diamond that you could give him, he will take as good care of you as I could myself."

"But why are all foreigners subject to arrest?" said Candide.

The Périgord Abbé here put in his word, and said:

"It is because a poor beggar of the province of Artois heard some idle words spoken, by which and nothing else he was instigated to commit a parricide, not such as that of the month of May 1610, but like that of December 1594, and like many others committed in other months of other years by other poor beggars, who heard people give vent to idle words."

The police officer then explained the matters thus hinted at, and Candide exclaimed:

"Ah! what monsters! Can such horrors be found among a people who dance and sing? Shall I not quit as soon as I can this country where apes provoke tigers? I have seen bears in my own land; men I have seen only in El Dorado. In the name of Heaven, Mr. Constable, take me to Venice, where I am to wait for Miss Cunegund."

"I can only conduct you into Lower Normandy," said the officer.

He instantly caused his fetters to be removed, saying that he had been mistaken, sent back his men, escorted Candide and Martin to Dieppe, and left them in his brother's charge. There happened to be a small Dutch vessel in the roads, and the Norman, who had been rendered the most obliging of men by the aid of three other diamonds, placed Candide and his attendants on board this ship, which was about to set sail for Portsmouth in England. This was not the way to Venice, it is true, but Candide thought it was a deliverance out of hell, and he intended to resume his journey to Venice on the first opportunity.

CHAPTER XXIII

Candide and Martin Arrive on the English Coast: what they See there

"Ah! Pangloss, Pangloss! Ah! Martin, Martin! Ah! my dear Cunegund! What kind of a world is this?" said Candide, when he was safely on board the Dutch vessel.

"Something very mad, and altogether abominable," answered Martin.

"You are acquainted with England. Are the people there as mad as in France?"

"Theirs is another sort of madness," said Martin. "You know that the two nations are at war about some acres of snow in the neighbourhood of Canada, and that they spend in that war far more than all Canada is worth. To tell you precisely whether there are more people who ought to be shut up as lunatics in one country than in another is beyond my feeble capacity; I only know that, as a general rule, the people whom we are about to visit are exceedingly morose."

While conversing thus, they came in sight of Portsmouth; a multitude of people lined the shore, and had their gaze fixed attentively on a stout man, who was kneeling, with eyes blindfolded, on the deck of one of the men-of-war; four soldiers, stationed opposite this man, discharged three bullets each into his skull, in the calmest manner possible; and then all the crowd returned home, very well satisfied with what they had seen.

"What now is the meaning of all this?" said Candide, "and what demon exerts dominion everywhere?"

In answer to his inquiry who that stout man was who had just been put to death with so much ceremony, he was told that he was an admiral.

"And why do they kill an admiral?"

"Because," said his informants, "he has not caused enough people to be slaughtered; he gave battle to a French admiral, and it has been found that he did not come to sufficiently close quarters."

"But," said Candide, "the French admiral must have been as far from the English admiral, as he from the other!"

"That cannot be disputed," was the reply; "but in this country it is thought a good thing to kill an admiral from time to time in order to put some courage into the others."

Candide was so astounded and shocked at what he both saw and heard, that he had no wish so much as to set foot on land, and made a bargain with the Dutch skipper (though he might rob him like his compatriot of Surinam) to carry him without delay to Venice.

The skipper was ready in a couple of days. They sailed along the coast of France; they came within sight of Lisbon, and Candide shuddered; they passed through the straits, and entered the Mediterranean; at last they reached Venice.

"Heaven be praised!" said Candide, embracing Martin; "it is here that I shall see my fair Cunegund again. I can rely on Cacambo as on myself. All is well, everything goes right, nothing could possibly be better."

CHAPTER XXIV

Treats of Paquette and Brother Giroflée

As soon as Candide was at Venice he instituted a search for Cacambo in all the taverns and coffee houses, and amongst all the women of pleasure, but he could not be found. He sent every day to reconnoitre all the newly arrived vessels; still no tidings of Cacambo.

"What is this?" said he to Martin; "I have had time to go from Surinam to Bordeaux, from Bordeaux to Paris, from Paris to Dieppe, from Dieppe to Portsmouth, to sail along the coasts of Portugal and Spain, to traverse the Mediterranean, and to pass some months at Venice; but the fair Cunegund is not yet arrived. In her place I have met only a ridiculous counterfeit and a Perigord abbé! Cunegund is doubtless dead, and there is nothing left for me to do but to die also. Alas! It would have been far better to have remained in the paradise of El Dorado, instead of returning to this accursed Europe. You are perfectly right, my dear Martin, there is nothing but disappointments and calamity."

He fell into a melancholy of the deepest dye, and took no interest either in the operas then in vogue, or in any other of the amusements of the Carnival; there was not a pretty face or figure that offered him the slightest temptation. Martin said to him:

"You are really very simple if you imagine for a moment that a mongrel valet, with five or six millions in his pockets, would go to the ends of the earth in search of your sweetheart, in order to bring her to you at Venice. He will take her for himself, if he finds her; if he cannot find her, he will take some other charmer. I advise you to forget your servant Cacambo and your mistress Cunegund."

Martin was not a good hand at giving consolation; Candide's melancholy grew worse, and Martin never ceased proving to him that there was little virtue or happiness on earth, except perhaps in El Dorado, to which nobody could go.

Whilst they were still discussing this important topic and waiting for Cunegund, Candide observed a young Theatine friar in the piazza of St. Mark, with a wench hanging on his arm. The friar looked fresh complexioned, plump, and vigorous; his eyes were bright, he carried his head high, and stepped along with a proud and confident air. The girl, who was very pretty, was singing and casting amorous glances at her friar, while from time to time she pinched his fat cheeks.

"You will at least allow," said Candide to Martin, "that this couple are happy. Up to the present time, throughout all the habitable globe, I have found only unfortunate wretches, except in El Dorado; but as for this wench and her Theatine friar, I warrant you they are happy enough."

"I will wager they are not," returned Martin.

"We have only to ask them to dine with us," said Candide, "and you will see whether I am mistaken."

He accosted them there and then, and after having paid them his compliments, invited them to his inn to eat macaroni, Lombardy partridges, and sturgeons' roe, and to drink the wine of Montepulciano, lachryma Christi, and the vintage of Cyprus and Samos. The damsel blushed, the friar accepted the invitation, and the girl, as she followed him, regarded Candide with eyes in which surprise and confusion were mingled with tears which made them dim. Scarcely had she entered Candide's apartment, when she said to him:

"What! Does Mr. Candide no longer recognise Paquette?"

At these words Candide, who had not hitherto noticed her with any particular attention, because his thoughts had been occupied with nothing but Cunegund, replied:

"Ah! my poor child, was it you then who reduced Dr. Pangloss to the fine condition in which I saw him?"

"Alas! sir, it was I indeed," said Paquette; "I see that you have been informed of everything. I have heard of the terrible misfortunes which have overtaken the whole household of my lady the Baroness, and especially the fair Cunegund, but I solemnly assure you my fate has been hardly less wretched than hers. I was innocence itself when you saw me first, but a Franciscan friar, who was my confessor, seduced me without much difficulty. The consequences were frightful, and I was obliged to quit the castle some time after my lord Baron had sent you off with some hearty kicks on your hinder quarters. If a celebrated physician had not taken compassion on me, I should have lost my life. I remained his mistress for some time out of gratitude, but his wife, who was mad with jealousy, beat me unmercifully every day; she was a perfect fury. The doctor was the ugliest man that ever was seen, and I was the most unfortunate of women to be continually beaten for a man whom I did not love. You know, sir, how dangerous it is for a cross-grained female to be the wife of a physician. The husband, driven out of all patience by his wife's proceedings, gave her one day, to cure her of a slight cold, a medicine so efficacious, that she died in dreadful convulsions before two hours were over. The lady's relations instituted a criminal prosecution against the gentleman; he betook himself to flight, and, as for me, I was thrown into prison. My innocence would not have saved me, if it had not been for my good looks. The judge set me at liberty on the condition that he should succeed the doctor, but I was soon supplanted by a rival, cast out of doors without any compensation, and forced to carry on this abominable trade, which seems to you men so pleasing, but which is for us nothing but a pit of misery. I came to Venice to practise my profession. Oh! sir, if you could only fancy what it is to be obliged to bestow caresses with equal impartiality upon old shopkeepers, lawyers, monks, gondoliers, and abbés; to be exposed to every kind of insult and outrage; to be often reduced to borrowing a petticoat to go and have it torn off one's back by some disgusting fellow; to be robbed by one customer of what has been earned with another; to be fleeced by the officers of justice, and to have no better prospect than a hideous old age, a hospital and a dunghill, you would be convinced that I am one of the most unfortunate creatures that the world contains."

Thus did Paquette open out her heart in response to Candide's kindness, in a small chamber, where Martin was also present. The latter said to Candide:

"You see I have already won half the wager."

Brother Giroflée meanwhile had remained in the dining-room, and was having a drink while waiting for dinner.

"But," said Candide to Paquette, "you had so jocund an air, and seemed so contented, when I met you, you were singing so gaily and fondling the friar with such apparently genuine complacency, that you seemed to me as happy as you assert that you are wretched."

"Ah! sir," answered Paquette, "there again is one of the miseries of my calling. Yesterday I was robbed and beaten by an officer, and today I must needs appear good-humoured to please a monk."

Candide had no wish to hear any more; he owned that Martin was right. They sat down to table with Paquette and the friar; the repast was tolerably entertaining, and, towards the end of it, they became quite confidential in their talk.

"Father," said Candide to the monk, "you seem to me to enjoy a lot which all the world might envy; the bloom of health shines on your countenance, your looks proclaim your happiness, you have a very pretty girl to amuse you, and you appear very well contented with your vocation."

"Upon my word, sir," said brother Giroflée, "I could wish that all Theatines were at the bottom of the sea. I have been tempted a hundred times to set fire to the monastery, and to go and turn Mohammedan. My parents forced me, when I was only fifteen years of age, to put this detestable habit on my back, in order to leave a larger fortune to a cursed elder brother of mine, whom Heaven confound! Jealousy, discord, and rage inhabit the convent. It is true that I have preached some bad sermons which have brought me in a little money, though the Prior robs me of half of it; the rest serves me to entertain the girls of my acquaintance. But when I return to the monastery in the evening, I am ready to dash my head against the walls of the dormitory, and all my fellow friars are in the same case."

Martin turned towards Candide with his usual composure, and said:

"Well now, have I not won the whole wager?"

Candide gave two thousand piastres to Paquette, and one thousand to brother Giroflée.

"I warrant you," said he, "that this will make them happy."

"I do not think it at all likely," said Martin; "those piastres of yours will perhaps render them more wretched than ever."

"Be that as it may," said Candide, "still one thing gives me consolation; I see that we often meet with people whom we never expected to see any more, it may very well come to pass that after having found my red sheep and Paquette, I may find Cunegund again also."

"I sincerely wish," said Martin, "that she may some day make you happy, but I strongly doubt it."

"You are very incredulous," said Candide.

"That is because I have seen what life is," retorted Martin.

"But look at those gondoliers," said Candide; "are they not always singing?"

"You do not see them at home, with their wives and their brats of children," said Martin. "The Doge has his vexations, the gondoliers have theirs. It is true that, taking everything into consideration, the lot of a gondolier is to be preferred to that of a Doge; but I deem the difference so insignificant, that it is not worth the trouble of examination."

"I hear people speak," said Candide, "of the senator Poco-curante, who resides in that fine palace on the Brenta, and entertains foreigners with such magnificence. They say that he is a man who has never known an annoyance."

"I should like to see so rare a specimen," said Martin.

Candide immediately sent a request to Signor Pococurante, that he might be allowed to pay him a visit on the morrow.

CHAPTER XXV

A Visit to Signor Pococurante, a Noble Venetian

Candide and Martin went in a gondola on the Brenta, and arrived at the palace of the noble Pococurante. The gardens were well laid out, and adorned with beautiful marble statues, and the palace itself was a magnificent building. The master of the house, a man of some sixty years of age, received the two inquiring travellers very politely, but without any demonstrative welcome, which somewhat disconcerted Candide, but was by no means displeasing to Martin.

First of all two pretty maids, neatly dressed, handed round chocolate, which they poured out with a fine froth upon it. Candide could not refrain from complimenting them on their beauty, their graceful carriage, and their cleverness.

"They are very good creatures in their way," said the senator; "I sometimes admit them to my caresses, for I am quite tired of the ladies of the town, with their coquettish airs, their jealous quarrels, petty humours, pride, and silliness, not to speak of the sonnets which one must make or order for their delectation; but, after all, these two girls begin to bore me a good deal."

After lunch, Candide strolled up and down a long gallery, and was surprised at the beauty of the pictures which were hung there. He inquired by what master the two first were painted.

"They are the work of Raphael," said the senator; "I paid a large sum for them several years ago, merely out of vanity. They are considered the finest in Italy, but they do not please me at all; the colouring is too dark, the figures are not well proportioned, and do not stand out enough, the clothing has no resemblance to real drapery. In a word, whatever people may say of them, I do not find there a true representation of nature. I only care for a picture when I can fancy that I am looking upon nature herself, and there are none of that sort to be seen. I have plenty of pictures, but I no longer take any notice of them."

While they were waiting for dinner, Pococurante provided them with a concert. Candide thought the music exquisite.

"This noise," said Pococurante, "may serve to while away half an hour; but if it lasts longer, it wearies everybody, though no one dares confess it. The music of the present day is nothing but the art of executing difficult tasks, and what has no other merit than difficulty fails to give pleasure in the long run.

"I might perhaps like the opera better, if the secret had never been discovered of making it such a monstrous absurdity that my reason revolts at it. Let those who like them go and see inferior tragedies set to music, where the scenes are made only to bring in by hook or by crook two or three ridiculous songs in which the voice of some actress may be employed to the best advantage; let all who will or can do so die away in raptures at hearing a eunuch trill out the part of Cæsar or of Cato, as he struts upon the stage with awkward air. For my part, I have long since given up these poor amusements, which constitute the glory of the Italy of today, and for which monarchs are wont to pay so high a price."

Candide said a little by way of opposition, but discreetly withal: Martin was quite of the senator's opinion.

They sat down to table, and, after an excellent dinner, they entered the library. Candide, catching sight of a splendidly bound Homer, commended the good taste of his illustrious host.

"There," said he, "is a book which gave delight to the great Pangloss, the first philosopher in all Germany."

"It affords me none," was Pococurante's cold reply. "I was once so far imposed upon as to fancy that I took pleasure in reading him; but that constant repetition of battles one exactly like another, those gods who are always meddling and never do anything decisive, that Helen who is the cause of the war, and yet plays hardly any part at all in the action of the poem, that Troy which is besieged and never taken,-all this bored me most infernally. I have sometimes inquired of learned men whether they grew weary as I did in reading him; all those who were sincere confessed that the book was apt to drop out of their hands, but that they were obliged to keep it in their libraries as a famous monument of antiquity, like those rusty old coins which are no longer of any use as money."

"Your Excellency surely does not think the same of Virgil?" said Candide.

"I am convinced," answered Pococurante, "that the second, fourth, and sixth books of the Æneid are excellent; but as for his pious Æneas, the brave Cloanthus, the trusty friend Achates, the boy Ascanius, the foolish king Latinus, the commonplace Amata, and the insipid Lavinia, I think there is nothing more frigid and disagreeable. I like Tasso better, and the drowsy tales of Ariosto."

"May I venture to ask you, sir," said Candide, "whether you do not find great pleasure in reading Horace?"

"He has maxims," replied Pococurante, "from which a man of the world may derive some profit, and which, being compressed into vigorous verse, are easily graven on the memory; but I care very little for his journey to Brundisium, or for his description of a bad dinner, or for his blackguardly quarrel between Persius and a certain Rupilius, whose language, as he says, was full of poisonous filth, and another fellow whose words were steeped in vinegar. I have never read without the utmost disgust his indecent lines against old women and witches, and I do not see to what merit he can lay claim in telling his friend Mecænas that if he is placed by him in the rank of lyric bards, he will strike the stars with his exalted head. Fools admire everything in a celebrated author; I read only to please myself, and I like nothing but what answers my purpose."

Candide, who had been taught never to judge of anything for himself, was very much astonished at what he heard, but Martin thought Pococurante's way of thinking not at all unreasonable.

"Oh! here is a Cicero," said Candide; "now as regards this great writer, I do not suppose you ever grow tired of reading him?"

"I never read him at all," answered the Venetian. "What difference does it make to me whether he pleaded for Rabirius or for Cluentius? I have quite enough causes to decide myself. I should have more inclination for his philosophical works; but when I saw that there was nothing about which he did not doubt, I concluded that I knew as much about them as he, and that I had no need of anybody to teach me ignorance."

"Ah! There are eighty volumes of transactions of the Academy of Science!" cried Martin. "There may be something good there."

"So there might be," said Pococurante, "if a single author out of all who have accumulated this lumber had so much as invented the art of making pins; but in all these books there is nothing but empty systems, and not a single thing of any use."

"What a number of plays I see there," said Candide, "in Italian, Spanish, and French!"

"Yes," said the senator, "there are three thousand of them, and not three dozen of any merit. As for these collections of sermons, which, taken all together, are not worth a page of Seneca, and all these big folios of theology, you may be sure I never open them,—neither I, nor anyone else."

Martin noticed some shelves filled with English books.

"I think," said he, "that a republican may well be pleased with most of these works, written, as they are, with such admirable freedom."

"Yes," answered Pococurante, "it is a fine thing to write what one thinks; it is the privilege of a human being. In all this Italy of ours, no one writes anything but what he does not really think true; those who inhabit the country of the Cæsars and the Antonines do not dare to entertain an idea without the permission of a Dominican friar. I should be well enough pleased with the liberty which inspires the works of English genius, if passion and party spirit did not spoil all that that precious liberty holds worthy of esteem."

Candide, perceiving a Milton, asked him if he did not regard that author as a great man.

"Who?" exclaimed Pococurante, "that barbarian, who writes a long commentary upon the first chapter of Genesis in ten books of ragged verse? That rude imitator of the Greeks, who disfigures the creation, and, whilst Moses represents the Almighty producing the universe with a word, makes the Messiah take a great pair of compasses out of the celestial cupboard, to trace the outline of his work? Can I set any value on an author who has spoiled the hell and the devil of Tasso, who disguises Lucifer sometimes as a toad, and sometimes as a pygmy, who makes him repeat a hundred times the same speech, who puts into his mouth theological discussions, and who, imitating in all seriousness Ariosto's comic introduction of firearms, represents the devils as cannonading heaven? Neither I, nor anyone else in Italy, can take any pleasure in these deplorable extravagances. The marriage of Sin and Death, and the snakes which Sin brings forth, are enough to make anyone sick who has the least delicacy of taste; and his lengthy description of a lazar-house is fit only for a grave-digger. This obscure poem, fantastic and revolting, was despised when it first made its appearance, and I treat it now as it was treated in his own country by his own generation. In fine, I say what I think, and I care very little whether others think as I do, or not."

Candide was distressed at these remarks; he had a respect for Homer, and a little liking for Milton.

"Alas!" said he aside to Martin; "I very much fear that this man has a sovereign contempt for our German poets."

"He would not be far wrong if he had," said Martin.

"Oh! what a superior person!" said Candide again in a low voice. "What a great genius, to be sure, is this Pococurante! Nothing can please him."

After having thus examined all his books, they went down into the garden, and Candide praised all its beauties.

"I know nothing in worse taste," said the owner; "everything here is vulgar and gaudy, but I am going to begin to have a garden laid out tomorrow on a more noble plan."

When the two inquirers had taken leave of His Excellency, Candide said to Martin:

"There now you will agree with me is the happiest man in the world, for he looks down upon all his possessions."

"Do you not see," returned Martin, "that he is disgusted with everything he has? Plato remarked long ago that it is not the healthiest stomach which rejects all food."

"But," continued Candide, "is there no pleasure in criticising everything, in perceiving faults where all other men think they see beauties?"

"Which is as much as to say," answered Martin, "that there must be some pleasure in never being pleased."

"Ah, well," said Candide, "then nobody is happy but myself as soon as I shall see Miss Cunegund again."

"It is always a good thing to be hopeful," said Martin.

Meanwhile days and weeks passed by; Cacambo did not return to him, and Candide was plunged into such deep distress, that he did not even make the reflection that Paquette and friar Giroflée had never come so much as to thank him for his kindness.

CHAPTER XXVI

*Treats of a Supper at which Candide and Martin were
Present with Six Foreigners, and Tells who they Were*

One evening, when Candide, followed by Martin, was about to
sit down to table with the other guests who were staying at the
same inn, a man, whose face was as black as soot, accosted him
from behind, and, taking him by the arm, said:

"Be ready to start with us,—do not fail."

He turned round, and saw Cacambo. Nothing but the sight
of Cunegund could have surprised and pleased him more, and
he was almost wild with joy. Embracing his dear friend, he
exclaimed:

"Is Cunegund here? Where is she to be found?—Take me to
her, that I may die with joy in her presence!"

"Cunegund is not here," said Cacambo; "she is at
Constantinople."

"Good Heavens! At Constantinople!—But were she in China,
I would fly to her.—Let us be off."

"We will start after supper," replied Cacambo. "I cannot tell
you anything more; I am a slave, my master is expecting me,
and I must go and wait upon him at table. Do not say a word,
take your supper, and hold yourself in readiness."

Candide, divided in his feelings between joy and disappointment, delighted to have seen again his faithful agent,
but astonished at finding him a slave, full of the idea of
recovering his mistress, with agitated heart and distracting
thoughts sat down to table with Martin, who regarded all these
occurrences quite calmly, and with six foreigners, who were
come to pass the carnival at Venice.

Cacambo, towards the end of the meal, as he was pouring
out wine for one of these six strangers, whispered in his new
master's ear:

"Sire, Your Majesty may start when he pleases; the ship is
ready."

Having said these words he left the room. The company looked at each other with surprise, but without uttering a single word, when another attendant, approaching his master, said to him:

"Sire, Your Majesty's carriage is at Padua, and the boat is ready."

The master made a sign, and the servant retired. All the guests stared at each other again, and the general surprise grew greater. A third footman, in like manner, went up to another of the strangers, and said:

"Sire, believe me, Your Majesty should not remain here any longer; I am going to get everything ready"—and he immediately disappeared.

Thereupon Candide and Martin came to the conclusion that this was doubtless some carnival masquerade, when a fourth servant said to his master—"Your Majesty can start when he pleases," and left like the others.

A fifth footman said much the same to a fifth master; but the sixth addressed the last stranger, who sat beside Candide, in a different manner:

"Upon my word, sire," said he, "people here will trust neither Your Majesty nor me any longer, and we run a great risk of being locked up in gaol tonight, so I am going to look after my own business. Farewell."

All the servants having taken their departure, the six strangers, Candide, and Martin sat on in profound silence, which Candide at last broke by saying:

"Gentlemen, this is a singular piece of pleasantry on your part. How is it you are all Kings? As for Martin and myself, I must confess that neither of us is of royal rank."

Cacambo's master gravely replied to his question, saying in Italian:

"I at least am not joking. My name is Achmet III., and I was Grand Sultan for a good many years. I dethroned my brother, and my nephew has done the same to me. My viziers have all had their heads cut off, and I am eking out the remainder of my days in the old seraglio; my nephew the Grand Sultan Mahmud allows me to travel sometimes for my health, and I am come to spend the carnival at Venice."

A young man seated by Achmet spoke next, and said:

"My name is Ivan; I was Emperor of all the Russias, but was dethroned in the cradle. My father and mother were closely confined, and I was brought up in prison; I am sometimes permitted to travel, accompanied by those who are responsible for my safe keeping, and I am come to spend the carnival at Venice."

The third stranger said:

"I am Charles Edward, King of England; my father has resigned to me his title to the kingdom, which I have fought to maintain. Eight hundred of my followers have had their hearts torn out and thrown in their faces, and I have myself been cast into prison. I am on my way to Rome, to pay a visit to the King my father, dethroned like myself and my grandfather; and I am come to spend the carnival at Venice."

The fourth then spoke as follows:

"I am King of Poland, but the fortune of war has deprived me of my hereditary dominions; my father experienced the same reverse, and I am resigned to Providence, like Sultan Achmet, the Emperor Ivan, and King Charles Edward (to whom God grant a long life!), and I am come to spend the carnival at Venice."

The fifth said:

"I also am King of Poland; I have twice lost my throne, but Providence has bestowed on me another State, in which I have done more good than all the Kings of Sarmatia together have been able to effect upon the banks of the Vistula. I too resign myself to Providence, and am come to spend the carnival at Venice."

It only remained for the sixth monarch to speak.

"Gentlemen," said he, "my royalty is of less exalted rank, but for all that I have been a sovereign like yourselves. I am Theodore, whom the Corsicans chose as their King. I have

206

been styled 'Your Majesty,' and now they hardly call me 'Sir.' Money has been struck in my name, and at present I do not possess a farthing; I have had two secretaries of State, and now I can scarcely be said to have any longer a valet; I have sat upon a throne, and, since then, have lain for long upon straw in a London prison. I very much fear I may be treated in the same way here, though I am come, like Your Majesties, to spend the carnival at Venice."

The five other Kings listened to this speech with generous compassion, and each of them gave King Theodore twenty sequins to buy himself shirts and other clothing, while Candide made him a present of a diamond, the value of which was not less than two thousand sequins.

"Whoever can this man be," said the five Kings, "who is in a position to give away a hundred times as much as any one of us, and who actually does it. Are you, sir, also a King?"

"No, gentlemen, and I have no desire to be one."

At the moment when they were leaving the table, there arrived at the same hostelry four Serene Highnesses who had likewise lost their territories by the fortunes of war, and were come to pass the remainder of the carnival at Venice, but Candide paid no heed to these new arrivals, being altogether absorbed in the thought of going to Constantinople in search of his beloved Cunegund.

CHAPTER XXVII

Candide's Voyage to Constantinople

The faithful Cacambo had already obtained permission from the Turkish captain, who was going to take back Sultan Achmet to Constantinople, for Candide and Martin to be received on board his vessel, where they both presented themselves, after having done obeisance to His miserable Highness. On their way to the ship, Candide kept saying to Martin:

"What a singular thing it is now that we should have supped with six dethroned kings, and that out of these six monarchs moreover there should be one on whom I have bestowed alms! It may be that there are many other princes yet more unfortunate. As for me, I have only lost a hundred sheep, and now I am flying into the arms of Cunegund. My dear Martin, once more let me tell you, Pangloss was in the right, and all is well."

"I wish it may prove so," said Martin.

"But what an adventure we have had here at Venice," pursued Candide, "and how extremely improbable it would have seemed beforehand! When was it ever seen or heard of that six dethroned sovereigns supped together at a tavern?"

"It is not more extraordinary," said Martin, "than most of the things that have happened to us. It is a very common occurrence for kings to be dethroned; and as for the honour we have had in supping with them, that is a trifle unworthy of our attention. What matters it with whom we sup, provided we meet with good cheer?"

Candide had no sooner reached the vessel than he fell on the neck of his old servant and friend Cacambo.

"Tell me now," said he, "how is Cunegund getting on? Is she still a prodigy of beauty? Does she love me as much as ever? Is she well and happy? You have doubtless bought a palace for her at Constantinople."

"My dear master," answered Cacambo, "Cunegund washes

dishes on the shore of the Sea of Marmora for a prince who has very few of such articles; she is a slave in the house of a foreign sovereign, named Ragotski, to whom the Grand Turk grants a pension of three crowns a day in his retirement; but, what is far more melancholy, she has lost her beauty and is become horribly ugly."

"Ah, well! handsome or ugly," said Candide, "I am a man of honour, and it is my duty to love her under all circumstances. But how came she to be reduced to a state so low, when you left me with five or six millions?"

"Oh! for the matter of that, was I not obliged to give two millions to Señor don Fernando d'Ibaraa y Figueora y Mascarenès y Lampourdos y Souza, Governor of Buenos Ayres, to obtain his permission to get back Miss Cunegund? And did not a pirate gallantly rob us of all the rest? And did not that same pirate take us to Cape Matapan, to Milo, to Nicaria, to Samos, to Petrias, to the Dardanelles, to Marmora, to Scutari? Cunegund and the old woman are slaves in the household of the Prince I have mentioned, and as for me, I am a slave of the dethroned Sultan."

"What a chain of frightful calamities!" said Candide. "But after all I have still some diamonds left, with which it will be easy for me to ransom Miss Cunegund. It is a great pity she is become so ugly."

Then turning to Martin, he said:

"Which, think you, is the most to be pitied, the Sultan Achmet, the Emperor Ivan, King Charles Edward, or I?"

"I cannot tell," said Martin; "it would be necessary for me to look into your hearts to know that."

"Ah!" said Candide, "if Pangloss were here, he would know all about it, and could tell us at once."

"I know not," said Martin, "in what scales this Pangloss of yours would have weighed the misfortunes of mankind, so as to estimate their relative sufferings. All I presume to assert is that there are millions of men upon the earth more to be pitied than King Charles Edward, the Emperor Ivan, and the Sultan Achmet."

"That may well be so," said Candide.

In a few days they arrived at the Bosphorus. The first thing that Candide did was to pay a heavy ransom for Cacambo, and, without any loss of time, he went on board a galley with his companions, to coast along the shore of the Sea of Marmora in search of Cunegund, however ugly she might prove to be.

Now there were among the crew two galley-slaves who rowed very badly, and to whom the Levantine skipper applied the lash from time to time on the bare shoulders. Candide, from a natural feeling of sympathy, regarded them with more attention than the rest of the crew, and approached them with a look of pity. Their faces, disfigured though they were, seemed to him to bear some resemblance to those of Pangloss and the unhappy Jesuit Baron, Miss Cunegund's brother. Touched with sorrowful emotion at this idea, he observed them still more attentively.

"Truly," said he to Cacambo, "if I had not seen Dr. Pangloss hanged, and if I had not had the misfortune to have killed the Baron, I could believe that it is they who are rowing in this galley."

At hearing the names of the Baron and of Pangloss, the two galley-slaves uttered a loud cry, ceased rowing, and let their oars fall from their hands. The Levantine skipper hurried up to them, and applied the lash with redoubled vigour.

'Stop! Stop, my good sir!" exclaimed Candide; "I will give you as much money as you like for them."

"What! Is it Candide?" said one of the two slaves.

"What! Is it Candide?" said the other.

"Is this a dream?" said Candide; "am I asleep or awake? Am I really in this galley? Is this my lord Baron, whom I killed? Is that Dr. Pangloss, whom I saw hanged?"

"Yes, indeed, it is we ourselves whom you see before you," they answered.

"What!" exclaimed Martin; "is this the great philosopher of whom I have heard so much?"

Candide again accosted the Levantine skipper:

"Sir," said he, "how much money will satisfy you for the ransom of my lord Thundertentrunk, one of the first barons of the Empire, and of Dr. Pangloss, the most profound metaphysician in Germany?"

"Dog of a Christian," answered the Levantine skipper, "since these two Christian dogs of galley-slaves are barons and metaphysicians, which is, no doubt, a high dignity in their country, you shall pay me for them fifty thousand sequins."

"You shall have them, sir; only take me back like a flash of lightning to Constantinople, and you shall be paid on the spot. But no; take me to the house where Miss Cunegund lives."

The Levantine skipper, on Candide's first offer of ransom, had already turned the vessel's prow towards the city, and now made his crew row more quickly than a bird cleaves the air.

Candide embraced the Baron and Pangloss a hundred times.

"And how was it I never killed you, after all, my dear Baron? And, my dear Pangloss, how is it you are alive, after having been hanged? And why are you both galley-slaves here in Turkey?"

"Is it really true that my dear sister is in this country?" asked the Baron.

"Yes," replied Cacambo.

"Do I then indeed behold once more my dear Candide?" cried Pangloss.

Candide then presented Martin and Cacambo; they all embraced each other, and all began to speak at the same time, while the galley flew on, and soon brought them back to the harbour. A Jew being sent for, Candide sold him for fifty thousand sequins a diamond worth a hundred thousand, though the Jew swore to him by Abraham that he could not in conscience give more for it; and Candide immediately paid down the money to ransom the Baron and Pangloss. The latter threw himself at his deliverer's feet, and bathed them with tears; the other thanked him with an inclination of the head, and promised to return the money on the earliest opportunity.

"But can it indeed be possible that my sister is in Turkey?" said he.

"Nothing is more certain," replied Cacambo, "since she scours the dishes and plates in the house of a Transylvanian prince."

Two other Jews were immediately summoned, to whom Candide sold more diamonds, and they all started again in another galley to go and release Cunegund from bondage.

CHAPTER XXVIII

What Happened to Candide, Cunegund, Pangloss, Martin, etc

"I crave your pardon once more," said Candide to the Baron; "forgive me, reverend father, for having run my sword through your body."

"I beg you will never speak of it again," said the Baron; "I was a little too hasty, I own. But as you wish to know how it came to pass that you found me a galley-slave, I must tell you that, after having been healed of my wound by the brother apothecary of the College, I was attacked and carried off by a party of Spaniards, who threw me into prison at Buenos Ayres just after my sister had left the city. I asked and obtained permission to return to Rome to the Father General, who nominated me to go and serve as chaplain to the French Ambassador at Constantinople. I had not been a week in my new post, when I met one evening a very handsome young Icoglan. The weather was very warm, the youth wished to bathe, and I took the opportunity of doing the same, not being aware that it was a heinous crime for a Christian to be found stark naked with a young Mussulman. A Cadi ordered me to receive a hundred blows on the soles of my feet, and sentenced me to the galleys. I do not believe that a more horrible act of injustice was ever committed. But I should like to know how it came about that my sister is kitchenmaid to a sovereign of Transylvania who has taken refuge with the Turks."

"And you, my dear Pangloss," said Candide, "how can it have happened that I see you again?"

"It is true," said Pangloss, "that you saw me hanged; I should, in the ordinary course of things, have been burned, but, as you will remember, it rained in torrents when I was about to be roasted. The storm was so violent that there was no hope of lighting the fire, so I was hanged because nothing better could be done. A surgeon bought my body, carried me home with him, and began to dissect me, by making in the first place a crucial incision from the navel to the neck. Now it was impossible for anyone to have been hanged more unskilfully than I was; the executioner of the high decrees of the Holy Inquisition—a sub-deacon—was indeed a perfect adept at burning people, but hanging was not in his line of business; the cord was wet, and, not slipping properly, failed to form a tight noose. In fact, I was still breathing when they cut me down, and the crucial incision made me utter such a piercing scream, that the surgeon fell flat on his back, and, believing that it must be the devil he was dissecting, rushed off in a panic of fear, and fell down again on the stairs in his hurried flight. His wife came running out of an adjoining chamber on hearing the noise, and, seeing me stretched out upon the table with the crucial incision made on my body, she was struck with even greater consternation than her husband, took to her heels, and tumbled on the top of him. When they had recovered a little from their fright, I heard the surgeon's wife say to her husband:

"'My good man, what were you thinking of to dissect a heretic like that? Don't you know that the devil is always in the bodies of such people? I'll go directly in search of a priest, that he may come and exorcise the corpse.'"

"I shuddered at these words, and, gathering up the little strength I had left, cried out:

"'Have pity on me!'

"At last the Portuguese barber-surgeon took courage; he sewed up my skin, and even his wife was prevailed upon to nurse me, till at the end of a fortnight I was on my feet again. The barber then found me a situation, and I became serving-man to a Knight of Malta who was going to Venice; but my master not having the wherewithal to pay me my wages, I entered the service of a Venetian merchant, and followed him to Constantinople.

"One day the fancy seized me to enter a mosque; there was no one there but an old Imam and a very pretty young devotee of the fair sex, who was saying her prayers. Her neck was quite uncovered, and in her bosom she had a beautiful nosegay of tulips, roses, anemones, ranunculuses, hyacinths, and auriculas. She let fall her nosegay; I picked it up, and put it back in its place for her with eager but respectful attention. I was so long in replacing it properly, that the Imam grew angry, and, seeing that I was a Christian, shouted for assistance. I was brought before the Cadi, who sentenced me to receive a hundred blows of a stick on the soles of my feet, and sent me to the galleys. I was chained in the identical galley and to the very same bench as my lord Baron. There were also among our number four young men from Marseilles, five Neapolitan priests, and two monks from Corfu, who told us that such adventures as ours are a matter of everyday occurrence. My lord Baron maintained that he had suffered greater injustice than I had done; I, on the other hand, insisted that it was far more excusable to replace a nosegay in a woman's bosom than to be found stark naked with an Icoglan. We kept up a constant dispute on the question, and we were receiving twenty lashes a day, when the chain of events in this universe brought you on board our galley to redeem us from bondage."

"Well, my dear Pangloss," said Candide, "now that you have been hanged, dissected, and thrashed black and blue, with all your experience as a galley-slave, have you continued to think that everything happens so well that it could not be better?"

"I have always retained my original opinion," answered Pangloss, "for am I not a philosopher? It does not become me to retract my words. Leibnitz cannot possibly be wrong; besides, the 'pre-established harmony' is the finest thing in the world, as well as the 'plenum' and the 'materia subtilis.'"

CHAPTER XXIX

How Candide Found Cunegund and the Old Woman again

Whilst Candide, the Baron, Pangloss, Martin, and Cacambo were recounting their adventures, and reasoning upon the contingent or non-contingent events that occur in this world; whilst they were disputing about causes and effects, moral and physical evil, free-will and necessity, and particularly the sources from which consolation may be derived when one is a galley-slave on Turkish waters, they reached the shore of the Sea of Marmora at the point where the house of the Transylvanian Prince was situated. The first objects that presented themselves were Cunegund and the old woman, who were spreading out towels to dry on a clothes-line.

The Baron turned pale at the sight. Candide, fond lover as he was, on beholding his fair Cunegund's complexion ruined, her bloodshot eyes, withered neck, wrinkled cheeks, and coarse red arms, started back a step or two in horror, but immediately afterwards advanced as good manners dictated. She embraced Candide and her brother, and after the old woman had been embraced also, Candide ransomed them both.

There happened to be a farm vacant in the neighbourhood, and the old woman proposed that Candide should take it until something better should turn up for the whole company. Cunegund was not aware that she had grown ugly, and no one was so impolite as to tell her so; she reminded Candide of his promises in so confident a tone, that the good-natured fellow did not dare to refuse her. Then he gave the Baron to understand that he was going to marry his sister.

"I will never," said the Baron, "tolerate such a low connection on her part, nor such insolent presumption on yours; I will never incur the reproach of infamy so great; my sister's children would be unable to enter the privileged circles of Germany. No, my sister shall never marry anyone but a baron of the Empire."

Cunegund threw herself at his feet, and bathed them with tears, but he was inflexible.

"Sir fool," said Candide, "I have rescued you from the galleys, I have paid your ransom and that of your sister; she was washing dishes here till I came, she is ugly, I am kind enough to make her my wife, and yet you still presume to oppose the match! Were I only to consult my indignation, I would kill you again."

"Kill me again, if you will," said the Baron, "but you shall not marry my sister so long as I am alive."

CHAPTER XXX

Conclusion

Candide in his secret heart had no desire to wed Cunegund, but the extreme impertinence of the Baron made him determined to conclude the marriage, and Cunegund pressed him so earnestly that he could not go back from his word. He consulted Pangloss, Martin, and the faithful Cacambo. Pangloss drew up a fine treatise, in which he proved that the Baron had no right of control over his sister, and that she was free, according to all the laws of the Empire, to form a left-handed marriage with Candide; Martin concluded that it would be best to throw the Baron into the sea; and Cacambo's decision was that he ought to be given back to the Levantine captain, and made a galley-slave again, after which he might be sent to Rome and the Father General by the first available vessel. This advice seemed very good, and met with the old woman's approval, but nothing was said to his sister about the matter. The scheme was carried into execution for a certain sum of money, and they had the satisfaction alike of entrapping a Jesuit, and of punishing the pride of a German baron.

One would naturally suppose that, after so many disasters, married to his mistress, living with the philosopher Pangloss, the no less philosophic Martin, the shrewd Cacambo, and the wise old woman, and having moreover brought so many diamonds from the country of the ancient Incas, Candide would now lead an existence the most agreeable in the world; but he had been so cheated by the Jews, that nothing was left him but this little farm; his wife, growing uglier every day, became intolerably peevish as well; the old woman was feeble, and even more ill-tempered than Cunegund. Cacambo, who worked in the garden and went to Constantinople to sell vegetables, was worn out with incessant toil, and cursed his fate. Pangloss was dejected because he could not shine at some German university. As for Martin, he was firmly persuaded that one is equally badly off everywhere, and so he took things patiently. Candide, Martin, and Pangloss sometimes continued their disputes on moral and metaphysical philosophy. Boats were often seen passing under the windows of the farm laden with Effendis, Pashas, and Cadis, who were being sent into exile to Lemnos, Mytilene, or Erzeroum; they saw other Cadis, other Pashas, and other Effendis, who came to take the places of those who had been banished, only to incur the same fate in their turn; they saw heads neatly packed up in straw, ready to be presented at the Sublime Porte. Such sights gave a fresh impetus to their discussions; and, when they had nothing to dispute about, they found their life so excessively tedious, that, one day, the old woman ventured to address them as follows:

"I should like to know which is worst, to be ravished a hundred times by negro pirates, to have a buttock cut off, to run the gauntlet among the Bulgarians, to be scourged and hanged at an *auto-da-fé*, to be dissected, to be a galley-slave, to experience, in short, all the wretchedness through which we have all passed, or to remain here doing nothing."

"That is an important question," said Candide.

This speech of the old woman's gave rise to new reflections, and Martin in particular concluded that men were born to live either amid the convulsions of anxiety, or in the lethargy of dulness. Candide did not agree with this view, but he felt sure of nothing. Pangloss confessed that he had never been free from horrible sufferings, but, having once taken up the position that everything went on wonderfully well, he continued to assert the same opinion, without really believing it.

There was one incident that completely confirmed Martin in his detestable principles, that made Candide hesitate more than ever, and embarrassed Pangloss himself. This was the sight they one day had of Paquette and friar Giroflée landing at their farm in a state of extreme destitution. They had very quickly consumed their three thousand piastres, had parted from each other, had been reconciled, had got into trouble, had been put in prison, had escaped, and finally brother Giroflée had turned Turk. Paquette continued to ply her trade everywhere, but gained nothing more by it than before.

"I was right in my foreboding," said Martin to Candide, "that your gifts would soon be squandered, and would, only serve to increase their misery. You and Cacambo have been gorged with millions of piastres, yet are no happier than brother Giroflée and Paquette."

"Ah!" said Pangloss to Paquette, "Heaven then brings you back among us here. My poor child! Do you know that you have cost me the tip of my nose, an eye, and an ear? What a fine woman you have grown, to be sure! Ah! what a world this is!"

This fresh adventure set them to work philosophising more deeply than ever.

Now there dwelt in the neighbourhood a very celebrated dervish, who was held to be the best philosopher in Turkey; him then they went to consult, and Pangloss acted as spokesman, saying:

"Master, we are come to beg that you will tell us why such a strange animal as man has been created?"

"Why should you meddle with the matter?" said the dervish; "what business is it of yours?"

"But, reverend father," said Candide, "there is a dreadful amount of evil in the world."

"What does it signify," replied the dervish, "whether there be evil or good? When His Highness sends a ship to Egypt, does he concern himself whether the mice on board are comfortable or not?"

"What is to be done, then?" asked Pangloss.

"To hold your tongue," said the dervish.

"I was hoping to have the pleasure," continued Pangloss, "of arguing a little with you on causes and effects, the best of all possible worlds, the origin of evil, the nature of the soul, and the pre-established harmony."

The dervish at these words shut the door in their faces.

While this conversation was being carried on, the news was

spread that two Viziers of the Bench and the Mufti had just been strangled at Constantinople, and that several of their friends had been impaled. This catastrophe created a great ferment for some hours. Pangloss, Candide, and Martin, as they were returning to their small farm, came upon a good old man who was enjoying the fresh air outside his door under a bower of orange trees. Pangloss, who was as inquisitive as he was argumentative, asked him what was the name of the Mufti who had just been executed.

"I know nothing whatever about it," answered the good man, "and I never yet knew the name of any Mufti or of any Vizier. I am absolutely ignorant of the event to which you refer; I presume that those who mix themselves up in public affairs generally perish some time or other in a miserable manner, and that they deserve it; but I never seek information about what goes on at Constantinople; I am content to send thither for sale the fruits of this garden which I cultivate."

Having said these words, he invited the strangers to enter his house. His two daughters and his two sons offered them many different kinds of iced sherbets, which they made themselves after the Turkish fashion and flavoured with candied citron peel, oranges, lemons, pineapples, dates, pistachio-nuts, and Mocha coffee free from admixture with the inferior produce of Batavia and the West Indies. Afterwards the daughters of this good Moslem poured fragrant essences over the beards of Candide, Pangloss, and Martin.

"You must have a vast and magnificent estate," said Candide to the Turk.

"I have only twenty acres," he answered, "which I and my children cultivate; labour keeps aloof from us three great evils,—dulness, vice, and want."

As Candide returned to his farm he reflected deeply upon what the Turk had said, and remarked to Pangloss and Martin:

"This excellent old man appears to me to have cut out for himself a lot far preferable to that of the six kings with whom we had the honour of supping."

"Great positions," observed Pangloss, "are highly dangerous, as all philosophers are agreed: for, let me remind you, Eglon, King of the Moabites, was assassinated by Ehud; Absalom was hung up by his hair and pierced with three darts; King Nadab, the son of Jeroboam, was slain by Baasha, King Elah by Zimri, Ahaziah by Jehu, Athaliah by Jehoiada; the Kings Jehoiakim, Jechoniah, and Zedekiah became slaves. You know the miserable ends of Crœsus, Astyages, Darius, Dionysius of Syracuse, Pyrrhus, Perseus, Hannibal, Jugurtha, Ariovistus, Cæsar, Pompey, Nero, Otho, Vitellius, Domitian, Richard II. of England, Edward II., Henry VI., Richard III., Mary Queen of Scots and Charles I., the second, the third, and the fourth Henry of France, the Emperor Henry IV. You know—"

"Yes," said Candide, "and I know too that we must attend to our garden."

"You are right," said Pangloss; "for when man was put into the Garden of Eden, he was placed there '*ut operaretur eum*,'—to dress it and to keep it, which proves that man is not born for idleness and repose."

"Let us work without arguing," said Martin; "that is the only way of rendering life tolerable."

All the little company entered into this praiseworthy resolution, and each began busily to exert his or her peculiar talents. The small orchard brought forth abundant crops. Cunegund, it could not be denied, was very ugly, but she became an excellent hand at making pastry; Paquette embroidered; the old woman took care of the linen. There was no one who did not make himself useful, not even friar Giroflée; he was a first-rate carpenter, and actually turned out an honest fellow. Pangloss used sometimes to say to Candide:

"All events are inextricably linked together in this best of all possible worlds; for, look you, if you had not been driven out of a magnificent castle by hearty kicks upon your hinder parts for presuming to make love to Miss Cunegund, if you had not been put into the Inquisition, if you had not roamed over

222

America on foot, if you had never run your sword through the Baron, or lost all your sheep from the fine country of El Dorado, you would not be here now eating candied citrons and pistachio-nuts."

"Well said!" answered Candide; "but we must attend to our garden."

NOTES

Voltaire despised novels. Tragedian, epic poet, philosopher and historian: these were his titles to contemporary honour. *Zadig* and *Candide* were written as entertainments. But Candide and Pangloss stand alongside Don Quijote and Hamlet, while Voltaire's *Henriade* (epic) and *Zaïre* (tragedy) are opened only by scholars. Voltaire was born François-Marie Arouet in 1694. A bourgeois who originally intended to live by his pen, he acquired a vast fortune through speculation and "insider dealing", and was eventually able to relieve impoverished European royals with his loans. Twice imprisoned in the Bastille, cudgelled by the henchman of a vindictive aristocrat, constantly in fear of persecution, by 1765 he was able to make the *affaire Calas* resound through Europe, forcing the French state council to remedy an anti-Huguenot injustice and overturn the verdict of the Toulouse *parlement*. When exiled from France, he took the opportunity to write about England, and his *Lettres philosophiques* (1734) are credited with introducing Shakespeare, Locke and Newton to the French. For this publication, he was again in danger of the Bastille. He learnt to escape censorship by multiplying his printers and having editions published in many different countries, thus presenting the censors with a *fait accompli*. After accusing the Regent of incest, he contrived to dedicate his tragedy *Oedipe* (1718) to the Regent's mother; he sent his tragedy *Mahomet* (1742, an allegory of Christian fanaticism and hypocrisy) to the Pope, and received a favourable response. Long exiled from Paris, he lived peacefully at Ferney, cultivating not only his garden but his connections throughout Europe. When he died, in 1778, he was mourned not only as a tragedian but as the great enemy of state injustice: "the Calas-affair man".

Zadig reflects the disabused courtier. Voltaire wrote much of it in enforced clandestinity at the castle of the Duchesse de Maine at Sceaux (see note to p. 183). Zadig, like Voltaire, rises to prominence on his merits, but they cannot prevent his downfall. Providence, the theme of both *Candide* and *Zadig*, eventually rewards Zadig's merit, but inspires little confidence. And Voltaire takes care to leave the story open; Zadig and Astarte live happily "ever" after, until the next episode. *Zadig* is set in what Pomeau calls "the philosophical Orient of the 18th century". Montesquieu, in his celebrated *Lettres persanes* (1721) was not the first to site social criticism in those safer latitudes. And the reign of Louis XV (1715-1724) was not propitious for those who directly criticised either religion or authority. Voltaire, though he believed in a God, regarded Christianity, and the Old Testament in particular, as little better than superstition; he sought absolute freedom of speech; and though he favoured the notion of an "enlightened despot" (this was one of the attractions of Frederick II of Prussia) he saw in the government of France little but incompetence, favouritism and inflexibility. His wit and free speech made him a dangerous enemy of state and religion. In *Zadig*, neither court nor *magi* are spared. When Missouf orders the master of horse to make a tart, we hear the royal mistress of the hour recommending her favourite for a promotion he does not deserve. The quarrels between Jesuits and Jansenists are mercilessly treated, along with the absurdity of condemning a man to death for his beliefs about mythical entities. Voltaire's picaresque narrative moves from allegory to allegory, settling personal scores as it goes. Could the French church complain that, in Babylon, a course of instruction by two *magi* had resulted in the pregnancy of their student? Only by suggesting that the allegory referred to the French church. And what could make one think that?

Candide, like *Zadig*, proceeds apace. Like *Zadig*, it has a thematic refrain to structure it. Today's reader can barely glimpse the scandalous nature of this narrative, which seems, like Voltaire's *Lettres philosophiques*, scarcely to deserve the opprobrium it incurred. But its heads of offence were manifold. Voltaire is sexually outspoken, without a hint of pornography. His anticlericalism is given free rein; avarice, cruelty and cupidity seem to identify the servants of God. His technique of *ostranenie*, "making strange" by omitting contextual explanation, allowed him to ridicule even as he avoided direct criticism. Could anything be more monstruous than to burn a man for not eating bacon with his chicken? Could anything be more absurd than two nations "at war over a few acres of snow"? The Admiral shot "to encourage the others" has entered both English and French languages. But Voltaire's principal target here is Leibniz, and the Providentialist views Leibniz had set out in his *Essais de theodicée* of 1710. The occasion of Voltaire's attack was the Lisbon earthquake of 1755. Voltaire had been a Providentialist himself, but this event put him at odds with his creator. It seemed particularly ironic that the inhabitants of Lisbon had gone out to Mass, leaving food to cook, when the earthquake struck; the fires that resulted did almost as much damage as the earthquake itself. Initial reports were of 100,000 deaths. It is arguable, of course, that no individual incident could ever disprove the notion of Providence. Of misfortune is good fortune born; man cannot penetrate the divine dispensation. This is not the impression left by a reading of *Candide* But pessimism is not unconfined. Human nature is not as depraved as Martin declares: Cacambo and Cunegund keep faith with Candide, and Candide himself learns to question the words of his philosophical master. Behind Pangloss, incidentally, stands a sad figure, that of Louise-Dorothée, Duchess of Saxe-Gotha, whose principality was constantly overrun and plundered during the Seven Years War; it was, she said, automatic with her "to love, to idolatrize Providence". Voltaire gently mocked her as the "best of all possible Princesses".

Candide and *Zadig* were bestsellers. Voltaire's struggle to impose Newtonian science on a reluctant French establishment passed over the heads of the many. The estimated 50,000 people who saw his tragedy *Alzire* (1743) remembered a tragedy of conventional kind. But those who read one of the

20,000 copies of *Candide* printed in the first year of its existence had in their hands one of the seeds of the French revolution. The freedom of Voltaire's spirit is released like a bacillus from which the pretentions of oppression might never recover. *Force majeure* would return. But there was no longer any excuse for credulity.

ZADIG

p. 9   *Certificate of Approval*: this text accompanies *Zadig* in all but the first and last editions published during Voltaire's lifetime. It is a satirical reference to the practice of censorship in France. *Zadig* was published in 1747, under the title *Memnon, histoire orientale*; it was printed in Amsterdam, the traditional location for the printing of subversive works, owing to its relative freedom of the press and religious tolerance. This edition seems not to have reached France, despite Voltaire's request to the marquis d'Argenson to smuggle some copies from Amsterdam to Paris, hidden in military baggage. The date of *Zadig*'s eventual appearance in Paris (10 September, 1748) is known to us through a denunciatory letter from the printer Bonin to the *Lieutenant de police*, Berryer. This 1748 edition was similarly anonymous, and Voltaire at first denied authorship. The direct object of censorship in Voltaire's time was the bookshop, which would undertake the printing and publishing of a volume. Censorship took the form of approval by the King, exercised through the office of Director of the Booktrade. The Director organised the allocation of manuscripts to readers, and, following their reports, issued them with a royal approval or some less commendatory permission. The censors were themselves men of letters; among them were well-known authors such as Fontenelle, Crébillon *fils*, and Condillac. But many were minor figures, submission to whose judgement Voltaire might reasonably resent; personal enmity might enter into the case. The 1748 edition of *Zadig* was to be limited to 1,000 copies, and since *Zadig* was already known in certain circles, Voltaire was afraid that the printers might run off a pirate edition. He therefore confided the first half of the manuscript to Priault in Paris and the second to Lefèvre in Nancy. Neither part could be sold independently. When Priault and Lefèvre each requested the other half, Voltaire refused. He then obtained their worthless print-runs and had them bound together. The Solomonic judgements of Zadig are of a piece with this ingenious ruse.

p. 9 *cadi*: a judge in an Islamic community.

p. 11 *Zadig ... Sultana Sherah ... Sadi*: the name Zadig would seem to derive from Herbelot, *La bibliothèque orientale*, a work which Voltaire consulted for his *Essai sur les moeurs*. Herbelot gives the Arab *sadik* meaning "truthful"; another likely source is the Hebrew *zadik* ("just"). The question debated in *Zadig* is whether merit is rewarded in this life; on this point Zadig is both example and witness. Zadig may be said to remain true to his principles of natural justice even when (it seems) they do him nothing but harm. The *Sultana Sherah* has often been identified as Mme Pompadour (1721-1764), the rich *bourgeoise* mistress of Louis XV, a patroness of the art and a meddler in politics. The attribution of the dedicatory epistle to *Sadi* is a homage to the Persian poet Saadî (c. 1215-?1292), who, as Price points out, shared certain characteristics with Voltaire, notably a fondness for allegory and a hatred of fanaticism and regal injustices. There had been translations of Saadî into French in 1634 and 1704.

p. 11 *Hegira*: the tale is thus set in 1433. The Hegira (Arabic *Hijra*: migration) took place in AD 622 and marks the start of the Islamic calendar. In that year, Mohammed, the Prophet and Founder of Islam, was forced by opposition in his native city of Mecca to emigrate to Medina. This "paved the way for the conquest of Mecca ... and the final settlement of Islam in Arabia from whence it would emerge to become a major world religion" (Netton).

p. 11 *Chaldee*: Chaldaea is a region of Babylonia between the Euphrates delta, the Persian Gulf and the Arabian desert; it is first mentioned in the Assyrian annals of Ahurnasirpal II (884/883–859 BC). But its association with learning comes by association with Babylon, and with Babylonian traditions of astronomy and astrology, which were proverbially advanced. The language itself was a dialect of Babylonian.

p. 11 *Sultan Oulook*: during the reign of Ulugh (Oulook) Beg (1394–1449), the grandson of Timur (Tamberlaine), the Timurid dynasty of Iran and its capital Samarkand reached their cultural apogee.

p. 11 *Thousand and One Nights, Thousand and One Days*. Antoine Galland's translation of the *Thousand and One Nights* had appeared in (1704–1717). Known in English as *The Arabian Nights*, this collection of stories is largely Persian in origin, with Arabian and Indian stories woven into it. Underpinning the collection is the situation of Scheherezade. The Persian monarch Shahriyar has ceased to trust women, taking a new wife every night and having her executed in the morning. Scheherezade tells tales within tales, and the monarch can never bear to interrupt them by her execution. The *Thousand and One Days* (1710–1712) consists of Persian stories translated by François Pétis de la Croix (1653–1713) in association with the novelist Alain-René Lesage (1668–1747). Under *etc.*, René Pomeau cites the "translation" of the *Thousand and one quarter-hours* (1723–1753) written by Thomas-Simon Gueulette (1683–1766).

p. 12 *Thalestris ... Alexander ... Queen of Sheba ... Solomon*: the story of the Queen of Sheba and King Solomon is told in I Kings, 10, and 2 Chronicles, 9. Hearing of his wisdom, the Queen of Sheba visits Solomon, and is overwhelmed to find his reputation more than borne out by his replies to her questions. Thalestris, Queen of Amazons, is supposed to have sought out Alexander and asked him to father her child.

p. 13 *King Moabdar ... Babylon*: it is possible that Voltaire touches here on his quarrels with the Regent of Louis XV, Philippe, duc d'Orléans, and his daughter Marie Louise, duchesse de Berry. Both were notoriously licentious, and it was rumoured that the father was one of his daughter's lovers. An epigram on this subject, calling Marie Louise *mère des Moabites* in reference to the conduct of Lot's daughters (see Genesis, 19, 31ff.) was attributed to and acknowledged (to a police informer) by Voltaire, who was consequently exiled from Paris in May 1716. By the time that *Zadig* was composed, Louis XV had taken over the reins of power, but the name Moabdar is related to these old quarrels. Herbelot gives the meaning of *dar* as "house, palace, residence, sojourn, place", and in Price's view, Moabdar would thus mean "King of the House of Moab", "King of the House of the Descendants of Lot". *Babylon* is, of course, in certain respects, Paris, as we shall see; Fougeret de Monbron made the same analogy in his *La Capitale des Gaules, ou la Nouvelle Babylone* of 1759.

p. 13 *Zoroaster*: Zoroaster, also known as Zarathustra, was born c. 628 BC, probably in Rhages, Iran, and died c. 551. His monotheism was a reaction to the class-oriented polytheism around him. He preached the worship of Ahura Mazda, a god surrounded by some six or seven beneficent immortals. In Ahriman, Ahura Mazda faced an opponent akin to the Devil. But this was not yet the fully fledged dualism of Mazdaism, a later development of his teachings, in which Ahriman was made equivalent in power to Ohrmazd (Ahura Mazda); Zoroaster taught that Ahura Mazda was the father of both good and evil. The Zorastrian scriptures are contained in the *Avesta*. Certain Zoroastrians left for India when Islam was enforced in Persia from the 8th century onwards, and formed the sect known as Parsees. Groos states that Voltaire was unacquainted with the Zoroastrian scriptures, having read only a summary called the *Sadder*, and that his references to these scriptures are invented. He read the *Sadder* in Hyde's *Historia religionis veterum Persarum*. Zorastrianism in *Zadig* and Manichaeism in *Candide* are integral to their theme of Providence.

p. 13   *leading magi*: the term *Magus* is a Greek transcription of the Iranian term for a Persian clan specializing in cultic activity. After the 1st century AD, the term also came to be applied to Babylonian magicians and soothsayers, with connotations of superstition and charlatanry. This ambiguity perfectly suits Voltaire's allegory of the Catholic priesthood, most of whose doctrines Voltaire regarded as little better than superstition. This passage has particular relevance to the debate about the theories of Sir Isaac Newton (1642–1727) concerning gravity and planetary motion. The church had opposed all astronomical advances, in particular Copernicus's *On the Revolution of the Celestial Sphere* (1543), condemned in 1616, and Galileo's *Dialogue concerning the Two Chief World Systems*, which Galileo was forced to retract in 1633. In 1734, Voltaire's *Lettres philosophiques* had given an account of Newton's theories; the volume had caused a considerable scandal (not only on account of its Newtonian content), and Voltaire had only just escaped arrest. Attacks on religion were regarded as directly subversive of the state in general and the divine right of kings in particular, while the church's official doctrines were the geocentric theories of Aristotle; so science and politics were irrevocably bound together.

p. 14   *Orcan*: this episode may be thought to echo the *bastonnade* (beating) administered to Voltaire by henchman of the chevalier de Rohan, a member of one of the great aristocratic families of France. In 1725, Rohan had twice verbally assailed Voltaire in public and been (predictably) worsted. The chevalier stood by to watch his henchmen administer the beating. Voltaire was unable to obtain justice; his aristocratic friends regarded the indignity administered to a mere man of letters as quite natural. When he sought a duel, and, failing that, to mount a similar operation against the chevalier, he was briefly imprisoned, and liberated only on the condition that he leave for England immediately. The incident is here revised in a manner greatly more satisfactory for Voltaire.

p. 14   *Mount Imaus*: there is no Mount Imaus. The name is used indiscriminately by ancient geographers of a great Asian mountain range. It may refer to the Altai - mountains.

p. 15   *Memphis ... Hermes*: Voltaire here turns his satire on contemporary medicine. The name Hermes, associated with the city of Memphis, inevitably suggests Hermes Trismegistus. Memphis was the capital of Ancient Egypt during the Old Kingdom (2575–2130 BC); it stood on the west bank of the Nile not far from today's Cairo. Hermes Trismegistus was the name given by Neoplatonists and alchemists to the Egyptian god Thoth, while "hermetic" philosophy was the name given to alchemy. None of this sounds like medical science, but Price cites a Doctor Borelli, named in Voltaire's correspondence, who held precisely Hermes' view of the right eye.

p. 17   *Arnoult*: Arnoult advertised his cures in the *Mercure de France* in 1747 and 1748. In the *Lettres philosophiques*,

Letter 25, Voltaire discusses Pascal's wager, and compares it to the claims of this Arnoult: "There is no proof that my sachets do not sometimes cure apoplexy; you should therefore wear them just to be sure".

p. 17   *the bridge Chinavar*: Zorastrians believed that the dead had to cross the bridge Chinavar, or the Bridge of the Requiter, to enter the afterlife. Azrael is the (Islamic) angel who separates the body and soul of Muslims at death. The angel said by Hyde to oversee traffic on the Zoroastrian bridge is Mohr Izad.

p. 18   *stream*: in his *Sottisier* Voltaire records a Chinese version of this story, in which the new lover is be cured by the brain of the not-so-very-late husband. The most famous version is "the Widow of Ephesus", given in the *Satyricon* of Petronius (1st century AD).

p. 19   *put away*: this has the sense of "repudiate". Formal divorce could be achieved by the husband under the terms prescribed by the Koran, which involved two repudiations under oath, followed by a third and definitive statement of the formula "I divorce you". These provisions have at times been abused; it was not expected that the three repudiations should be spoken at once, and among the sayings of Mohammed is one that of all things that are permitted, divorce is most hateful in the eyes of God. The provisions are set out in *Surat al-Baqara* and *Surat al-Talaq*.

p. 19   *cubic line ... silk ... porcelain*: Voltaire is satirizing contemporary scientific research. The porcelain jibe refers to René-Antoine Réaumur (1683–1757), a physicist and naturalist, best known for the invention of the Réaumur thermometer. Measurement of the speed of flow of water was undertaken by Pitot, La Hire and others were working on rain-gauges, and Bon de Saint Hilaire attempted to produce silk from cobwebs.

p. 20   *Grand Desterham ... knout*: Voltaire's spelling is entirely original. Herbelot had written *Defterdar*, and defined this post as "having charge of the police and finances among the Persians and Turks". A knout is a whip.

p. 20 *for having said that he had not seen what he had seen*: Voltaire's brushes with the Babylonian (Parisian) authorities generally involved his having said that he had seen what he had seen. It seems likely that this episode again refers to the Regent, the duc d'Orléans. The formulation (p. 19) "It is a bitch, not a dog" [*C'est une chienne, et non pas un chien*] is suspiciously close to one of the epigrams for which Voltaire was imprisoned in the Bastille. The epigram begins "It is not the son, it is the father / It is the daughter, and not the mother," and refers again to the rumoured incest. Voltaire contrives to utter his sentiments without inhibition. The king's horse is often identified as Boyer, tutor to the Dauphin, and the former Bishop of Maurepoix; he used to sign himself *anc.[ien évêque]* de Maurepoix (for[mer Bishop] of Maurepoix). Voltaire on this basis dubbed him the *âne de Maurepoix* (ass of Maurepoix) or "the king's ass". Voltaire may have killed two birds with one stone here. Another of his enemies was the poet Roi, who was a knight *chevalier*, and whose name could be written *cheval*ier de Roi (*horse*/Sir Roi/of [the] King). The story itself derives from *Le voyage et les aventures de trois princes de Sarendip, traduits du persan* ['The voyage and adventures of three princes of Sarendip', 1548, French translation from the Italian 1719], as one of Voltaire's enemies, Élie Fréron (1718-1776), discovered; he accused Voltaire of plagiarism in the *Année littéraire*, which he edited (1716, v. 1, Letter VIII). Fréron notes that Voltaire merely replaced a camel with a horse and a dog. Voltaire had, as we have seen, his reasons.

p. 22 *looked out of the window*: one of the satires of which Voltaire was suspected when exiled by the Regent in 1716 was a poem on the reign of Louis XIV, known as *les*

J'ai vu" ["I have seen"]. It enumerated the failures of the reign, ending "I have seen all this, and I am not yet twenty". In fact, Voltaire was not the author, and this may be an ironic reference to the fact.

p. 23   *griffin*: Voltaire here seems to be making fun of Persian superstition. But in fact he is glancing at the Old Testament. The griffin is a mythological winged monster, with the head of an eagle and the body of a lion. The French Old Testament gives "the eagle, the griffin and the sea eagle" at Deuteronomy 14, 22, where the English reads "the eagle, the gier eagle, and the osprey". The griffin would in any case qualify for the interdict pronounced in Leviticus, 11, 27 "And whatsoever goeth upon its paws, among all the beasts that go on all four, they are unclean unto you", since it has a lion's paws.

p. 23   *Yebor*: Jean-François Boyer, the former Bishop of Mirepoix, was tutor to Louis XV's son and an important adviser to the King. He was also something of a *bête noire* for Voltaire, who, when seeking membership of the Académie française in 1743, had written to Boyer explaining that he (Voltaire) was, after all, a good Catholic. Frederick of Prussia mocked him for this, noting his surprise at seeing "the minister of truth [Voltaire] kneeling before the idol of superstition". Louis XV was personally opposed to Voltaire's election and selected a Cardinal in Voltaire's stead. Voltaire's fruitless self-abasement added a personal motive to his dislike of Boyer's reactionary influence at court. The reference to Yebor was added in 1752.

p. 23   *griffins ... rabbits*: Cador simply puns on the French word *griffes* (talons), to say that Zadig keeps poultry. Rabbits are explicitly condemned as unclean in Leviticus, 10, 5, but were a stock part of the French peasant diet.

p. 24   *a maid of honour*: Voltaire suspected Boyer of having mistresses among the pious women to whom he acted as confessor.

p. 24   *Arimaze* is generally identified as Pierre François Desfontaines (1685–1745), the French translator of *Gulliver's Travels* and contributor to the *Journal des savants*. He was a persistent thorn in Voltaire's side; his pamphlet against Voltaire, *Voltairomanie*, sold two thousand copies in two weeks. He had first come into contact with Voltaire when liable to death at the pyre for the crime of sodomy; Voltaire's influence allowed him to escape this fate. He is given a name close to that of the principle of evil (the devil) in Zoroastrianism.

p. 24   *harpies*: deriving their name from the Greek for "to seize or plunder", the harpies were birds with the heads of women. Virgil describes them in Book III of the Aeneid (Dryden's translation): "When from the mountaintops, with hideous cry / And clatt'ring wings, the hungry Harpies fly; / They snatch the meat, defiling all they find, / And, parting, leave a loathsome stench behind".

p. 25   *Hyrcania*: a province of the ancient Persian Empire, south east of the Caspian sea.

p. 25   *the most opprobrious libel*: Voltaire/Zadig could never, of course, be guilty of such a thing. See note to p. 13.

p. 28   *satrap*: a satrap was a provincial governor in ancient Persia. But the word is also used to describe a despotic or cruel governor, and the application is to Paris.

p. 30   *At last, then, I am happy*: Voltaire specifies his theme with this refrain.

p. 31   *divan*: the council of state of the Ottoman Sultan.

p. 33   *the doctrine of the monads and the pre-established harmony*: these are the doctrines of Gottfried Wilhelm Leibniz (1646–1716), who is Voltaire's principal victim in *Candide*. Monads are single substances, "the true atoms of nature", that have "souls", in the sense of having perception and appetition. The pre-established harmony establishes why cause and effect can never be physical, and changes merely arise from the nature of the substance mutating: "... God first created the soul, and every other real unity, in such a way that everything in it must spring from within itself, by a perfect *spontaneity* with regard to itself, and yet in a perfect *conformity* with things outside" (*New System, and Explanation of the New System* [1695–1696]).

p. 33   *Irax*: this name means "wrathful" in Latin, but it is also (Price) an anagram of "Archi", as in *Archimage*, Voltaire's orientalised version of Archpriest. The satire of "Whatever he says will be right" may therefore be directed at Papal infallibility. The episode was added in 1748.

p. 35   *temple*: Voltaire may be alluding to his much-desired and long-delayed election to the Académie. The two sects here should be identified with the Jansenists and the Jesuits. Their dissension, and their quest for supremacy at the court, attracted some of Voltaire's more stinging satires. The Jansenists preached a Calvinistic morality, the Jesuits were the principal agents in France of the Counter-Reformation.

p. 35   *wants imagination*: Voltaire's poem *La bataille de Fontenoy* was criticised by Desfontaines and the poet Roi (another of Voltaire's enemies) for its lack of epic similes. But the examples here are drawn from the Old Testament. Psalm 114: "The mountains skipped like rams" (4); "the sea saw it, and fled" (3); stars are cast down in Daniel 8, 10, and the day star falls in Isaiah 14, 12; the last reference is presumably a joke, since it describes manna: "And when the sun waxed hot, it melted" (Exodus 16,21). "The hills melted like wax" is found at Psalms 97, 5. Thus the Bible is equated with a work of imagination.

p. 36   *the white and the black magi*: again, Jansenists and Jesuits are the target. Like the griffin and temple episodes, this dispute shows Voltaire mocking those who fanatically uphold a dogma that cannot be proved in this life.

p. 36 *comedies that made them laugh*: this is a reference to the fashin for the "tearful comedies" of Pierre-Claude Nivelle de la Chaussée (1692–1754) and others, which were more laughable than comic; tragedies at which one wept might, of course, have come from Voltaire's pen.

p. 36 *Mithras and the Zendavesta*: Mithras was one of the gods of the Iranian polytheistic pantheon, associated with the sun and with contracts. He returned to favour in the Roman Empire. The *Zendavesta* is a book of Zoroastrian scriptures.

p. 39 *Astarte*: Voltaire names the Queen after Ashtart, an ancient Near Eastern goddess of love and war.

p. 41 *a blue bowstring*: the bowstring is the traditional instrument of the executioner sent by the oriental potentate to strangle the condemned man. By making the bowstring blue, King Moabdar apparently seeks poetic justice.

p. 44 *Canopus*: a port in ancient Egypt east of Alexandria.

p. 52 *worshipped the host of heaven*: this refers to the religion of the Sabaeans,who practised a kind of astral Neo-platonism.

p. 52 *the land of the Gangarides*: this features in Voltaire's tale *La Princesse de Babylone* as a sort of pastoral Utopia, set on the east bank of the Ganges.

p. 54 *Since that time...*: Voltaire continues to satirize the inconstancy of women, rehearsing the Petronian fable recounted of Azora. But the practice of suttee was a very real one, and was ended in India only by colonial legislation. In Voltaire's reflections on the children such widows "might have presented ... to the State" (p. 53), we hear overtones of his arguments against monast-icism for women, which may be the subject of his allegory here.

p. 55　*Bassora*: today's Basrah in Iraq. Voltaire ignores the information provided by Herbelot, that the town and its market-fair were established only in the 17th century. This is almost certainly because by its name it could represent the Low Countries (*Les Pays Bas*: French *bas* "low", Latin *ora* shore) in which religious tolerance was well established. However, the passage is notably similar to one in the *Lettres philosophiques*, Letter 6: "Enter the London Stockmarket, a place more respectable than many courts: you will find assembled there for the benefit of mankind the representatives of every nation. There Jew, Muslim, and Christian do business with each other as if they were all of the same religion, and only the bankrupt are considered infidels; there, the Presbyterian trusts the Anabaptist, and the Anglican accepts the word of the Quaker".

p. 56　*fish Oannes*: Voltaire borrowed his fish from *La Mythologie et les fables expliquées par l'histoire* (1739) by Abbé Bannier. Pomeau tells us that Voltaire merely added the daily preaching on dry land. The Celtic God Teutates, familiar to readers of *Asterix*, is also mentioned by Bannier.

p. 60　*the tower of Mount Lebanon*: a derisive reference to the Song of Songs, 7, 4: "Thy nose is like the tower of Lebanon which looketh toward Damascus".

p. 61　*Tidor and Ternat*: towns in the Molucca Islands.

p. 61　*Sheat ... Algenib*: stars of the constellation of Pegasus. These are, after all, the "priests of the stars", and know the stellar hours at which Almona's assignations are given.

p. 62　*Chapter XIV*: this chapter and the next are posthumous chapters, often printed as an appendix. The translator has saved appearances here by leaving out the last two paragraphs of the previous chapter, which see Zadig leaving Setoc to travel to Syria. The name Serendip appears in Persian fairytales, notably in *The Three*

Princes of Serendip, in which the heroes possess the gift of Serendipity, the "faculty of making fortunate discoveries by accident". In the *Arabian Nights*, the name refers to Sri Lanka.

p. 63   *people and books that deal in prodigies*: Zadig's words seem eminently reasonable, but on reflection can be seen to apply to such works as the Bible and the Koran; the "people that deal in prodigies" (such as resurrection) are therefore the priests of established religion.

p. 65   *you have rightly divined*: we are, it should be remembered, in the island of Serendip.

p. 66   *bonzes*: a "bonze" is a Japanese or Chinese Buddhist monk; Sri Lanka is a centre of Buddhism.

p. 68   βοωπις: Voltaire's Greek is defective. The Greek word shown here means "ox-eyed", which was indeed a compliment; the Greek for blue-eyed would be γλαυκοπις.

p. 68   *the bonzes, who owned half the revenues of the state*: the French church at this time paid no taxes, only a self-assessed contribution.

p. 69   *burnt, in all likelihood, in Arabia*: this is another difficulty raised by the insertion of the two posthumous chapters; at the end of Chapter XIII, "Zadig was saved" from the threat of the pyre. Without the explanation provided at the end of that chapter for Zadig's departure, the sudden eclipse of Setoc from the narrative and the arrival of Zadig in Syria are unexplained.

p. 70   *Arbogad*: Price notes that in Hebrew, *gad* means both "God" and "robber". Arbogad's character as described here is that of Frederick II, King of Prussia (1712– 1786), who corresponded with Voltaire and invited him to his court, rescuing him from disfavour (here, a battle against the odds) at the court in Paris A man of literary accomplishments himself, Frederick frequently compared Voltaire's works to treasures, and in particular to the Golden Fleece captured by Jason and the Argonauts. Frederick, in his relations with Voltaire, sought to extend his authority well beyond his own borders, a point touched on in Arbogad's first speech and in the Surinam episode of *Candide*. Finally, one cannot help hearing in this bandit's account of himself an account of the origin of kingship more accurate than Divine Right.

p. 72 *my customers pay nothing for rank*: in the light of contemporary doctrines of the sanctity of the Royal person, the subversive power of these words is worth noting.

p. 76 *but the fishes mock me as much as men do*: Voltaire mocks Christ's words (Mark, I, 17), "I will make you fishers of men".

p. 76 *You are an angel sent to save me*: Zadig's behaviour should be contrasted with that of the angel Jesrad, relating it to the argument about Providence that constitutes the "refrain" of *Zadig*.

p. 78 *cockatrice*: this is another name for the basilisk, a small dragon combining features of the cock and the snake, and said to be fatal by look or breath. The basilisk's only enemy was the weasel, but, like the unicorn, it was susceptible to the blandishments of virgin young women.

p. 78 *Ogul*: the name is a genuine oriental name, but is also an anagram of *gulo*, the Latin for "glutton". Price points out that Louis XV, when ill at Metz, had been persuaded to give up his mistress Mme de Châteauroux, on the grounds that his illness was the result of his sins. The parallel made here is with cure by a mythological creature, in this case, God.

p. 81 *Missouf*: the name is perhaps an anagram of *misosoph[ia]* or "hater of wisdom", which is the burden of another possible source, the mixture of English

"Miss" and French "fou" (mad). Voltaire here touches on the arbitrary allocation of privileges at the court, under the influence of the reigning mistress; functions were bestowed without reference to qualification.

p. 81 *the image in which I was confined*: the spectacle of a king haunted by the words of a graven image may seem risible, but behind them Voltaire is pointing to the absurdity of such events as the Metz illness. Behind the sentence of the god is always, he suggests, a human voice.

p. 82 *I had always heard it said*: Voltaire again observes that the person of a king or queen shows no sign of divine right.

p. 87 *Such a man as I*: the first letter Desfontaines wrote to Voltaire contained the words: "I am too well known in society for it to be appropriate for such a man as I to keep silent after so heinous an affront". Voltaire adopted the phrase as an index of presumption, citing it in the *Lettres philosophiques*.

p. 94 *They are the winds*: is this a reference to the philosopher David Hume (1711–1776)? In Book II, Section III of his *A Treatise of Human Nature* (1739–1740), Hume undertakes to prove that "reason alone can never be a motive to any action of the will". Hume does not feature in the *Lettres philosophiques*, but Voltaire was an admirer of his work.

p. 96 *Jesrad*: Herbelot gives the name Jez-Dad as that of the angel of goodness in Zoroastrianism.

p. 97 *But*: Voltaire's scepticism here is like that of his tale *Le blanc et le noir*, in which the hero, Rustan, finds the explanation of his guardian angel unsatisfactory, and of *Memnon*, in which Memnon's guardian angel is equally unsuccessful. The story Voltaire tells here has many precedents, and though he was accused of plagiarising Parnell by Fréron, he could have found it in many places, including the Koran (Al-Kahf, 62ff.).

p. 97 *tenth sphere*: in the Ptolemaic system, the earth is
surrounded by nine spheres; the tenth, the empyrean,
was thought by early Christians to be the abode of God
and the angels.

CANDIDE

p. 103 *Candide* was composed in 1757–1758. It was printed by
the Cramer brothers in Geneva; on 15 January 1759,
copies were sent to the Cramers' correspondents
throughout Europe. Voltaire counted upon pirated
editions being made, since print runs were generally
small. Editions were printed in Paris, Geneva, Lyon,
Avignon, Liège, and London; three English translations
appeared in 1759. The French *candid* means
"ingenuous".

p. 103 *Dr. Ralph*: the doctor is a fiction to cover Voltaire,
allowing him to disavow the work, which he at first did,
describing it in a letter to Vernes as "a schoolboy joke,"
and attributing it to various authors, notably the
apocryphal M. Démad. The "additional matter" is the
1761 additions, in particular the changes to the Parisian
episode, with which Voltaire, exiled from Paris, had
struggled. In 1759, Minden was the site of a battle
between English and French armies.

p. 105 *quarterings*: coats of arms massed on a shield, re-
presenting intermarriages.

p. 105 *Pangloss*: this name is normally interpreted as "All
tongues" from its Greek components, though, given the
philosopher's willingness to interpret everything in the
one light, his name might derive from the French *gloser*,
to "annotate or gloss" or "ramble on about".

p. 106 *It has been proved*: this refers to the *Theodicy* of Leibniz,
his most unyieldingly optimistic work.

p. 106 *sufficient reason*: in *A Specimen of Discoveries about
Marvellous Secrets of Nature* (c. 1686), Leibniz wrote:

"necessary truths can be reduced to identical truths ... but in the case of contingent truths ... the reduction proceeds to infinity. So the certitude and perfect reason of contingent truths is known only to God". And he adds in a note: "The true cause of the fact that these things exist rather than those is to be derived from the decrees of the divine will, of which the primary one is the will to do everything in the best manner possible ... God acts like the greatest geometer, who prefers the best construction of problems". This is sufficient reason; it is not the same as necessity, where God too would have been bound.

p. 108 *Two men dressed in blue*: Prussian press-gangs were dressed in blue. English press-gangs similarly sought to make their victims unwittingly "take the king's shilling".

p. 109 *king of the Bulgarians*: the French *Bulgares* may have overtones of "the king of Buggers" (*Bougres*) in reference to the tastes of Frederick II.

p. 109 *run the gauntlet*: at the Prussian court, Voltaire had met a Frenchman named Courtils, who, having been invited to the court of Prussia with the offer of a chamberlainship, was placed in a regiment; when he deserted, he was forced to run the gauntlet, and had his nose and ears cut off.

p. 110 *Dioscorides*: Dioscorides Pedanius is the name of a Greek army physician of the 1st century AD. His book, the *Materia medica*, was the first attempt to systematize the use of drugs, and was long regarded as the standard work on this subject.

p. 110 *Avarians*: the encounter, in French, of *Bulgares* and *Abares* sounds comical in itself. Though these two Scythian tribes both existed, and Voltaire had read of them in Pufendorf's *Introduction to the General and Political History of the Universe*, they here designate France and Prussia, who were then embroiled in the Seven Years War (1756–1763). The Greek word *barbaros* referred to all foreigners; by replacing the first "bar" by an alpha privative, Voltaire creates a word meaning "non-foreigners", i.e. the French.

p. 112 *the Pope is Antichrist*: the orator is a Protestant. The rhetoric of anti-Catholic hatred has survived intact to this day, for example, in the sectarian vocabulary of Northern Ireland.

p. 112 *Anabaptist*: the word "anabaptist" means "rebaptizer". Several groups of Anabaptists lived in Holland, notably Melchiorites and Mennonites. Their doctrines were various, but the tenet to which they owe their name is their non-recognition of infant baptism; they insisted on baptism of believers. They thus incurred the emnity of both Protestants and Roman Catholics, and were much persecuted. This episode is akin to the parable of the Good Samaritan (Luke, 10, 30 ff), with the Protestant appearing in the role of "a certain priest".

p. 113 *featherless biped*: Diogenes Laertius claims that Plato gave this somewhat otiose definition of man.

p. 113 *fabrics of Persia*: Holland was a centre of the textile trade; Voltaire refers to the practice of passing off Dutch goods as imported from the Orient, and charging premium prices in consequence.

p. 113 *the tip of his nose eaten away*: this is the proverbial symptom of syphilis. Tissue destruction is in fact a symptom of tertiary syphilis, the final stage of the disease.

p. 115 *Columbus*: syphilis began to be recorded after the discovery of the Americas by Columbus in 1492, and there is evidence that syphilis existed in the Caribbean before Columbus's voyage. But other diseases receiving the same treatment, notably leprosy, preceded Columbus's voyage.

p. 118 *a priori*: *a priori* reasoning is from a general principle to particular effects.

p. 119 *trampled ... on the crucifix*: Voltaire notes in his

Fragments sur l'Inde, sur l'histoire générale, et sur la France: "It is indeed true, that, early in the 1638 revolution [in Japan], the Dutch were obliged, like the others [i.e. like the Japanese] to trample the crucifix".

p. 119 *Lima*: Lima was devastated by an earthquake in 1746. The Lisbon earthquake was one of the greatest natural disasters to befall Europe in modern times. The quake was felt as far as Geneva. Whole towns in the Maghreb were destroyed. Voltaire, overwhelmed by the scale of the disaster, wrote a *Poème sur le désastre de Lisbonne* ('Poem on the Lisbon Disaster'), an attack on the optimism of Pope, which he had previously admired, and of Leibniz, the principal target of *Candide*.

p. 120 *the Inquisition*: the Inquisition came into being in 1232 under Pope Gregory IX. In 1252, Pope Innocent IV justified the Inquisition's use of torture in his papal bull *Ad extirpanda*. The Spanish Inquisition was set up in 1479 with papal approval by Fernando V of Aragon (1452–1516) and his wife Isabella of Castille, its role was highly political, as it was closely associated with the reconquest of Spain. Its first Grand Inquisitor (1483–98), Torquemada, was notorious for the number of those whom he condemned to death at the stake, estimated at around 2,000.

p. 122 *auto-da-fé*: the Portuguese term means "act of faith". The Inquisition tended to torture its suspects as a matter of judicial routine, which was not unusual at the time. Those who would not confess were burnt at the stake.

p. 122 *fellow god-parent*: the relation of godparent was considered to establish family relations, placing the relation within the interdict on incest. This is satirized in Voltaire's story *L'Ingénu*, in which *l'ingénu* falls in love with a woman who has acted as his godparent.

p. 122 *rejected the bacon*: after the reconquest of the Iberian peninsula from Islamic occupation, some converted Muslims remained. Non-converted Jews were expelled

247

from Spain. Muslims are forbidden "carrion, blood, and the flesh of swine" (Koran, Al-Ma'idah, 5.3); for Jews too, the swine is "unclean" (Leviticus, 11.7). Converted Muslims (Moriscos) and Jews (Marranos) were a particular target of the Spanish Inquisition. The rejection of bacon was thus a (possible) index of whether a Morisco or Marrano had, after conversion, apostasized.

p. 122 *sanbenito*: the garment worn by the victims of the Inquisition to their deaths. On the garment of those who had confessed, flames were depicted facing downward; on those who had not, the flames faced upward, indicating that they were to be burnt at the stake. The devils are not, oddly enough, of Voltaire's invention, but derive from an illustration in Dellon's *Relation de l'Inquisition de Goa* (1688).

p. 129 *miserere*: a section of the sung Mass invoking God's pity.

p. 132 *moidores*: a Portuguese coin; the name simply means "money of gold" (*moeda de ouro*).

p. 132 *side*: Voltaire is more explicit.

p. 132 *Hermandad*: the Brotherhood of the Inquisition, its official name.

p. 132 *the common sewer*: Don Issachar, as a Jew, could not be buried in a consecrated graveyard.

p. 133 *pistoles*: gold coins. The word is of French origin.

p. 133 *maravedi*: Spanish coins of copper or gold; copper is clearly meant here.

p. 133 *San Sacramento*: the Jesuits established communities in the Paraná and Uruguay basins in south east Paraguay. Between 1721 and 1735, their 30 *reducciones* governed the lives of some 150,000 Amerindians. In due course their power attracted the attention of the settlement at Asunción, which sought to subject the Jesuit communities, and in 1754-1757 a combined Spanish and Portuguese attack caused their settlements to be abandoned. In 1767 the Jesuits were expelled from South America.

p. 133 *having seen some service with the Bulgarians*: the Prussian army was considered the most disciplined in Europe.

p. 134 *what is behind*: the French is again more explicit: "if I were to show you my behind".

p. 136 *Palestrina*: Groos notes that the principality of Palestrina was ruled by the Barberini family, to which Pope Urban VIII (the last Pope of that name, 1623-44) belonged. Voltaire's note is posthumous, first appearing in the Beuchot edition.

p. 137 *Sallee rover*: a pirate vessel from the Moroccan town of Salé, once reputed as a centre of piracy.

p. 137 *in articulo mortis*: (Latin) "at the point of death".

p. 137 *nook and cranny*: the original is again more explicit: "What surprised me more was the fact that they inserted a finger in a place in which we ladies normally allow only enemas to be inserted".

p. 138 *Muley Ismäel*: Ismai'il Ibn Sharif (1665/6-1727), second Mawlay (Lord) of the Alawi dynasty of Morocco, a brutally efficient ruler, was said to have 700 sons. He kept both European powers and the Ottomans at bay.

p. 138 *tigers*: tigers are not found in Africa.

p. 139 *O che sciagura d'essere senza coglione*: (Italian) "O what a disaster to be without balls!"

p. 140 *rulers of States*: this is a reference to the *castrato* Farinelli (Carlo Broschi, 1705-1757), who rose to favour in the Spanish court of Felipe V, curing his melancholy by singing him the same five songs nightly for ten years.

p. 140 *exterminating the commerce*: in Chapter 18 of his *Le Siècle de Louis XIV*, Voltaire recorded an agreement of this kind.

p. 141 *Dey*: a commander of the Janissaries of Algiers (1671-1830).

p. 141 *an Aga of the janissaries*: an Aga is a military commander in the Ottoman Empire; the Janissaries were the infantry of the military slave force first raised by Sultans Murad I and Bayezid I. The Russians, under Peter the Great, besieged Azov in 1695–1697.

p. 142 *Imam*: an imam leads the prayers in a congregational mosque.

p. 142 *rump steak*: Voltaire discovered this story in the writings of Saint Jerome (c. 342–420).

p. 142 *boyard*: more commonly spelt "boyar", this is an ancient order of Russian nobility, ranking below princes. The order was abolished by Peter the Great.

p. 143 *yet to cling to it*: the daughter of a Pope has forgotten that she is recommending what was, in Catholic eyes, a mortal sin.

p. 143 *Robeck*: Johann Robeck, born 1672 in Calmar, Sweden, drowned himself in the Weser at Bremen in 1739.

p. 144 *convenient falsehood*: this refers to Abraham. Fearing he would be murdered on account of Sara's beauty, he told the Egyptians (Genesis, 12) that she was his sister; Sara was consequently taken into Pharaoh's household. Abraham repeated this stratagem with Abimilech, King of Gerar (Genesis, 20). Fortunately, God came to Abimelech "in a dream of the night" and corrected the misapprehension. Abraham's son Isaac perpetrated the same deceit, which Abimelech this time resolved on his own, after seeing "Isaac sporting with Rebekah" (Genesis, 26) and inquiring about the supposed incest.

p. 145 *alcalde ... alguazils*: (Spanish) a magistrate and his officers.

p. 145 *grey friar with the long sleeves*: Voltaire remarks on the dispute that arose within the Franciscan movement over the design of the habit. A scission about fashion is particularly ironic in an order vowed to poverty.

p. 148 *padres*: (Spanish) fathers, in reference to the Jesuits.

p. 150 *Saint Ignatius*: Saint Ignatius Loyola (1491/1495–1556) was the founder of the Jesuit order.

p. 151 *horribly salt*: exorcised and blessed salt is an ingredient in holy water.

p. 151 *Croust*: in 1754, Voltaire was staying in Colmar, and had been antagonised by Pierre-Antoine Krust, the director of the Congregation of Messieurs, and of the Brotherhood of the Agony of Christ. Krust and another Jesuit, Sébastien Mérat, were attempting to have Voltaire and his work *Abrégé de l'histoire universelle* condemned by the Conseil d'Alsace. Jesuit colleges had a reputation for homosexuality.

p. 154 *Trévoux Gazette*: the *Mémoires pour servir à l'histoire des sciences et des beaux-arts*, to give its full title, was generally known as the *Journal de Trévoux*. Founded at Trévoux in 1701, and transferred to Paris in 1731, it was an influential literary monthly that sought to defend religion from the attacks of the *philosophes*.

p. 155 *lovers*: Voltaire is unlikely to have made this allegation without some documentary source; in his *Essai sur les moeurs* he notes that homosexuality is practised among the "Brazilians", but does not mention bestiality in his chapter on Paraguay.

p. 156 *Oreillons*: this translates the Spanish word *Orejones* from the *Comentarios Reales* (1609–1617, French translation 1704) of the Inca Garcilaso de la Vega, from whom Voltaire took certain details of his account of El Dorado, notably the provision of free board at inns. The name was given by Garcilaso de la Vega to a tribe, the lobes of whose ears were artificially elongated. The French word *Oreillon* (earpiece, ear-flap) is somewhat comical as a name for cannibals, since it also means "mumps".

p. 156 *first-rate fare. Let us eat up the Jesuit!*: through Fréron, Voltaire had come across an anecdote in Muratori (1672–1750) about cannibals preferring Jesuit flesh, as the Jesuits were the only clerics in South America who ate salt. Voltaire refers in a letter to the slogan "Let us eat Jesuit!" being frequently heard in the streets of Paris after the publication of *Candide*.

p. 157 *offered them their daughters*: Voltaire probably refers here to Lot's conduct in Sodom. The Sodomites wished to sodomize the angels visiting Lot, and he offered them his virgin daughters instead (Genesis 19, 13: "Behold now, I have two daughters, who have not known men; let me, I pray you, bring them out unto you, and do ye to them as is good in your eyes: only unto these men do nothing"). Voltaire regarded both the Jews and the God of the Old Testament as barbarian, and equates them with the cannibals of his narrative.

p. 158 *Cayenne*: capital of French Guiana, founded in 1643.

p. 159 *large red sheep*: llamas were thus described in contemporary accounts.

p. 163 *El Dorado*: legendary ruler of an Amerindian town near Bogotá, who was supposed to coat himself in golddust (thus: "the gilded one") and plunge into the waters of Lake Guatavita. The legend multiplied, and soon an entire country of gold was supposed, with cities named Manoa and Amagua. Voltaire refers to this legend, and to a lake named Parima whose sands were of gold, in his *Essai sur les moeurs*, chapter 151.

p. 163 *Sir Walter Raleigh*: Raleigh (1552?-1618), sailor, soldier, freebooter and poet, was involved in various expeditions to the American content. Imprisoned under James I, he was freed to seek gold by sailing up the Orinoco to the presumed site of Manoa. He failed, and was executed on his return.

p. 163 *slay us all*: Voltaire had been impressed by the *Brevísima relación de la destrucción de las Indias* by Bartolomé de las Casas, which he had read for his *Essai sur les moeurs*. It is a history of genocide and torture motivated by the search for gold.

p. 168 *Surinam*: Surinam, then a Dutch colony; its capital, the town in question, is Paramaribo.

p. 169 *they cut off the hand*: Voltaire has transposed the *Code noir* of the French West Indies to the Dutch colony of Surinam (Dutch Guiana), but he is not exaggerating. In 1767, a ministerial decree went out as follows: "It is important for the preservation of order that the state of humiliation attaching to the black species is not attenuated ... His Majesty is determined to maintain the prejudice that must forever separate coloured people and their descendants from all the advantages attaching to whites". Provisions in the *Code noir* in favour of blacks were systematically ignored.

p. 169 *the cost at which you eat sugar*: Voltaire's words here reflect his reading of *De l'esprit*, in which Helvétius (Discours Premier, Ch. III, n. 11) discusses the cost in suffering of every barrel of sugar that reaches Europe; one of the components in Helvétius's calculation is the suffering caused by the slave trade and the treatment of slaves in the French West Indies. Criticism of French imperialist behaviour was current among the *philosophes* and contributors to the *Encyclopédie*. Diderot, with whom Voltaire corresponded, wrote the attacks on slavery and despotism in Abbé Raynal's *Histoire des deux Indes*, which appeared in 1770.

p. 169 *patacoon*: from the Spanish *patacon*, a piece of eight.

p. 171 *the Dutchman*: the name and nationality of Vandurendur are a clear reference to the Dutch publisher Van Duren, who had been given the right to publish the *Anti-Machiavel* (Anti-Machiavelli), a treatise written by Frederick II of Prussia shortly before he succeeded his father on the Prussian throne. No sooner was Frederick II on the throne than he recanted his anti-Machiavellian pronouncements, and asked Voltaire to buy the entire print-run from Van Duren. Van Duren, convinced that the publication would make his fortune, refused the successively larger amounts that Voltaire offered. When

Voltaire obtained the manuscript, and attempted to render it unpublishable by additions and crossings-out, Van Duren merely insisted he had a right to publish this second edition too. The upshot was a genuine second edition, which Frederick rejected as excessively altered. A second allegorical meaning is present in the "sheep", a meaning related to the episode of Arbogad in *Zadig*. When Voltaire left Prussia, he was arrested in Frankfurt-*sur-Main* (an anagram of Surinam), and his baggage searched for papers belonging to Frederick. Frederick having referred to Voltaires's literary works as his "Golden Fleece", and to his mind as a Peru (a legendary source of riches and gold), Candide's loss of his "luggage" (sheep laden with gold) takes on a particular resonance. The personal and autobiographical references are never allowed to constrain the archetypal value of the episode nor the swift progress of the narrative (unlike notes).

p. 171 *piastres*: from the Italian *piastra d'argento* (silver plate), this name was used of the Spanish piece of eight and its representatives in Spanish American countries.

p. 173 *Socinian*: the name is derived from those of two Italian religious teachers, Lelio Sozini (1525–1562) and his nephew Fausto Sozzini (1539–1604), both using the Latin name Socinus. Fausto denied the divinity of Christ, the Trinity, and the natural immortality of man. Socinianism lays stress on the example of Christ's life as a way to salvation. This was close to the deism of Voltaire.

p. 174 *Manichean*: Manes, or Manichaeus (c. 215–275), was born in Ctesiphon, the capital of the Persian Empire. He was forced into exile by the opposition of the Zoroastrians, spread the word throughout the Orient, and returned to Ctesiphon in 242. He was flayed alive under Bahram I. Manichaeists define human life in terms of the primeval conflict between light and dark.

As such, it corresponds to the Zoroastrianism of *Zadig* in its contribution to the debate about Providence.

p. 177 *convulsions*: this refers to the convulsionaries, extreme representatives of the Jansenists. The convulsionaries displayed behaviour like that of epilepsy, along with cures, prophesying, etc. around the tomb of the Jansenist François de Paris (1690–1727), at St.-Médard in Paris.

p. 178 *that the earth was originally all sea*: Groos sees here a reference to the first day of Creation, dry land having occurred only on the second day, at Genesis 1,9. A Bible was likely to be the ship captain's entire library, and Martin's answer, in which "idle dreams ... retailed to us for ever so long" probably refers to religions. Another possible target is *Telliamed, ou Entretiens d'un philosophe indien avec un missionaire français*, published in 1748 by Benoît de Mallet. Mallet asserted that mountains and mankind alike had arisen from the ocean.

p. 179 *a professor from the north*: Pierre-Louis Maupertuis (1698–1759), a French scientist of limited abilities and one of Newton's defenders in France, had been in high favour at Frederick II's court. Voltaire's quarrel with him was one of the reasons for his departure from Berlin. A calculation of this kind is found in Maupertuis's *Works*, on p. 45 of the 1752 edition, described as the fundamental principle of statics. Maupertuis believed that the existence of God could be mathematically proven, and this derisive reference may therefore embrace the metaphor of the Holy Lamb.

p. 180 *a bill payable to bearer to be repaid in the other world*: in 1750, the Archbishop of Paris had required that a signed note from the confessor of the dying was required, stating that the moribund subscribed to the anti-Jansenist bull *Unigenitus*, before the last rites could be administered.

p. 180 *a little abbé from Périgord*: in his *Lettres philosophiques*,

Voltaire remarks: "That indefinable entity, neither church nor layman, in a word, the *abbé*, is a species unknown to the English... When they learn that in France, there are young men, known for their debauchery and elevated to the prelacy by women's plots, who court in public, entertain themselves by composing erotic songs, every day give long and exquisite dinners, and go thence to implore the inspiration of the Holy Ghost, daring to denominate themselves the successors of the Apostles, they thank God that they are Protestants" (Letter V). *Abbés* were not required to belong to an order, and the definition of the state covered a multitude of sins.

p. 180 *he is a man who does not believe in innate ideas*: the tragedian is Voltaire, who had been one of the first French spokesmen for Locke's belief that all ideas come from the senses. This was contrary to the views of Descartes and Leibniz, and was condemned by the Sorbonne and the Parlement. The tragedy is Voltaire's *L'Orphelin de Chine* (1755); the title is given in the La Vallière manuscript, though crossed out. It is set in China, its author did not know a word of Chinese, and many pamphlets had been written against him.

p. 181 *a tolerably dull tragedy*: this is generally taken to be *Le comte d'Essex* (1678) by Thomas Corneille (1625–1709), the younger brother of the famous dramatist Pierre Corneille.

p. 181 *thrown them in the common sewer when they are dead*: this and the account of "Mlle Monime" overleaf, refer to the fate of Adrienne Lecouvreur, with whom Voltaire had a liaison, and whose acting he admired. "Mlle Monime" (this is the name of the role in Racine's *Mithridate* played by Lecouvreur) was refused burial in consecrated ground. Actors were *de officio* excommunicate in France, with the exception of those of the Italian company, who had made it a condition of their return to Paris in 1716 that they maintain their rights to the sacraments. Lecouvreur was buried on wasteland on the edge of the city without monument or ceremony. Voltaire was moved to write a poem of indignation at her treatment. The poem was, in its turn, criticised for contradicting the views of the French Church — and that of most theatre-goers of the time.

p. 182 *Fréron*: Élie Fréron (1718–1749), a critic and journalist, was the editor of the *Année littéraire*, which carried attacks on the *philosophes* and the *Encylopédie*. He was an object of ridicule in several of Voltaire's works.

p. 182 *Mademoiselle Clairon*: this was the stage name of Claire Legris de Latude (1723–1803), a tragic actress celebrated for her work in Voltaire's tragedies.

p. 183 *he had lost fifty thousand francs*: in 1747, Mme du Châtelet, Voltaire's mistress, spent two days gambling in the circle of the Queen at Fontainebleau. Cheating at cards was so much the custom there that certain leading aristocrats had taken lessons in sleight of hand. Mme du Châtelet lost forty-eight thousand *livres* over the course of the two days, a sum which she could by no means afford. Voltaire, exasperated, asked her in English: "Can you not see that you are playing with cheats?". He was overheard and understood; he and his mistress took flight, and Voltaire himself took refuge in the castle of the duchesse du Maine at Sceaux, where he lived a solitary and nocturnal life until the affair had passed over. The similarity of the sums (a franc was originally worth a *livre* or pound of gold) suggests that a reference to this event is intended. Another target is Jean-Jacques Rousseau. In his *Julie, ou La Nouvelle Héloïse* (1761), Saint-Preux succumbs to a rather low class of prostitution, and informs Julie in a sentimental letter. Voltaire felt that Rousseau/Saint-Preux displayed a lack of *savoir-vivre* in both his choice of temptation and his excessive contrition. Candide sets a better example.

p. 183 *Gauchat*: Gabriel Gauchat (1709–1774) had not written any novels at the time of *Candide*'s publication, but Voltaire suspected him of being the author of *L'Oracle des nouveaux philosophes*, as he says in a letter of Thiérot of 23 September 1760. The *Oracle* was in the fact the work of Abbé Guyon, and appeared 1759–1760. Gauchat's best-known work was the *Lettres critiques*. Given Voltaire's disparaging use of the world *roman*, he may be referring to the *Lettres*.

p. 184 *Trublet*: Abbé Nicolas Trublet (1697–1770), author of *Essais ce morale et littérature*, serves as an example of what happened to Voltaire's enemies. Voltaire pilloried him in verse: "L'Abbé Trublet avait alors la rage / D'être à Paris un petit personnnage / ... / Il nous lassait sans jamais se lasser" ("Abbé Trublet fiercely desired to be a somebody in Paris ... He wearied us unwearyingly"), and Trublet never really overcame the humiliation.

p. 185 *Molinists*: here used as a synonym for Jesuits, it refers more strictly to followers of the theologian Luis de Molina (1535–1560) and his doctrines concerning God's foreknowledge of human cooperation with the Divine gift of grace. Molinism was widely adopted by the Jesuits, and, though controversial, is still taught alongside Thomism.

p. 189 *a poor beggar of the province of Artois*: the beggar was Robert-François Damiens (1714–1757), who attempted to assassinate Louis XV on 5 January 1757. Damiens seems to have been a madman, and his death under atrocious torture scandalised Voltaire. The "parricide" (regicide) was unlike that of May 1610, in that François Ravaillac (1578–1610) had succeeded in his attempt to kill Henri IV. It resembled that of December 1594, in which Jean Châtel had failed in his attempt to kill Henri IV. Moreover, the two unsuccessful attempts were thought to have been fomented by the Jesuits. By the Edict of Nantes, Henri IV (1553–1610), himself a Protestant by upbringing, who had abjured Protestantism in order to secure his claim to the throne, had obtained some liberty of conscience for the Huguenots (the French Calvinists), and thus incurred the enmity of some parts of the Catholic church.

p. 191 *some acres of snow*: the war led to British acquisition of Canada, confirmed by the Treaty of Paris in 1763, the decisive battle being Wolfe's celebrated capture of Quebec in 1759.

p. 191 *an admiral*: Admiral John Byng (1704–1757) had been commander of the English fleet when the maréchal de Richelieu took Port-Mahon/Fort St. Philip (Menorca) from the English. Byng was relieved of his command and imprisoned by the government of the Duke of Newcastle. Voltaire heard of the affair via the brother of the new English Prime Minister, William Pitt, and obtained a statement from Richelieu justifying his opponent's actions. This was presented in court, but Byng was condemned to death for negligence under an amendment that he had himself instituted in 1739. He was executed on 14 March 1757, on board the *Monarch* in Portsmouth Harbour.

p. 194 *Theatine friar*: the Theatine order was founded in 1524 with a view to reforming the Church. One of its founders, Gian Pietro Caraffe, was Bishop of Chieti ("Theate") and later Pope Paul IV. The Theatine order required great austerity, and permitted neither property nor begging. It played an influential part in the Counter-Reformation.

p. 194 *lachryma Christi*: a flattering name (Christ's tear) for a wine from the bay of Naples.

p. 195 *torn off one's back*: the original merely has the petticoat "lifted".

p. 196 *Giroflée*: Voltaire's name for his Theatine friar does not suggest austerity; it means "gillyflower".

p. 197 *Pococurante*: the name means "caring for little".

p. 198 *Raphael*: Raffaello Sanzio (1485-1520) is widely regarded as one of the greatest artists of all time.

p. 199 *a eunuch trill out the part of Caesar or Cato*: the preeminence of castrato singers was such that the principal male role often fell to them, despite and because of their soprano voices.

p. 200 *the second, fourth and sixth books*: these are the books of Virgil's Aeneid in which: (2) Aeneas recounts the fall of Troy and his escape; (4) the love of Dido and Aeneas is recounted; (6) Aeneas is conducted by the Sibyl into the Underworld.

p. 200 *Tasso ... Ariosto*: Torquato Tasso (1544-1595), author of *Gerusalemme Liberata*, an epic combining romance elements with the story of the First Crusade. Ludovico Ariosto (1474-1533), author of *Orlando furioso*, a long poem featuring the heroes of French *chanson de geste* (Roland/Orlando, Charlemagne).

p. 200 *journey to Brundisium*: Quintus Horatius Flaccus, poet (65-8 BC), is best known for his Odes. Voltaire objects to the quotidian and sometimes sordid details of Roman life contained in Horace's Satires and Epodes. He described his journey to Brundisium (Brindisi) in Satires, I, 5; the dinner spoilt by a gastronomic pedant and a domestic disaster is recounted in Satires, II. 8; the quarrel between Persius and Rupilius Rex is described in Satires, I, 7; witches are described in Satires, I, 8 and Epodes, 5; an old woman is insultingly rejected in Epodes, 8; the compliment to Maecenas, Horace's patron, occurs in the last lines of Odes I, 1. Pococurante is mocked for his lack of appreciation, but his speeches give Voltaire an opportunity to declare his own preferences and his independence of conventional estimates.

p. 201 *Cicero*: Marcus Tullius Cicero (106-43 BC), celebrated orator, politician and author, was Roman Consul in 63 BC. His works include orations, and philosophical writings of Stoic tendency. Since many of Cicero's orations are courtroom speeches, Pococurante refers to his own causes (cases).

p. 201 *Academy of Science*: Voltaire refers to the French Academy of Sciences, founded by Colbert in 1666 for the study of mathematics, physics and natural history. In his *Lettres philosophiques*, Voltaire remarks that "It is entirely possible that such profound and thorough-going research, such exact calculations, such subtle discoveries and such far-ranging vision will eventually produce something of universal benefit"; apparently nothing of the sort had yet occurred.

p. 201 *Seneca*: Lucius Annaeus Seneca (born between 4 BC and AD 1, forced to commit suicide in 65) was a Roman philosopher and playwright of Spanish origin.

p. 201 *it is a fine thing to write what one thinks; it is the privilege of a human being*: this might be Voltaire's maxim; he defined liberty in these terms.

p. 202 *barbarian*: John Milton (1608–1674), author of *Paradise Lost*, receives one mention in Voltaire's *Lettres philosophiques*, which were credited with "introducing" English literature to France. There Voltaire describes *Paradise Lost* as *fort triste* ("very grim"). *Paradise Lost* is in twelve books, not ten, and concentrates on the first three chapters of Genesis, not the first only. The "ragged verse" is no doubt so deemed for being unrhymed. Moses is cited here as the author of the Pentateuch. Pococurante refers to the following sections of *Paradise Lost*: VII, 225–6 ("He took the gold'n Compasses, prepar'd / In Gods eternal Store"); IV, 799–800 ("him there they found / Squat like a Toad, close at the ear of Eve"); I, 778, where Satan is not in fact transformed into a pygmy; VI, 571 ff. (the cannonading of the celestial host); II, 790 ff (Death rapes Sin, his mother); XI, 472 (the vision of the Diseases resembles a "lazar-house" [leper-colony]).

p. 203 *Plato remarked*: Plato noted in *The Republic*, V, 475C, that a person finical about food is not hungry and not a lover of food, which is not exactly what Voltaire reports.

p. 205 *How is it you are all Kings?*: Voltaire's list of kings overthrown or even self-created is highly subversive. If kingship was a matter of divine right, there was clearly some confusion in heaven. Needless to say, this meeting of kings anonymous never took place.

p. 205 *Achmet III*: Ahmet III was the Ottoman Sultan from 1703–1730. His predecessor was Mustafa II, who ruled 1695–1703. He was succeeded by Mahmut I, who reigned 1730-1754. These are Sultans from the declining years of the Ottoman Empire. "Seraglio" is a variant of the Turkish word for palace, *sarayi*.

p. 206 *Ivan*: Ivan VI of Russia (b. 1740) inherited the throne at two months of age, was superseded by Elizabeth, daughter of Peter the Great, imprisoned, and finally put to death by Catherine the Great in 1764.

p. 206 *Charles Edward*: Charles Edward Stuart, the Young Pretender (1720–1788), grandson of James II of England, and son of James Stuart, the Old Pretender.

p. 206 *King of Poland*: Augustus III (1696–1763), Elector of Saxony and King of Poland, was overthrown during the Polish War of Succession (1733–1735), and replaced for the duration of the war by Stanislaus Leszczynski, after which he was restored. His father, Augustus II, was the Elector of Saxony. After election as one of 18 candidates to the Polish throne, he was crowned King of Poland in 1697. He was deposed by a Polish faction in 1704, and fled to Saxony. Saxony was then invaded by Charles XII of Sweden, and Augustus agreed to give up the crown of Poland under the terms of the the Peace of Altranstädt (1706); following Charles's defeat by the Russians at Poltava (1709), Augustus abjured the treaty and the Diet restored him to the throne of Poland.

p. 206 *King of Poland*: Stanislaus Leszczynski was elected King of Poland by the Polish Diet in 1704, after the expulsion of August II. He was driven from the throne in 1709 when Augustus II was reinstated, then restored to the throne by an overwhelming vote of the Diet during the War of the Polish Succession (1733–1735). His daughter Marie having married Louis XV, Louis sought to impose him against Russian and Austrian opposition. Louis failed, and Augustus III was reinstated. In 1738, Stanislaus was granted the Duchy of Lorraine and Bar and allowed to keep his royal title; he died in Lorraine in 1766. For Voltaire, Stanislaus was a loyal patron and his court a refuge.

p. 206 *Sarmatia*: the region between the rivers Volga and Vistula, now divided between Poland and Russia.

p. 206 *Theodore*: a Westphalian baron, and military adventurer, Theodore de Neuhoff helped the Corsicans revolt against their Genoese government and was elected King of Corsica in 1736. Forced to abdicate, he eventually found his way to London, where he was imprisoned for debt. He died shortly after his release, in 1756.

p. 207 *sequin*: French and English term for the Italian gold coin *zecchino*.

p. 209 *Ragotski*: François Leopold Racocy (1676–1735), Prince of Transylvania, led a Hungarian uprising against the Holy Roman Emperor Joseph II (ruler of the Austro-Habsburg dominions) with French and Turkish support. When it failed, he fled to Constantinople.

p. 213 *Icoglan*: a page of the Sultan's palace in the Ottoman Empire.

p. 214 *crucial incision*: the cross-shaped incision is thought by the surgeon to have expelled a devil.

p. 215 *Her neck was quite uncovered*: Pangloss is telling a most unlikely story. The sexes are segregated in mosques, and modest dress is required of Muslim women at all times.

p. 215 *plenum ... materia subtilis*: "All nature is a plenum," says Leibniz in his *Principles of Nature and of Grace, Founded on Reason* (1714), S.3. In a plenum, everything is affected by everything else. *Materia subtilis* is a more rarefied sort of matter, such as might be found in angels' bodies. For "pre-established harmony", see note to p. 33.

p. 218 *left-handed marriage*: another term for morganatic marriage, that is, a marriage between a high and a low ranking person, in which the low ranking person is not elevated to the higher rank of the spouse, and the issue have no claim on the succession of the higher party.

p. 219 *Effendis, Pashas*: "Effendi" is merely an honorific title; "Pasha" was placed after the name of a provincial governor, and indeed after that of the Grand Viziers.

p. 219 *Sublime Porte*: the court of the Ottoman Empire. Executioners were required to strangle their victim, place his head in a leather bag, and return with it as proof that the job had been carried out.

p. 220 *dervish*: a Muslim ascetic; the best known are the followers of Mevlana (Rumi), whose dance-meditation has earned them the name "whirling dervishes".

p. 221 *Mufti*: the preeminent religious leader within the Ottoman Empire.

p. 222 *Let me remind you*: the reader will need no reminding of the fate of these rulers of the Old Testament and Greek, Latin, English and French history, finishing with a German Emperor.

p. 222 *ut operaretur eum*: the quotation is from the Vulgate (*ut operaretur et custodiret eum*); in English (Genesis 2, 15) "to dress it and to keep it [i.e. the Garden of Eden]". Ironically, Voltaire brings *Candide* to an end with the accomplishment of God's purpose for man in the Garden of Eden. The formula "cultivate our garden" is customary in translating Voltaire/Candide's phrase.